The Treasures of
Darkness

Carol L. Anderson

BY

CAROL LEE ANDERSON

ISBN: 1453882359
ISBN-13: 9781453882351
LCCN: 2010915285

Table of Contents

Prologue

"The king! I must speak to the king!"

Towering, double doors groaned as they gave way to the strength of muscular sentries. The messenger, dusty and tired from his long journey, gazed upward in awe as he took in the vast luminescent interior of the high king's castle. Recovering his purpose, he hurried through the doorway and hailed a waiting servant.

Jubilee bent to listen to the rushed account, drew back in alarm, and beckoned to Mirth, high servant to King Zenith. Hearing the whispered message, Mirth sprinted toward the throne.

King Zenith leaned forward as he deliberated the matter before him, while a host of courtiers dressed in all the colors of the rainbow waited for what they knew would be a wise and just response. Mirth slowed his pace just before reaching the king and knelt.

"High and Sovereign King, a messenger has come with an important message." The king motioned with his scepter for Jubilee to bring the man forward.

The Treasures of Darkness

"What is it? What message do you bring?" asked the king.

"Your Majesty, you are a just and kind ruler. Your greatness is known in all the world. Your wealth also is beyond measure," panted the weary messenger. "I bring word from the far regions of your kingdom that one has turned against you and become your enemy. I am sorry to say that he has stolen from you, your great and valued Treasure and now uses it to destroy your kingdom."

The king's attendants gasped and began to murmur among themselves. Engulfed in soft folds of purple, the aged ruler sat still, his brow contracted into furrowed lines from the heaviness of this news. A tear ran down his cheek.

"My Treasure?"

At last, the king's face raised, and those before him could see the muscles harden with firm determination. He nodded his head in understanding. The attendants drew a collective breath in anticipation of his next move, and exhaled again as the wait continued. At last, the king rose from his seat, sweeping the train of his royal robes aside with a strong arm. A cloud of sparkling dust whirled in smooth circles high into the air and gently settled again to the floor. All fell to their knees, bowing with hands outstretched.

Standing tall and firm before them, like an ancient oak tree, he declared in a thundering voice, "The time has come."

"The time has come?" buzzed the crowd to one another, as they swarmed about the room.

"The time has come!" they shouted to one another, smiling for the first time since they heard the news.

"Send for my son," commanded the king. Mirth shouted the order to the entrance of the hall. "The prince! Send for the prince!" and then they all waited once more, this time with loud chattering comments about the past accomplishments of the young, future king.

Massive hinges on the heavy doors ground open again for a courtier who announced the arrival of the prince. The attendants parted into two groups, forming a narrow corridor between the doors and the throne. The king raised his scepter.

Prologue

"Bring him in!"

A younger man, dressed in a long, golden coat over a white gown, strode forward, wafting in the aroma of wild flowers and forest glades. The crowd on either side sank low, with faces to the clear glass pavement.

The prince was a valiant warrior, strong and firm. Upon his head rested a circlet of gold that sparkled with tiny jewels. Approaching the throne, he bowed and knelt on one knee before his father.

"Father, you called for me."

"My son, news has reached me that there is trouble in the south. My servant tells me that an evil pretender, with his magic arts, has stolen that which is precious to me. The time has come for all to know the true king. This pretender shall not succeed."

"Father, who is this evil ruler?"

"Once he was my beloved servant, but he has turned against me," replied the king in a sad voice.

"You don't mean...."

"Yes, it is him. My heart is broken that the one I favored has become my enemy. I fear that there is no hope of his return. It is too late for that now. He will meet destruction at my hand. For that, I have set a time and place and there is no going back."

"Father, what would you have me do?" asked the prince, as he searched his father's glistening eyes.

"My son, go! Destroy the magic. Bring back my Treasure! I know this is a dangerous mission, for the one who has done this is murderous and violent. He will stop at nothing to keep that which does not belong to him," warned the king. "And you, my son, are the only one I can count on to foil his plan."

"Father, I will. Shall I raise an army of armed warriors for a battle?" All those in the throne room nodded together in approval.

"No, this is much too great a contest for mere swords." The crowd drew back in shocked surprise. Knowing the wisdom of their lord, they awaited the revelation of a superior plan.

"What should I take with me then?"

"Son, take this." The king reached down to find a small, golden chest. Lifting it up, he handed it to the young man and said, "Use what you find according to the wisdom I have given you, and the battle will be yours." Upon opening the chest, a flare of multi-colored light shone out, so bright that the hosts present squinted and covered their eyes. The prince lowered the lid and tucked the chest under his arm.

"Son, I give you this as well." The king reached forward and clasped a yellow metal band on his son's wrist. "You will know what to do."

"I understand, Father" He stood for a moment, sighed, and then reached up to remove his own crown and place it at his father's feet.

A rumble spread through the crowd again. Why did the one who could command an army now remove his crown? Each tried to grasp the enormity of the task that had been given to the son. How could he possibly succeed?

The son bowed low, turned, and left King Zenith's presence to venture alone into the dark realms.

CHAPTER 1

Jip

A dark form crouched in the inky blackness. With cat-like stealth, it rose and moved forward in smooth, determined strides.

The early summer night air was cool and dry. Stars gleamed overhead in the moonless sky, offering faint light. Jip's eyes had adjusted enough to see the ancient vine he had tested countless times in the past. He grabbed it, carefully inserted his toes between projecting stones in the high wall, and then hurled himself up to stand on top. The jump to the ground in the garden was not difficult for a man of his youthful strength and agility. He landed with a soft thud and crouched again waiting for any movement or sound. Aside from a night dove cooing in the distance, all was still.

Jip ducked behind a stone warrior in full armor, glad for shelter to again scan the grounds before his last assault. No guards patrolled the east side of the great house. Creeping ever closer, Jip tingled with anticipation and wariness as his hand reached out for the gate. It was locked, as he expected it would be. He walked close to the exterior wall, inching along until he came to what he knew was her window. Its tall narrow frames, filled with hundreds of small panes of beveled glass, stood above his head. Jip raised his hand and felt along the stone edge until he was sure he held the bottom of the frame. His fingers worked to pry the unlocked window open enough to allow his body to enter. Heavily muscled arms pulled his bulk up and over the sill and into complete darkness.

Soft snoring reached the intruder's ears, whose first instinct was to judge the direction and distance, then slowly make his way to the opposite side of the room. *Where are you? Where would she hide you?*

CHAPTER 2

Julen

Blackness, struggling, and terror—a strong force pushed her screams for help back into her chest. Smothering darkness wrapped around her body; pushing, jabbing monsters choked out life. She fought with all her strength, but there was no use. No movement was possible. No one heard her cries. "Father, help me!"

"Uuaaghh!" A tousled head of dark, thick curls jerked this way and that. A sudden shock, a cold wooden floor, her body tangled in her musty quilt. Julen awoke to find she had again had the nightmare. She opened her eyes to let in the dim light that was the dawn of a new day. Raising her head, a wave of familiar sorrow passed over her again, as it did every time. She fought her way back onto the straw mattress, unwrapped the quilt, and rewrapped it around her shivering body. Her toes squirmed into the warm bedding as her head fell back to the mangled wad she used for a pillow. She wiped her eyes and reflected again on the nightmare, always the same. Julen pulled the covering over her

The Treasures of Darkness

head, momentarily shutting out the stark stone walls. The new day would not cease to demand her presence just because she did not welcome it.

"Is that you, Julen? Have you had one of your dreams?" rasped the weak voice of a very old woman. Bare walls and few furnishings produced an empty, hollow sound in the room. Its only coziness was afforded by the low, sloped roof that formed a ceiling, and the dormer window that brought in the morning light.

"Sorry. I'll be all right," she yelled so the nearly-deaf ears could not fail to hear. *The dream again. Always the same.* She shook loose the horror of the night and remembered that this was a day with its own worries and cares.

"Ahh, I am sorry, my love," the voice faded to a hoarse gasp for breath. "If I could make it go away I would."

"Please don't be troubled. I'm sorry to have awakened you so early. Forgive me," Julen apologized, as she struggled out of her bed clothes into an upright position.

"Don't fret, Child. I have not been sleeping," said Ralda with a tinge of resignation, "Enough time for that later."

Julen found her slippers, which were kept close to the mat, and put them on. Pulling back her black hair, she gathered, squeezed, and twisted until the mass, like the wild torrent of a spring waterfall, was tamed and confined to a fine string net, which she fastened behind her head. She changed into the rest of her servant's garb, donning a shapeless, gray dress with its sash tied in the middle. Around her slim waist, she added an apron.

The young woman crossed the small room and bent over the frail, shrunken form of her friend and companion. Looking for signs that would tell her how the old woman was faring this day, she saw only a look of weary resolve in the faded green eyes. Julen pondered how long it would be before the light in those eyes would be gone forever. She busied herself helping Ralda get ready for the day. "I must leave you soon, Ralda. I am sorry that I can't be with you today." Julen's voice was shaking.

"You look frightened, my dear. Don't let them frighten you. They will try, but you must be strong." Ralda reached out her hands to take Julen's.

8

Julen

"I am trying, Ralda. When I have that dream, I fear that something terribly is about to happen—if it wasn't bad enough reliving that part of my life."

"Something is going to happen, Julen. There is so much to tell you, Child. So many things left unspoken." Julen heard the tone in Ralda's voice and knew what she meant.

"I am frightened. I am worried about you. Noni said she would bring you bread and tea. Please send word if you need me."

"Julen. I am dying. I won't be here for you much longer and I am sad to leave you like this. I have tried to protect you and teach you everything you need to know." The old woman looked down with sadness. "Believe me. There is much to tell, even yet."

Julen remembered the Ralda she first knew when she was brought to the old stone mansion as a young slave. She had been strong then, and wise in the ways of the household. She was the only reason Julen had survived the harsh environment she had been thrust into against her will.

The young servant unlatched the window made from tiny panes of translucent, yellowed glass, and pushed. The aged wooden frame creaked open, allowing the early morning breeze to flood the room. A great longing in Julen's heart to go back and undo the past compelled her to this daily ritual. What was it she hoped to see in the great beyond? A ship sailing from her homeland, coming to take her away from her imprisonment? If only the dreams in daylight could vanquish the specters that haunted her nights. The metal band on her wrist brought her back to the reality of her Netherian slave status in the kingdom of Bellicosa.

From the dormer window high in the vast roof of the great mansion known as Arcana, she could see that the morning sun had not yet risen above the cliffs that flanked Graystone. Eons before, an enormous chunk of the coastal cliff had fallen away leaving an eroded depression, which much later became the main seaport town of Bellicosa. The house, build high on the steep hill, offered a view of the lower part of the city and the sea beyond. To the east and west was a jumble of broken crags topped by hilly plateaus. She had never seen the small farms and villages that dotted the countryside to the east, nor the quarries and mines that were said to mar the landscape like open wounds in the western part of the kingdom. Behind Arcana were steep mountains that went on and on into unknown lands. But from this southern view above the gray slate roofs, Julen was heartened to see the golden sea sparkle as the orange light of dawn spread westward.

"It is unusual for the mistress to choose one as young as you are to serve her. Bina has been her servant for many years. You must be careful today. Watch everything they do and make no false moves." Ralda's words came in short, breathless bursts.

"It is strange, Ralda. I don't understand why the mistress wanted me to serve her. I could have gone on scrubbing the floors on my hands and knees for many years. But here I am, learning how to be a lady's maid from that cantankerous Bina. This alone could give one nightmares!"

"Tell me again. What did the mistress say to you?" asked Ralda. Julen had told her many times what had transpired, and each time the old slave had applied all the experience and knowledge she could muster to find some plot or conspiracy behind it.

"The mistress saw me scrubbing then stopped. 'Julen, that's your name isn't it?'" Julen acted the part of the haughty mistress and, for a brief moment, enjoyed telling the story again. "She should remember my name. She is the one who took pity on me and bought me from the slave market!"

"You are right. Of course, she must remember your name. But, you have changed, Julen. You are grown now, though your looks are distinctly not Bellicosan," Ralda declared, observing Julen's olive skin and almond-shaped, brown eyes. "You will never be pale and fair-haired as they are, but you are beautiful nonetheless."

Julen blushed and smiled at her friend. "Maybe that is why she recognized me. She said, 'Stand up, child. I want to see what a young woman you have become.' So I got up and stood there. The mistress looked up and down and said something about how I had grown into a strong woman, but that I was awfully thin. She told me she liked my eyes. But my hair was too wild and my nose a bit long. On the whole, I guess she approved. I was stunned that she wanted me to work for her. 'I bought you and I should have the benefit of your services,'" Julen feigned the aloof manner of the wealthy. "'You will become an assistant to my servant Bina.'"

Ralda grinned at Julen's comical impersonation of the mistress. This was the Julen that she delighted in, the young girl who could be filled with wit and fun.

"'Bina, you will take the young Julen here and teach her everything she needs to know to assist you in your work. Is that clear?' You should have seen the look I got from Bina when she thought I would be moving to her quarters!"

The edges of Ralda's lips curled into a sly smile, as she knew what was coming next. "'No,' I said to them. 'I must stay with Ralda and look after her because she is my dearest friend.'"

Ralda beamed with delight hearing again of Julen's love for her. But she warned, "Be careful, my dear. Bellicosa is the land of treachery." Ralda focused on Julen's foreign beauty, which in the recent years had bloomed before her eyes. "My poor child, torn from your home and brought to this house to live out your days in hard work—may you fare better than I have done. I'm leaving soon. You know that, don't you?"

"Don't say that!" Julen chided. She knew that death would come one day and things would change. "You can't leave me. With whom will I share my joys and sorrows? You are my only friend."

Ralda thought for a moment and then said softly, "When my time comes, my dear, I have a gift for you. It is something very special that I have saved for a long time."

"What could that possibly be? Haven't I seen everything you own in this room?" inquired Julen. "What small things you have I would be glad to own, though, to remind me of you."

Lowering her voice and trying to contain her excitement, Ralda continued, "Ah, but I do have something you do not know about, Julen, my dear child. It is very precious. I didn't deserve to have it." Julen smiled tenderly, wondering if this was some kind of delusion. The old slave waited for a look of curiosity to appear on Julen's face, but none came. She went on in a whisper looking from side to side, as if to make sure no one could hear her. "It is very secret. No one can know."

Loud creaking from across the room stopped the conversation and the old oak door burst open. A short, round-bodied women with arms akimbo glared from the passageway.

"So what are you going on about this morning, old woman?" asked Bina as severely as she could. Her spotless apron with large pockets stood out prominently over the shapeless, gray uniform. Silver-streaked brown hair pulled back into a netted bun accentuated dark-circled, puffy eyes. On her pasty cheeks, she had dabbed a bright pink preparation in hopes of distracting attention from the toll her forty years had taken.

"Telling secrets? What is so important that you keep Miss Mophead from her day of working for me?" Bina taunted, triumphing in her moment of surprise like a cat with a frightened mouse.

Ralda sunk down in her rocker, avoiding the stare from the infamous Bina. She turned her eyes to Julen, silently clenched her jaw and hoping Bina had not overheard her last words to Julen.

"Let's get on with the day, shall we, Your Laziness?" Bina urged through pinched lips in a studied effort to sound authoritative. She rolled her eyes and tossed her head as she turned to make her exit. Pointing a finger to the place behind her where Julen was to follow, she hurried away down the stairs.

Ralda held Julen's hands in her own, looked into the young woman's face, and said, "We will talk of this again later. I don't have long."

Julen smiled with tenderness and sympathy, "I must go now. Don't worry."

CHAPTER 3

Dismalia

As Julen made the last turn of the staircase, she found Bina at the bottom, standing with arms crossed and scowling, trying to control her rapid breathing and failing strength. Julen slowed her pace and stepped in behind in subservience.

It was still early in the morning, but the kitchen was already alive with bustling activity. Not many in the household were awake yet, so the two women had stopped to eat a simple meal of cheese and coarse bread.

"Ah, look who we have with us today, Noni. It is that pretty, young scrub girl." Bessie, the rotund cook shouted to her assistant, bellowing in laughter that even Bina's withering glare could not stifle. "I hear you are moving up in the scheme of things in this old house. Sit down and have some of my best porridge to start the day off right." Julen smiled, welcoming the hot, brown gruel and the friendly gesture.

"Did you hear about the visitors?" Bessie asked as she wrenched the wings from a headless goose on her butcher block. Other fowl, having met a similar fate, hung overhead waiting for the cooking fire.

"All right, Bessie, who is it now?" asked Bina, annoyed with the cook she could not intimidate. She groaned in distaste for the gossip of the kitchen, but Julen could see that she reveled in its suspense nonetheless.

"I heard from the coach driver that Mistress Violencia Mortifa and that bunch have come for the week before the Festival of the Moon. They will be dining with the master this evening. Oh, I would love to be in your place to see it unfold," she said with evil glee. "Noni, fetch me more water!"

"No! I want to hear!" scowled Noni. The young serving girl turned a spit over the fire that suspended an enormous leg of bobbit for the evening's dinner. "How do YOU think the mistress will enjoy her supper tonight?" Noni asked, scooting toward the door to fetch water. Bina's eyebrows raised and she shook her head slightly in response to the question. Her mouth remained twisted into the contemptuous sneer that had come to be known by all, but gave no answer. Everyone seemed to know the answer—except Julen. Bessie raised her cleaver with a threatening gesture and bellowed a loud, hearty laugh that echoed through the kitchen and out into the Great Hall.

When they had finished their meal, Bina turned, pointed to the floor beside her, and faced the corridor. The trainee obeyed and found her place. Walking side by side down the wide hallway, Julen struggled to slow her pace to that of Bina's.

"Now that's an odd couple—one short and stout the other tall and lean," Bessie snickered and ignored the threatening sneer from Bina.

"Watch out for that one, missy," said the cook with a wink and a comical smile.

The house was silent and cold. As they approached the mistress' apartment, Julen whispered to Bina, "What did Bessie mean about Mistress Mortifa coming to dinner?"

"It won't be pretty," predicted the cynical servant.

Dismalia

"Why?"

"You'll see."

Dismalia's rooms did not appear to be a new addition, but were of a different style than the main part of the house. The ceiling was lower and the heavy beams a different color of wood. Tapestries hung on the stone walls of the central room holding out the chill and providing a distraction from the dull gray of the stone. Julen could see that the ancient needlework scenes had once been of brilliant colors, but were now worn and faded—pale apple trees in gardens of gray flowers, surrounding pallid children who played near thread-bare cottages—scenes insulating Dismalia from everyone but her servants. Julen had wondered why someone who was free would choose to stay cooped up in the gloomy apartment.

In the center of the room was a circular divan piled with an assortment of luxurious cushions and pillows. "These are to be neatly arranged and tidy at all times," snapped Bina affecting a cold and impersonal presence. "You will see that there are few visitors. Master Chiselstone never comes. The children seldom stay for long." She paused before adding in a lower voice, "There is only need for one servant here." Julen shriveled at the intimidating words.

Bina led her into the bedroom where an enormous bed, with enough room for six people, filled the space. Dismalia Chiselstone lay in the center, barely visible under heavy quilts and puffed pillows. One arm lay draped across her face.

"Rubina, is that you?"

"Yes, Mistress."

"What should I wear to dinner this evening?"

"I think the black gown with silver sash, Mistress."

"Yes, black fits the occasion," she replied in a resigned monotone.

Bina and Julen retreated from the room temporarily when the elder servant pointed out the cavernous closet where the lady's clothes were stored. When they were out of earshot, Bina explained, "The mistress long ago gave up any color but black. Invitations to social events are as scarce as bobbit beaks."

A pang of sympathy surfaced in Julen. Though she had worked in the house for many years, the affairs of its members were still a mystery to her. Pausing just a moment to gauge Bina's mood, Julen whispered, "Why is the mistress so sad?"

Bina closed her eyes and furrowed her brow, as she realized that it was now her job to prevent this naïve upstart from making position-threatening blunders. Grudgingly, she determined to educate her unwanted minion.

"The mistress was a fine lady when they met. I remember it all. She was beautiful in her own way and very quiet. The master took one look at her and I could tell he was intrigued. He thought she was mysterious." There was sharpness in Bina's voice, a hateful tone. Julen found herself fascinated hearing about the master and mistress, Dismalia and Harrasster Chiselstone. They seemed to come alive and be more real than they had before, when her only view was from the paving stones of the Great Hall.

"She was flattered by all the fuss and bluster—thought he was daring and funny. Don't we all know better now?" Bina laughed, though scorn and bitterness lay just below the surface. "Once they married, all that changed. She turned out to be moody and cold. His daring was nothing more than foolishness. And his humor? You will see."

"Why does she live in this small suite?" Julen asked.

"It has been two years. The mistress overheard him speaking with one she trusted as a friend. He said awful things about her, and when she confronted him, he only laughed. After that, she no longer trusted any friends, or her husband. Now she licks her wounds in the solitude of her own quarters. And by law, she must remain married to him no matter what he does."

"Maybe I can encourage her," Julen offered.

"Don't you dare!" Bina demanded. "It is not your place."

Julen drew back in fear and touched her wristband, remembering Ralda's words to her that morning. *This is a place of treachery.*

"Who are you talking to? Is that my new servant? Bring her here." Dismalia called out impatiently from the bedroom. The two hurried back to their charge. Julen attempted a curtsy as Bina shoved her toward the mistress.

16

"Ah, Julen, welcome. I am glad to see you this morning. At least some-one is smiling. Bina is such a sourpuss." Bina's face hardened into a false smile while looking at her rival. She motioned with a snap of her fingers for Julen to draw the heavy drapes from the high windows to let sunlight fill the room. Obediently, Julen darted forward; she was blinded when the sun flared into the room. Squinting, Dismalia looked away. Bina's attention was drawn to the cool breeze blowing in her face. Who had opened the window? Certainly not the mistress, who had slept like the dead all night. A hurried survey of the room showed nothing out of place.

"I thought you said Bessie's bad knee predicted rain today," complained the mistress.

"Bessie's bad knee has never missed yet, Mistress. It will rain by tomorrow."

"What is it? Why are you staring out the window, Bina? Come here and help me." Bina shut the window with a deft shove as she continued scanning for clues.

"It is nothing. You there, Girl!" Bina yelled. "Come with me to the closet. I must show you the mistress' gown for this evening." Having left the mistress in her bed, they approached the closet. Bina wheeled about and flung her harsh whisper at her young protégé. "Did you open the window?"

Julen recoiled at the illogical question. "No. I have only just come into this room for the first time. Perhaps the mistress was too warm and opened it after you left her last evening."

"She would never do that. She doesn't stir once she has fallen asleep."

"Bina, come in here now," came the whining voice of Dismalia, as she rose and put on her morning robe.

"Oh, bother. Something isn't right." Bina complained as she turned and waddled back to the bedroom.

Julen peered into the closet's dark space where gray lumpy forms piled on top of each other on either side faded into blackness. It was an uninviting place. She pondered how she would find the exact gown that Bina had recommended.

A tinkling bell broke the silence. Julen waited not knowing what to do. Dismalia, attempting to float regally into the room, stumbled over every third step, and seated herself on the divan. A quick flick of the mistress' hand in Julen's direction sent the servant springing into action and, in an instant, opened the tiny eye-level window. Wide-eyed twin faces bobbed up and down with impatience.

"Hurry! Open the door! We don't want to stand out here all day!"

"Mistress, it is your daughters who wish to see you."

"Ah, Nichola and Alumina." Dismalia gave a deep sigh and instructed Julen to usher them into the room. Two young women struggled in the doorway, both trying to enter at the same time. Nichola succeeded in elbowing out her sister and, arriving first, blurted out, "Mother, Father says we shall not have new dresses for the Festival of the Moon. You must help us. He is so unreasonable."

Dismalia looked at them through a dull haze and said nothing.

"What will happen if we do not make an impression on the 'right' people?" pouted Alumina. "This could be the most important event of our young lives!"

"Girls, girls. What influence do you think I possess? Do you think your father listens to me?" she asked in a tone of self-pity. "Run along and leave me alone. My head hurts and I can't think."

"Mother!" screeched Nichola. "Why do you lock yourself up in this room? What kind of mother are you?" Dismalia steadied herself against the pillowed couch and tried to focus on the two angry daughters. Ignoring the outburst, she asked, "Will Damon be coming to dinner tonight?"

"Is he all you care about? Come on, Nichola. I know who we can ask for help," Alumina sniped. With that, the exasperated twins turned and fled from their mother's presence.

At the mention of Damon, Julen's attention was diverted from the family quarrel. Damon had been an object of fascination since the first time she had seen his face. For years, she had watched him from her crouched position in the Great Hall. Now he was grown and seldom seen any more.

She treasured recollections of his blonde head bent over a book. While Julen had watched from the shadowy corridors, the girls dressed up in gowns and danced with pretend lords. Damon, on the other hand, walked back and forth, talking to himself, acting out the stories he read. Flashing an invisible sword, he vanquished invisible foe, then bowed and received his reward before an invisible king. The memories made her laugh.

"I feel very tired. I will rest a while. Go tell Coldstone I will have my breakfast late."

"Yes, Mistress," Bina shouted, bringing Julen back to attention.

CHAPTER 4
Surprise Visit

Bina and Julen opened the door of Dismalia's apartment and stepped out into the corridor just as a flash of movement caught their attention. Bina turned and walked toward the far end to see who had business in this part of the house. A darkly tanned, muscular young man rounded the far corner of the corridor. Both women's eyes widened in shock.

"Jip! What are you doing here?" Bina snarled in a loud whisper, signaling him to stay out of sight. The three scurried around the corner.

"Why, Mother, aren't you glad to see me?" the young man teased. "Your own flesh and blood! Come to visit his mother?" Jip grinned in his own mischievous but boyishly handsome way. He had brown eyes like his mother, but a lighter shade of brown hair—wavy and tousled. His frayed clothes were ill fitting, far too tight for his well filled out frame.

"You good for nothing wastrel…you know you can't come in here. Was it you who opened the window in the mistress' room?" Bina demanded.

"Do you forget, Mother, that I grew up haunting these corridors. I know every stone and crack in the place," Jip whispered.

Jip's young life had been spent running between Arcana, where he kept out of sight, and the streets of Bellicosa, where he was known as a misbegotten Netherian. Finally taken to work by the Chiselstone Blade Company, he shoveled coal into fires and later learned to work the metal for the famous Chiselstone blades.

"You were the one. You came in the window last night, didn't you? You have no business here now. You may work for the master, but not in his house! If you don't leave now I'll…I'll…." she couldn't think what she would do, so she shoved her hands into her empty apron pockets.

"What will you do? Yell at me? That should work." he laughed at his mother's inability to frighten him. Julen saw for the first time that Bina did not know what to say. She was powerless before her son, who had little love or respect for his mother. She knew Jip from her younger days as a tease and bully. He hardly knew how to sit still, let alone carry on a conversation.

"There is one thing you can do to make me go away. I need money. Can you loan me ten coppers?" he asked holding out a small bag slung under his arm. He put his lower lip out, fluttered his eyes, and feigned a forlorn expression. Julen snickered.

"Go! I will give it to you later. Only get out of here now before your mother loses her head because of her irresponsible son." Bina was beside herself with anger. Jip dashed forward and gave her a quick peck on her pink cheek.

"Julen? Not scrubbing floors now?" he asked, taking in the changes since his last sight of her. He grinned and winked. Then as quickly as he had appeared, he leaped away and was gone.

CHAPTER 5
Dining at Arcana

Julen leaned over the railing of the balcony, high above the gray slate rooftops of Bellicosa. The double doors of the dining hall faced the sea and were open to let in the last of the summer breeze before nightfall. The beauty of the setting sun and the spectacular view of the town and rocky shoreline lured her away from her duties. The sun, off to her right, had dipped below the edge of the sea, and thin slivers of orange lining were quickly fading from the blue-gray clouds. Darkness was rising up from below and soon it would reach high into the house. Above and behind Arcana, craggy hills dotted with low shrub-like trees rose a short distance, and high above the hills were the rugged, stony mountains. It was a bleak, barren land compared to her faded memories of childhood.

Somewhere out across the sea was a place she longed for and wished her dreams would carry her back to—that beloved land—instead of the dark, shadowy, fearsome places that haunted her nights.

The sound of the sea could not be heard, but she could still see the lighter gray shades of breaking waves on the beach. She beheld the wide bay, spread out before her with stone jetties reaching far out into the deep, accommodating ships of all sizes. At the edges of the bay on either side, the beach ended, and high, stone cliff walls stood to attention like immovable guardians.

"Julen, get in here!" demanded Bina. Julen turned her head to the threatening look and quickly scurried back from the balcony into her place beside the senior servants.

All were at attention, awaiting the entrance of Master Chiselstone and company who were due to arrive in the enormous dining hall. With bowed heads, they looked up and down the line to make sure all was in order. Bina straightened her apron and prompted others to rectify small imperfections in their uniforms.

A sound of laughter echoed through the Great Hall and soon the bustle of dresses and social banter was heard by all who waited for their cues.

"And then the fool tripped over his own feet and went crashing past pots and plates, ending up flat in the fireplace." A high-pitched female voice tittered.

Master Chiselstone, arm in arm with an elegant visitor some years younger than he, advanced through the high arched entrance to the dining room. The curious Julen was able to steal a glance of the couple as they entered. Master Chiselstone was wearing his formal dinner attire—a chartreuse, long-tailed coat buttoned at the top with metal buttons bearing the family crest. Protruding prominently from beneath the buttoned section of the coat was his round belly, covered with a light-brown, loose-fitting tunic. His brown breeches were almost eclipsed between the low hanging tunic and knee-high boots. Below the prominent bulge of what was once a waistline, the raw metal of a belt buckle, like a centerpiece of a great round table, could almost be seen. Julen had seen the buckle from her floor-scrubbing vantage point of the past. Standing in the dining room, she could not see it well, especially since the master's girth had expanded over the years and eclipsed its view. On it was the image of a fearsome, silvery-green dragon with ruby-red glowing eyes.

The master looked at first to have a merry face with round, red cheeks. But Julen detected the negative turn in his temperament and was wary of what had been reported as a malicious tint.

"And then, there he was," the visitor continued though gales of laughter, "covered in bobbit stew and ash, hobbling about like a blind baboon."

The lady on Chiselstone's arm pranced into the room knowing her presence gave the room an air of refinement and gaiety. The darkness of her full head of hair contrasted with the pallid tone of her skin. A touch of pink on each cheek brought some warmth to a face otherwise as cold as ice. On her long, dark red gown, shiny stones had been fastened into patterns of swords and knives around the hem. As she twirled this way and that, the sparkling weapons came to life and danced as if locked in battle. The master looked on in approval and winked at his companion. Julen was shocked. Everyone knew that Chiselstone's highly successful business making such weapons had been his primary interest. In fact, Chiselstone blades had made the family the richest in the kingdom. What would happen when Lady Chiselstone entered the room?

A pair of male servants stepped behind the master and his lady friend and pulled a heavy chair out, waiting for him to be seated. On the back of the chair was the Chiselstone trademark, the letter "C" carved like an open mouth of a reptile. From the top of the C hung incisors between sharp canines, with a matching set on the bottom of the C. At the table, knives and spoons all bore the same emblem of ownership.

"Lady Violencia, I swear I am laughing so hard I don't think I shall be able to eat. Let's talk about something with more intrigue, like how I shall capture the heart of Hilbert Stonehurst at the Festival of the Moon." The voice belonged to Nichola Chiselstone. She and her twin, Alumina, entered in their usual style, with neither content to let the other be first. Julen thought they were both very beautiful, though each in a different way. Both had their father's dark blonde hair and hazel eyes. Nichola was taller, taking after her mother, while Alumina was heavier, favoring her father. They were always dressed in gowns of the finest imported cloth, and of such wondrous colors! Tonight Nicola wore a fine ensemble of orange of cooked cumquat, and Alumina's dress was the green of squashed zinger berries. How Julen envied them.

The servants, in contrast, in their shapeless gray attire melted into the background by design. A narrow sash around the waist provided the only relief from the gray, each servant having a color-coded sash for their position in the household. Julen's sash indicated the least of those in her class. She comforted herself with the thought that at least she was no longer assigned to floors. She could stand there and imagine being dressed in such wonderful clothes.

"We don't want to talk about your intriguing plans for Lord Stonehurst, Nichola. How about my plans for one Master Copperblow?" Alumina sneered at her sister and turned to her father with a wink adding, "What we want to talk about is what we will wear to this festival. Everything we have has been seen over and over again. You must allow us to purchase something more grand, Father. This may be the moment we capture the hearts of those who will make our future fortunes!"

"There, there, girls. You are each as unimpressive as you think the other," Master Chiselstone scolded in mock seriousness, seating Violencia in a vacant chair close to his own place at the table.

"Don't be hard on them, Master Chiselstone. They are creatures like me. We are vain and beautiful, but you love us just the same, do you not?" Violencia asked playing the diplomat. "I do hope you will permit me to help you look your best when the time comes, my dear girls."

Other guests drifted into the room, each pair in their own conversation, and then came the silent figure of Mistress Dismalia Chiselstone. She wore the recommended black gown made from a fine, draping fabric. Her face revealed no emotion and she did not make eye contact with anyone in the room. She was oblivious of the conversation that had gone on to this point, though at the last comment by Violencia, there was a slight raising of her eyebrow.

Her pace was halting as she approached her chair near the dining room entrance. As she passed Bina and Julen, the two servants fell in behind her and laid a protective cloth on her lap. Each holding a side, they moved the chair closer to the table. On cue, they took two steps backwards to stand under the arched doorway, with heads bowed, and waited for their next summons.

"Good evening, Mistress Chiselstone," crooned Violencia in a seductive voice. "It is good to see you again. It has been months, has it not? I do hope you are well. You are not quite looking yourself these days," Violencia's dark brown eyes pierced into those of Dismalia to detect a response. Mistress Chiselstone shifted in her chair, looking as if she had been sitting on something sharp. "Good evening to you as well, Violencia. I am quite well, thank you," she lied.

The final family member to enter was Damon who had been running. He slowed to a walk just as he came through the stone portal, and was out of breath. The servants braced themselves to see what the response would be to his hasty entrance. Master Chiselstone cast a stern glance his way. He opened his mouth to speak. Violencia laid her hand on his arm as if to signal that restraint was in order.

"Greetings to you, Damon. I thought I might not see you this evening, and here you are, looking fit as ever," said the red mistress. Damon looked in her direction and nodded but chose not to reply.

"What do you think, Lady Violencia? My daughters fancy themselves beautiful and my son believes himself invincible," said the master in the same mocking tone. Turning to his daughters he said, "Neither one of you is a very fine prize, my little matched set of toads. New dresses could not cure your ills, I'm afraid." Master Chiselstone followed his with harsh laughter. The other guests laughed politely, uncertain of the point of the humor.

Two faces fell as one in anger and frustration, and remained speechless. Julen winced as she heard the stinging words and felt sorry for the twins. She knew herself to be an orphan and had missed the kind attention of her father of long ago. Julen knew that this was no way for a father to behave.

As the steaming platter heaped with joints of bobbit was brought from the kitchen and placed in front of the family and their guests; eyes were wide with excitement. Bobbit was a delicacy served at the very best of dinners. It was a difficult animal to catch, being large and fast, but its enormous hind legs, when turned on a spit for two days, was the most tender and most flavorful meat in the land.

Julen paid no attention to the meal, as she knew that none of this fare would be given to the servants. Instead, she let her mind drift to the other side of the table. Soon she felt the glaring eyes of Bina out of her peripheral vision and she knew she had done wrong. She was doing her best to learn the role of lady's maid from one who had been doing it for many years, but it was difficult not to turn her eyes toward the handsome son of the house. His green shirt in close proximity to his hazel eyes and face, with its fine features, was too great a temptation. How could she not stare and imagine his face turning toward her with a smile? But Bina would make sure that she did not go far wrong in her behavior.

As Julen shifted her line of vision away from Damon, she saw that Nichola was just about to speak to her father. Julen wanted to warn her that it was hopeless but, of course, she had to remain silent. A brief syllable was all that came from Nichola's mouth when her father cut her off and shot a question to his son.

"Now, with one batch of nonsense out of the way, we move to the next. Damon, are you going to tell us about your latest fancy—your proposed voyage?"

Nichola's ears turned red and her eyes flashed with offense. Julen suspected that the question was a trap and wondered how Damon would handle it.

"I wish to accompany a shipment of weapons aboard the Mirage. We have lost much due to *mishandling*," replied Damon, emphasizing the last word spoken. "I think my going along might assure that the goods actually arrive!" braved Damon to his father in front of the guests. The muscles in his face were contorted and he found the words difficult to utter. Julen could see him brace himself for the next volley.

"My misguided boy…how noble of you. Do you, for a moment, think you could stop a pirate ship, or deal with rogue seamen on such a voyage? Are you not but a puny runt of a lad compared to the lot you will travel with?" Master Chiselstone laughed in derision. "And what's more, I hear you plan to…work…WORK…on board?" Chiselstone looked around at his audience and gained the response he sought. Everyone at the table broke up into wild laughter. Damon ground his teeth together with hardened jaw.

"And have you ever encountered the fierce Leviathan?" continued the master, with his hands raised like the front legs of a monster about to strike and his face shaped in a hideous grin. "Leviathan, God of the Sea and, therefore, god of all prosperity, is not to be trifled with."

The master rose, wobbling from side to side from his strong drink, and pointed for all to look at the belt buckle with the dragon image. The guests emitted nervous chuckles and forced smiles. "I suppose you could throw one of your books at him," the master blustered with fresh laughter and dropped back into his chair.

Mistress Chiselstone's head rose from staring at her meal. She had heard all the conversation. The attack on her favorite child was not to be born. She was not going to let her boy be bullied by his father. The master saw the tightening of her face as she opened her mouth to speak. He was too quick for her.

"And tell us all when you plan to make this voyage, my inexperienced offspring," Chiselstone looked around the room to make sure everyone present heard the request.

Damon hesitated, as he knew that the next shipment would take weeks of travel and would possibly be endangered by an early storm season. The seas would be rough and challenging for one so young and untrained. He had been on voyages before, but it was with calm conditions and of short duration. He loved the sea but had to admit that he had never really seen it in all its varieties of behavior.

"I know what I am doing. For one thing, that whole Leviathan legend was just made up to scare little boys. I am no longer a little boy, in case you hadn't noticed."

All motion froze while the icy words still hung in the air. It was dangerous, indeed, to make such statements about a god, especially when one is in the Chiselstone line of business.

"Sooner or later I must learn more about shipping, don't you agree? This seems like a perfect opportunity to learn. And why not do the work of a sailor? Someone in this household should be working and not throwing away their fortune at gaming tables all day long!" Eyebrows were raised all around the table, waiting for the master's response.

"Ho, boy! Are you not aware that my gaming has put a fine roof over your head! Huh? Look around you. Arcana! Taken from under the nose of Lord Arcane himself!" The guests fawned and fussed over the master and his great talents, trying to divert any further outbursts.

Damon fought to subdue an angry wave full of dredged debris building inside him. This wasn't the time or place for it to crash upon the present company, he knew, but this was too much for him to endure.

Another at the table saw the growing intensity and interrupted the interchange before the next escalation. "What a wonderful idea, Damon. Before long, your father will have to be looking for things to do. He will have so much spare time once you have taken over more of the business." Violencia shifted her gaze toward the large figure to her left and again placed her small hand on his beefy fist.

Mistress Dismalia grimaced and closed her eyes. Julen saw the mistress struggling for words, but no words came from her mouth. Bina had told her that the law of the land dictated that Harrasster Chiselstone was bound to his wife even if they no longer spoke to each other. *What did Mistress Mortifa stand to gain by treating Mistress Chiselstone this way?* she wondered.

Dismalia had eaten very little, as she had lost her appetite. Rising, she pushed back her chair just as Damon spoke in a sudden rage. The two servants were distracted by the outburst from the son, but managed to jump forward to help their charge with the chair.

"I plan to go and will prepare the cargo in the next few days. You can continue blathering about festivals while I at least attend to what is important!" Leaving his plate of food half-eaten and knocking over his tankard of ale, he rose and pushed aside his chair. As he turned to stomp out of the room, he rushed right into the tall, thin figure whose attention was on the mistress. She saw him coming, but he was so intent on leaving in a hurry, there was no time to get out of the way. Damon lost his balance for a moment but regained his footing. The impact sent Julen flying backward grasping for anything she could catch to stay upright. This turned out to be Bina, who also fell, together toppling onto each other on the hard stone floor with arms and legs flailing in all directions.

Damon's fierce anger would not allow him to stop, but in that brief moment, his eyes met Julen's and saw the hurt and terror there. Memories flooded him and he saw again the scene from his childhood, those haunting eyes—the small, pitiful girl shivering in the cold on the slave block. He pulled his eyes away and rushed past, fighting the pang of conscience. *This is no time to worry about servants,* he thought to himself.

Master Chiselstone, Violencia, and the guests laughed until their sides hurt and tears rolled down their faces. Composing himself once again, the head of the household said, "Where were we? Oh yes...what will I do with all my spare time?"

CHAPTER 6

Discovery in the Closet

Having risen from her chair, the offended wife stepped over the fumbling figures, shooting indignant glances as they rose and straightened their clothing. Julen and Bina stepped out of the way to let her pass and then turned to follow, looking sheepish and pathetic. Julen could hear the laughter, and her eyes filled with stinging tears. How could she have gotten herself into such trouble? The vision of a life of scrubbing endless floors loomed before her.

Down the corridor, the threesome walked, heading toward Dismalia's apartment. The sounds of swishing gown followed by rumpled muslin were all that could be heard as the servants crept behind their mistress. Julen was limping from pain in her leg; she imagined the sight of a bruise that must be forming from her collision and fall. Bina, inspecting her apron, which had been torn in the scuffle, cast a menacing look out of the corner of her eyes as she ran her fingers over the damage.

All at once, Dismalia stopped her forward movement, and Julen, preoccupied with her pain, almost had a second collision for the evening. She caught herself, just in the split second before disaster. Bina let out an exasperated sigh and bit her lip. Still staring at the stones, the two servants heard the mistress speak.

"Good evening, Coldstone," came Dismalia's quavering voice.

"Mistress," grumbled the head housekeeper, Obdura Coldstone, as she fondled her heavy set of iron keys. "I heard the news of your unfortunate experience. Of course, we know it was these two incompetent, undeserving wretches you call your servants that caused this whole thing," she hissed and cast the two a look that would just as soon have them both hanged.

Julen's cheeks burned with the heat of indignation. Why were they being blamed? Wasn't it the master on whom the servants should heap insults? She remained with bowed head, unable to see the look from the head housekeeper. She heard enough in her voice to know that punishment awaited them.

"Ah, yes…an unfortunate accident," Dismalia returned, still recovering her composure after the insult of the dining room. Coldstone's patronizing smile melted into contempt.

"I know that the servants are under your care and observation at all times, but these two are my responsibility. If they deserve to be punished, I shall make sure that it is carried out. You needn't trouble yourself. You may go back to your duties," said Dismalia. Both servants shut their eyes and exhaled with relief.

"Right enough, Mistress," Obdura intoned in false agreement then brushed past them on Bina's side. "But if you need my help giving them what they deserve, I am here at your call. Good evening." The sound of clinking keys and the rustling skirts faded behind them.

Inside the apartment, Julen and Bina lit the lamps from the night candle left for them, then stood cowering as the mistress turned to face them.

"I could punish you both for the shocking display in the dining room. Because of your lack of proper attention, you caused a commotion that was completely unacceptable."

"I'm terribly sorry, Mistress." Julen stammered.

"Silence, girl! I know what I saw. My son was wronged. And, of course, the responsibility for this lies with the person who made him angry." Dismalia closed her eyes and put her hand to her head to soothe the ever-present pain.

"And we both know, I can't afford to let you go," she said looking at Bina as if they held some secret between them. The senior servant smiled in a half-hearted way hoping the danger was past.

"Coldstone means well. She knows my suffering." Dismalia continued with a decided note of anger and more massaging of her temple.

"I may let this incident go. Never let anything like this happen again," she warned. The servants bowed and whispered their thanks.

Turning away from them, Dismalia snapped her fingers again and commanded, "Prepare my bath."

Bina called for fire to heat the mistress' bath while Julen stepped into the private salon to light perfumed candles. Julen knew a long soak in her pool would calm the mistress' nerves.

"Sing to me, Bina," commanded Dismalia; Bina began to croon some mournful tune Julen had never heard.

Our lives are dreary and our days are long
Soon it will be over and there'll be no more song,
And though our hearts are lonely and the ache is sore,
Soon it will be over and we will know no more....

Though the song was not cheerful, the clear, high soulful notes drifted on the night air and took the chill off Dismalia's cold chamber as they waited for the pool to heat.

Having learned the routine that the mistress expected, Julen took Dismalia's gown and proceeded to hang it in the closet. Outside the bed-chamber, she limped far back in the dark room where Bina had shown her the place this particular gown was to be hung. Reaching that place, she felt around in the dim light. With the oil lamp in one hand and the gown slung over her arm, she felt along the familiar wall for the empty space. Finding it, she placed the lamp on the floor while she hung the dress and prepared to return to the bed chamber. Temptation overtook her and she picked up the lamp, raising it higher while looking over the many magnificent items that belonged to the wealthy woman. The light caught the sparkling treasure of stones that ornamented scarves, belts, shoes, and gowns. It was almost overwhelming to see such beautiful things there in the dark—things that would never again see the light of day unless Mistress Chiselstone had a change of heart and ventured outside her room more often. They would stay secluded in this room, hidden away with no one to appreciate them.

Julen ran her hand over a row of sashes hanging in the very back of the room and, as she did, one fell to the floor. She snatched it up and was about to rehang it when she noticed in the place from which it had fallen, a three-fingered hinge. Her curiosity surged and she let the sash drop once again to the floor. She raised her hand to brush aside the other sashes to see if there were other hinges top and bottom. Finding three in a row, she knew that there had to be a handle or latch somewhere within reach. Sure enough, she felt a door handle under one of the sashes just a short distance to the right.

She was due back in the bedchamber so couldn't stay long. The presence of a hidden door pulled at her to the point she thought she would burst if she didn't open it. But there was no time and, if she was caught, she knew toiling over floors would look good compared to what she would face. She re-hung the sash and retreated.

"Pleasant dreams, Mistress," Bina attempted a soothing tone but found her panic difficult to hide. Dismalia smiled as one expecting ecstasy and replied, "Ah, yes…wonderful dreams!"

Lifting the small silver tray, she backed away and turned toward the interior wall. Julen entered just as Bina was lowering the tapestry and smoothing it out. Coming alongside Bina, Julen whispered, "When will you show me how to prepare the mistress' bed time drink?"

Bina turned toward her and Julen looked into her face. A change had come over her countenance. Her eyes were wide with alarm and her cheeks were fiery red. Fearing that she had done yet something else wrong, Julen, cowering, asked, "What's wrong? What have I said now?"

"Don't ask," Bina whispered holding a finger up to her mouth and shooting a quick glance back at the figure in the bed. Mistress Chiselstone was almost asleep, but awake enough to overhear the sibilant sounds.

"Wonderful dreams…" she slurred with a short chuckle, and then silence. Soft snoring followed and they knew the Dismalia would not trouble anyone until morning.

Julen waited for more of a reply as she could see that something was wrong. Bina just shook her head in her characteristic way and muttered, "What has he done?"

"What has who done?" asked Julen. Bina closed her eyes and continued to mutter, "No, no. I'll kill him when I find him."

There was silence in the room for several minutes. Bina said no more, but continued her nervous pacing.

"Bina," Julen continued to whisper even though they both knew the Dismalia would not hear. "I found something in the mistress' closet."

"What are you doing rummaging around in the closet? That is NOT part of your work. You find only what the mistress tells you to find. Do you hear me?" Bina spat out the words as emphatically as she could muster without speaking loudly. She grabbed Julen by the arm and pulled her out of the chamber. She gave the wooden door a gentle nudge to close it, trying not to let the squeaky hinges disturb the sleeper.

Bina resumed her tirade. "Haven't you made enough trouble for one night? It is wonder we aren't on our way to the gallows after your little stunt." Her round figure lunged forward with each phrase, both hands raised in the air. Her fierce, hardened look frightened Julen, who thus far had never seen her in such a rage. Bina burst into tears and headed for the sitting room crying, "It's gone. He has stolen it!"

"Did Jip steal something?"

"This is the last time. His life is over," raged Bina. "And so is mine!"

Chapter 7
A Night on the Town

Jip smiled with an evil grin. It was hard to hide his amusement and excitement. He was about to meet his friends and what a tale he had to tell. They had bet him that he did not have the nerve to go into the great house and into the very bedchamber of Dismalia Chiselstone. But he had done it with ease, and only his mother would know what he had done. He was not afraid of her. He would stay out of her way for a while and she would forget all about it.

Brown eyes that darted back and forth under a shock of tousled light-brown hair hinted at the impatient energy he possessed. His soiled work clothes were frayed and outgrown. He was strong and fit, and prided himself on his ability to make his way in the world, whether by brute strength or by cunning. Being born into the Netherian class should have ended all his independent thoughts. Instead, he acted as if no man would ever own him. He was enslaved to a master for the work that had to be done, but Jip had learned to navigate the rough waters of slave life to his advantage, and did so at every opportunity. None of his class would dare challenge him, though most thought him mad for taking the chances that he did.

"Jip, you brick head!" other slaves yelled at him. "Why the foolish stunts? You will be caught some day and then what?" Laughing at the warnings, he pursued even more danger.

In a small bag under his tunic, he held a small treasure that would yield him enough in coins to enjoy life for some time to come. In his real life, he was paid a minimal amount to stay alive. Jip had already made up his mind that the men who now controlled his life would not have the privilege for long. He would show them all someday that he was made for a better life than this.

He waited outside the Rock Rat Inn at the corner of the building. When he saw several young men approaching, he fell in with them, drawing alongside with a wink and a sly grin. They returned his look of triumph, smiled as if to proclaim, "You did it!" Jip shook his head in the affirmative and they all broke out in loud laughter, swaggering along the road like drunken men. They ducked inside the inn door and looked for a secluded place to sit. In the far corner, they found a spot and ordered ale to be brought to their table.

"So let's see it," Landon muttered, hardly daring to move his lips lest anyone learn their business. "Are you crazy?" asked Jip. "It's right here in my tunic, enough for all of us. Now who will be first to pay up?"

Each man reached into pockets and purses to produce coins, avoiding any clinking sounds that might draw attention. Collecting the coins one at a time, Jip stowed them in a cloth bag. The big moment arrived when he would divide the spoils. Jip brought out five more small bundles, each held in a square of rag and tied with rough string, distributing them into eager hands. The men sat hunched over the table, their faces close, emitting low murmurings and muffled laughter. Each cast sidelong glances over a shoulder, conscious that they may be attracting unwanted attention.

Pewter mugs of ale were brought by the grizzled Innkeeper, who glared suspiciously through his one good eye with a look that defied the young to make trouble in his establishment. He turned and left. Quietly, the men raised their cups at the center of the table and then drank to their friend for his daring success. Jip gloated and puffed up his chest like a war hero, and they all laughed again in unison.

From across the room, in another corner, there was one who saw their celebration. The dark figure was wrapped in a black cape and hat. He had come in after the others and seated himself in order to watch them. Being an experienced observer of men, he quickly saw that they were celebrating something secret. His curiosity rose and he knew that he would have to know what it was they were up to. Was he not the Chief of Intelligence in the town of Bellicosa?

Jip rose to leave. His friends pushed and shoved one another playfully and drifted toward the door with high spirits helped by the inn keeper's ale. Each went his own way out into the night. It was very late, but the sense of elation kept Jip alert as he made his way along the dark streets and alleyways until he reached the boarding house where he had a tiny ground floor room of his own, no bigger than a closet. *Here I am again in this rotten hole. Maybe now those lump heads will want my company more often*, he thought to himself, unaware of the silent, dark figure who watched his every step and marked the location of his dwelling.

Though it was late and Jip knew he must report to his duties at the iron blade works early in the morning, he could not resist taking just a small amount of the stolen powder. He brought out the bag and poured out a spoonful into water. He downed it with loud gulps hoping that it didn't taste bitter, and found instead that it was sweet. He squatted down on the floor where his disheveled bedding lay in a heap and waited for the effect of the substance to begin. He was not disappointed. Within a few minutes, he began to feel a sense of joy. He felt safe and warm, and suddenly very sleepy. He rolled over on the bed, not even undressing or straightening out the rumpled mess of blankets; he fell fast asleep.

Through a small, dingy window, the silent figure watched. He saw Jip take the powder and drift into peaceful slumber after drinking it. He recognized the effects of Koma and smiled, knowing that there were not many sources for this illegal powder. In fact, he knew of only one.

The dark figure searched the visible part of the room. He noted the rough-hewn door was only partially locked. With a bit of ingenuity, he thought, he could unfasten the door and secure the evidence. Stealthily, he pulled a twig from a bush close by and bent the soft wood around the edge of the door. Soon the latch raised enough to be pushed with his hand. With great care, he pushed the door open and entered. The sleeper would not be woken easily, as he was far too drugged to know anything until the light of dawn. The black cape glided past his hanging jaw, out of which loud snores were cast into the room. *The powder and the coins—what could be better than taking both to prove the crime?*

In a moment, he was gliding down the dark street, imagining the coins falling into his already vast collection, hidden deeply in the dark of his secret chamber. *Like taking from a child—too simple,* he thought to himself

Jip lay as one dead to the world, with a grin on his face, off in the land of dreams that were the sweetest of all imaginable, and they would be the last peace of mind and safety that Jip would know.

CHAPTER 8

Discovery

Julen retreated to her room weary after a long day. Bina's words weighed heavily as she crept up the dark flight of steps. Upon opening the creaking door, the light of a small oil lamp shone. Julen held up her candle to see the face of Ralda more clearly. She had not thought about her old friend and her needs for many hours. The old woman was sitting up in bed waiting.

"Ralda, my dear, I am sorry. I have forgotten about you for so long today. What a day it has been." Julen decided not to burden the old woman with the tales of the day. She needed nothing new to upset her or threaten her fragile hold on life.

Ralda looked weak and ghostly pale by the dim light. She had eaten all of the food that Julen and Noni had left for her. Julen helped her prepare for sleep and made her comfortable before seeing to her own needs. Before the light was blown out, Ralda said in her thin, reedy voice, "Don't forget Julen, my child. Don't forget."

What should she not forget? She couldn't remember what Ralda said. The worries of the night were enough. Julen wondered how she would sleep this night after Bina's dire warnings. What did Bina mean that their lives were over?

The next morning, the promised rain was falling and the day was cool and dreary. The whole routine began again, except that Julen managed to finish her work with Ralda before Bina came looking for her. She was determined to make it downstairs before being summoned. Gliding down the steps, skipping to the kitchen, she arrived to find that Bina was not there ahead of her. Perhaps she had not slept well, she thought. Julen stood there not knowing what to do.

"Don't believe all that hoity toity goings on with Bina," said Bessie out of the corner of her mouth in a raspy voice. From the other side of the kitchen, she waddled over to Julen, her apron already soiled from cutting up the leftover leg of bobbit from last evening's meal.

"She's an orphan, she is. Just like you." Julen felt a pang in her stomach at the word *orphan*.

"Goes on and on about being the daughter of servants. They died on her they did. Got sick with the plague and died. She was sick too for a long time but she came out of it. Ah, she's a fighter, that one."

Julen was shocked at this sudden revelation about Bina's background. "Did her parents work here at Arcana?"

"No, no, nothin' high class like that. She was won in a game by the master, she was," whispered the old cook. "He's got a real weakness for that sort of thing."

Julen had seen over the years how much time the master spent in his private library with his men friends. She had heard how Arcana had been obtained in a similar way from the prominent family who had owned it for many generations. The master was obsessed with gambling. So delighted was he to obtain the house as part of his winnings that he did not change its name to his own. The house, with its history and name, became a trophy of his prowess.

A scuffling was heard and Bina arrived in the kitchen looking drawn and tired. Her eyes were bloodshot and she staggered to the table. The food was put before her, but she pushed it away in disgust. She was too upset to eat.

"Bina, are you ill?" asked Julen. Bina did not respond but hung her head in despair. Julen waited for several minutes, but the stout woman remained slumped over the table. Bessie winked knowingly at Julen and began to wrench apart joints of meat for her stew.

Finally, Julen prepared to leave, for it was time to be in the mistress' chamber. Bina followed, limply dragging her feet. Tears welled up in her reddened eyes and she looked as if she were being led away to the gallows.

"Master Damon. It is time to rise," Shale, Damon's personal servant, declared loudly once he had drawn the heavy drapes and lit several lamps to brighten the room. Damon woke and looked instinctively toward the window.

"Ah, rain and clouds. Not what I hoped for today but the next few months will be sunny and hot for my voyage, don't you think?"

"Yes, Master Damon."

"I've thought it through, you know…and we should be back well before the bad weather of autumn arrives."

"Yes, Master Damon," came the monotonous reply.

"Speaking of storms, I don't suppose you heard about last night." Shale detected the anger and dismay in the young man's voice.

"Yes, Master Damon. I have heard of it."

"Nothing I do makes my father happy. He will be sorry some day, because I plan to succeed where he has failed. I'll show him."

"Hmmm," replied Shale.

"They had a pretty good laugh after I left. I could hear them all the way up the stairs. My father would have me look foolish and I guess I gave him the opportunity he wanted," Damon continued, trying to get some more revealing response from Shale, but the tight-lipped servant nodded his head in disciplined subservience.

"Yes, Master." This time Damon was sure he had detected understanding in the servant's voice. This, in itself, was a comfort to one who had few friends he could trust.

"Did you hear about the part where I sent the pair of my mother's servants flying?" he asked, knowing there would be little returned. He gave a brief laugh before the picture came back to him—those eyes, the pitiful girl cowering on the floor. He felt a pang of shame and embarrassment but dismissed it.

"Oh, well. They must be used to being knocked around, don't you think? And that other bunch at the table, none but my father's lackeys who bow and scrape to earn his favor all the day long." Damon cast a sideways glance at Shale, whose face muscles tensed.

"I don't know what to think of my mother. She looks so sad these days. She used to be so active and alive. Now she is like one that's dead, but still moving, keeping to herself, cutting herself off from the family. What happened, I wonder, to make her this way?"

Shale did not reply. Damon had hoped to find out more from the trusted servant, but it was not to be. They both knew the answer already.

"Help me dress, Shale," said Damon, changing the subject. "On a day like this, who wants to fret about such things?"

Thoughts about business to be done, people to meet, and places to go displaced his negative thoughts and filled him with exuberance and energy.

"I think the white, loose shirt, Shale." said Damon wanting just the right touches for his new adventure.

"Here are your shooting breeches, Sir." said Shale. "Which boots would you prefer today?"

When the outfit was complete, Damon declared with pride, "I will wear my sword." He motioned to his servant to bring the sheathed weapon and fasten it around his waist. With raised eyebrows, but studied disinterest, Shale obeyed his master. The young man looked into the polished metal mirror, positioning the prominent Chiselstone trademark so it could be seen. Being thoroughly satisfied with the whole look, Damon gulped down the breakfast on his morning tray and headed for the door.

Today was one of those days he could have slid down the grand banister if he hadn't been afraid of old Obdura Coldstone, who was likely lurking somewhere with a broom to swat him away. It was almost worth it but, as he now heard voices in the Great Hall below, perhaps this was not the time.

One voice belonged to his father, he was sure. Wishing to avoid additional abuse, Damon changed his plan. He darted to the right and went to the end of the long upstairs corridor. Around another corner, there was a back stairway that led down to the kitchen. He would make his escape and not give any cause for more of his foolish father's jests or insults.

Just as he arrived in the kitchen, he recognized the two women who were leaving, though their backs were turned to him. *What a pair,* he thought. The tall, slender one was limping. *Another change of plans,* he said to himself, and sought to duck out the kitchen door.

"Those were pretty dangerous words from an upstart like you," called out Bessie from the counter. She swung her cleaver down with a thud on the wooden block. Noni shuddered as she pulled bread from the oven.

"Well, Bessie, what words would those be?" asked the young master, who knew the cook well after years of flattering and coaxing her to reward him with extra snacks. "Word travels in this house, Master Damon. Let me tell you that gods are not to be trifled with. You don't know them, but they know you. Watch out!" she warned. Damon smiled and kept on going through the door.

"Old women!" he muttered.

Julen and Bina had to cross the Great Hall to get to Mistress Chiselstone's quarters down the long corridor. The two walked unnoticed past the present company, their gray uniforms blending into the gray floor and wall. Violencia was, at that moment, sweeping in from the dining room with the twins, one on each side. The servants could not help but overhear the conversation.

"Oh, Alumina, darling, don't worry if that mean papa of yours won't buy you a new dress," she added, tipping her head to one side. She knew Harrasster was within a distance to hear, and hoped he had heard. Violencia was confident that she had not lost her powers of beguiling any man she chose; and she chose Master Chiselstone.

"What's that I hear?" he asked with a wry smile, turning away from his visitors toward the brightly dressed woman who accompanied his daughters.

"Why, look! It's the enchanting Violencia herself come to brighten our cold, wet morning. What can I do for you, Lency, my dear?" he added with a wink and a bow and all the appearance of a good nature.

"Good morning, Harrasster. My dear friend here tells me that you won't let these daughters of yours have new gowns for the ball. That can't be true can it? Doting father?" Violencia asked, knowing just how to make herself the most attractive and influential.

"However did you come by that information, dear lady? Would one such as I deprive my sweet daughters of anything their hearts desired for such an important occasion?" came the reply with oily smoothness. "Why don't you help them choose something in the town? There is a very fine shop they already know," he said, glaring at the two girls, "in which I am sure they will find the right dresses."

"Brilliant!" cried Violencia who held the master in her gaze. "Oh, girls, your father is the finest man I know. I knew he would not let you down when so much depends on your beauty at this season of your lives!" The girls looked at each other with amazed glee.

"Yes, beauty...season of their lives...of course," and he turned back to speak to the black-caped man before him who was waiting for the master's attention.

"Now, Chief Legerdemain, gentlemen, shall we get on with our game?" Master Chiselstone asked as he drew away his visitors toward his private library.

The two entered the suite and went about their usual duties. Julen pulled back the drapes. It was all so strange. Bina was exhausted and could not keep up with her work. When it was time for Dismalia to get up from her bed, she was already awake and visibly tense and angry.

"Bina, where are you? What is the meaning of this?" she stammered having awakened wracked with pain and discomfort.

At last, Bina had no choice but to speak up and confess to her mistress the reason for her less than pleasant night of dreams and miserable awakening.

"I am sorry! I have to report a theft of your property. When I went to prepare your tea last evening, I noticed that your powders were reduced to a very small amount. That is why you are not well this morning, no doubt." Bina said in a barely audible voice.

"WHAT?" screeched Dismalia from her bed. "WHAT have you done? You wretch, you fiend! You will hang. You will be torn limb from limb!" she bellowed but then caught herself and closed her mouth; she had remembered that no one in the house knew about the powder except Bina. If she made a fuss, they would all hang together. She broke out in loud wailing and buried her head in pillows.

"Why didn't you tell me last night? WHO?" she cried. "Does someone know about my koma?" At the mention of the name, a tiny flash of recognition registered in Julen's mind. Had she heard this word before? Bina's mind was searching for answers. "Mistress, I am as ignorant as you. I do not know who could have done this. No one knows of this, not even this humble wretch at my side." Julen, on cue, flashed a look of complete surprise and innocence, though she was now troubled at a strange familiarity.

"I shall never sleep again! I must know who did this. Who knows? I am in mortal danger, do you understand? And you both are as well!" she screamed at them. "We must let no one know of this but watch everyone. Has Coldstone had any access to my chambers?" she asked in a hysterical voice.

"Not to my knowledge," coughed Bina, who was now choking on her own hysteria.

CHAPTER 9
Faded Dreams

Blurred vision and a dull ache greeted Jip as he surfaced in the middle of the morning. The faint memory of fantastic dreams could still be brought back, but soon faded as the reality of the morning sunk into his brain. What time was it? The day had begun; it was dull and rainy outside his window. He groaned at what he knew would result from his truancy. He had to face the punishment or risk something even worse—prison! Such a small thing it seemed to be late for work. Jip was all too aware that his status at the iron works was as low as one can get. He eked out an existence in his tiny quarters, even managed to have a social life. But at the end of the day, his services were claimed exclusively by a powerful and cruel master. He had cut it too fine this time and trouble awaited him.

The inside of his mouth tasted bitter, so he drank from a cask of wine he had stashed under his low bed. Finding no relief, he brushed away a gang of busy cockroaches then gnawed at a hunk of stale bread he had left on the table the night before. As he tore into it, he looked around for the bag of coins and his envelope of powder. What had he done with it? Jip tossed bedding into the air and brushed aside the crusty remains of his meal, but could not find either the coins or the powder.

Impossible, he thought. *Was I so overcome by the powder? It has to be here somewhere. Oh, this is a waste! I had better look later.* He fled as fast as possible to the iron blade factory. He dreaded the blows of the whip, or worse, but there was no way around it. *What an amazing night of dreams,* he thought, and was surprised to find that he could remember none of them. Then he began to think about how and when he would risk taking the powder again. The thought of it gave him the courage to face the day.

"Well, well. Looks who's showing up to work late." The guard at the gate of the factory recognized Jip and hated him. He knew Jip was one of those who defied authority and pushed the limits. He knew as well what awaited the errant worker, and opened the gate with a flourish to let him in.

Inside, a task master grabbed his arm and checked the number on his wrist band. When the number was duly registered, he shoved Jip toward the guard who held the whip.

"Twenty lashes for the brute who shows up when the work is half done!" he shouted to the enforcer. With teeth clenched, Jip bore the lashes though he felt he would die. When at last it was over, he had now to endure the day's work with his back laid open and bleeding.

With each swing of his heavy hammer on the anvil, he groaned with pain while imagining the face of the master on the metal surface. When that no longer yielded any relief, he began to go over plan after plan for escaping. This occupied his thinking throughout the rest of his shift. By the end of the day, thinking about the wondrous powder made him long to sail away on the sea of dreams like he had the night before. *Perhaps just a bit more this night would help ease the pain and if I take it early,* he thought, *I won't sleep so late.*

"Whatever you did to earn that beating was not worth it," said his work mate quietly as they were headed out into the dusty street. Jip shook his head and weighed in his mind the pain and the pleasure; his wretched servitude and the magic of temporary escape. He shoved the negative thoughts to be back of his mind in favor of the notion that soon he would be home and find what he had misplaced.

CHAPTER 10
The Hidden Room

Julen had been stunned by the turn of events. The unsettled chaos had been rivaled by the wonderful discovery.

The powder, the deep sleep, and Bina, right in the middle of a crime; the mistress burying her sorrows and pain in an unreal and temporary world of dreams—what else could go wrong? Julen had heard about such things from the cooks in the kitchen. They always knew what was happening in the kingdom. Julen was sure they had informed her that the king, who saw koma as a way to escape from work and true loyalty, had banned its possession. The royal family alone qualified for the privilege to use such "medications."

"Is there none left?" cried the desperate woman.

"Mistress, I can find none in the usual place. I may have a small amount in a second hiding place," she said hesitating to judge the reaction of this revelation. Bina had not told anyone, but she had put aside some of the powder for her own use.

"You must bring it now!" she demanded. "Where is it?" Dismalia launched herself from her bed as if propelled by a spring; with dilated eyes and outstretched arms, she jerked forward. Bina shrank back and contemplated her next move. She did not want to divulge her hiding place but now had no choice. She turned and, with difficulty, pushed a chest from its place next to a stone wall. With a small pick hidden in her clothes, she teased out a smaller stone placing it on the floor. Reaching into the space, she pulled out a pouch with a drawstring.

"Give it to me!" the mistress bawled. She grabbed at it, but realized that she was shaking too hard to prepare the drink. She threw it back at Bina and commanded her to mix the potion. There was no thought about what would come after that, there was just the urgency of the moment, as her body felt the pangs of hunger for the tranquilizing effect to begin and her terror to cease.

Bina was also beside herself with terror and foreboding. She too was in the midst of craving, having given up her regular dose of the mistress' supply the night before. Bina turned her back to prepare the secret drink making sure none saw how much was in the bag. There would be enough to last for quite some time if she was careful.

With trembling hands, Bina measured the powder. "Hurry!" yelled Dismalia. Bina tilted the bag and shook it. All at once, a large amount spilled into the water, dissolved, and turned the liquid a faint yellow. Her whole body shook as she watched the drink disappear. Dismalia consumed half then paused to give a loud belch. Bina's eyes bulged with thirsty passion. She grabbed the cup and, without hesitation, finished what remained.

Julen stood in awe and disbelief at the behavior of the two women. Mistress Chiselstone fell back on the bed in peace at last. Bina stumbled to the sitting room, crumpled onto the divan into the plush cushions and passed into a land of bliss.

Standing in the middle of the sitting room, having followed Bina there, Julen was at a loss.

"Bina, wake up! What are we to do? You can't sleep now. We may be in danger!" pleaded Julen to no avail. She dropped down on the divan and tried to think. Both women were asleep and would be for some time.

The tiny bell suspended above the door jumped, sending its tinkling sound to shake Julen out of her thoughts. She leaped up and began straightening and stacking pillows to cover Bina. She opened the door the width of the breakfast tray. "Here you go, scrubby," Noni teased. She raised her eyebrows with a questioning look when the door was not opened further, but thought no more of it and left.

"Thank you!" Julen said, trying to hide her panic. Shutting the door, she realized that there was no one to eat the breakfast and it would look strange to send the tray back still loaded with food. She sat down and began to take a bite here and there, and finally consumed it all with delight. Trouble or no trouble, the stolen morsels were like none she had ever before eaten.

Julen closed her eyes and savored the final crumbs. Her reverie was interrupted by the nagging thought, *What should be done next?* Should she run away and hope never to be found? Being unable to think of any location to run to, she concluded that it was not a good idea. Her mind turned to what would happen when the two awoke. Julen had had no part in the crime. Would anyone believe her? She had to stay in the room, as leaving early would spark curiosity and questions. She sat for some time waiting for something to come to her and hoping the knot in her stomach would disappear. The image of a dark door crept unbidden into her thoughts. *The secret door. What was behind it?* She tried to think of something else, but an indelible image had been left there and it wouldn't go away. Julen stood, checked on the sleepers, and then proceeded to the closet. She hesitated and went inside.

It was dark. There was no means to light the lamp during the day as the light was passed out by the maids in the evening. She saw that she would have to feel her way along and hope for the best.

With arms held out in front of her, she groped at the gowns and sashes once again. Reaching the back, Julen felt along the wall until the hinges were again under her fingertips. Moving to the right, she reached the other side of the hidden door. There it was—a small handle. She turned it, producing a rusty, grinding sound, as if it had not been opened in a very long time. She pushed gently but nothing happened. She pushed harder and then harder still. Finally, the door yielded to her strength and flew forward until it hit the inside wall with a bang and stopped. She grabbed it to muffle the sound, but it was too late. She stood still, suppressed a cough from the heavy dust, and waited to hear if anything stirred outside the closet. All was quiet.

Inside, there was solid blackness. Julen's eyes began to adjust and a vague outline appeared. She leaned forward and felt a cold stone wall in front of her. She searched with her hands until she determined that there was a stairway leading upward to her right. A chill passed over her as she contemplated going up the stairs. Where might they lead? What if she was discovered by one of the house servants? Julen took a deep breath and began going up one stone step at a time until she stood at the top. A faint light revealed a door open the width of an arm. She crept in after pushing it open all the way. The light came from a narrow window built into the stone wall.

Looking around, she saw what appeared to be an ancient study room. There was a desk and books. The closer she looked, the more she noticed. Some of the books were on shelves, and some were scattered about on the floor as if thrown. Torn pages lay crushed on the desk. The chair was overturned and broken in pieces. A blackened splash dripping tentacles of oil marred the wall behind the desk while cobwebs and dust obliterated the crumpled remains of a lamp and wick that rested below the stain.

Julen felt a chill of fear as she gazed over what must have been a violent scene when the final occupant departed from the room. What had these old plaster covered walls seen? A tapestry hung on the far side of the room. Here at least was something that had not been disturbed. A brown fuzz of dust obscured the picture. Julen raised one corner and gave it a shake. She waved away the cloud of dust and coughed. As it cleared, she beheld a familiar image—the green dragon, Leviathan, god of the sea. She hated the sight of it, for it was an ugly, threatening creature, covered with green scales, menacingly rearing its head, with teeth bared and claws ready to strike, its tail long and curled. The eyes were wide open like the other images of this creature she had seen scattered around the Chiselstone estate—intimidating, powerful, red eyes. She did not want to stare long at it, as she felt it wanted to jump off the wall and tear into her flesh.

When she had lifted the edge to shake the needlework picture, something had caught her eye underneath. Again, she picked up the edge and held it higher this time. On the wall behind, someone had painted strange characters. She removed the tapestry altogether in order to get a better look, hoping no one would come inside this room to discover her brazen act. Standing on the corner of the desk, she managed to detach it from the pegs driven into plaster between stones of the wall. She lowered the wall hanging and looked at the swirling characters. They formed words written in a form that was, at first, difficult to decipher. She was not an educated person, having learned to read only a little from her father when she was young. She tried to make out the words.

CRY OUT TO THE ONE.
YEA, CRY OUT AND HE WILL RESCUE.

℔

How strange, thought Julen, as a nervous tremor rattled through her body. The word "rescue" pulled at her spirit and the pain of her slavery pushed her down again. The symbol at the bottom looked like initials of the one who had painted the message. *What is the meaning of this? Who painted these words and then covered them with the fearsome Leviathan?*

With mixed emotions, she replaced the tapestry as best she could, noting that she had left fingerprints of dust on the wall. She looked around for a cloth or something to wipe them off but could find nothing for the job. Thinking that no one was going to find this room for many years to come, she felt some measure of safety in leaving things as they were.

Her eyes were drawn to the books on the floor with their various bind-ings, shapes, and sizes. She had not seen any books like this since she was very small in her father's house. Bending down, Julen touched the books and ran her fingers over the rich covers. She felt the raised print of the titles. Her hand stopped on one volume that carried a strange symbol. Turning to the wall, she saw that the markings were the same—"♍."

Opening to the middle, she beheld the strange hand-written pages. After attempting to read it, she realized that she had forgotten too much. The words were very unusual and seemed to be in another language, or perhaps the language of more educated people. She longed to be able to decipher the words, feeling that they held secrets locked away long ago. Julen wondered if perhaps more sense could be made of it after further study, and concluding this, blew as much dust away as she could and then slipped the volume into her apron pocket.

She took a last look around and backed out of the room, leaving the door at the top of the stairs open to provide light for her descent. When she reached the bottom, she pulled the door in the closet closed. In the dark, she felt around to make sure all the sashes were hung as usual and nothing else seemed to be disturbed.

Entering the sitting room once again, she saw Bina splayed out on the divan looking like she was in a heaven of unaccustomed comfort. Before long, it would be time for the mid-day meal and Noni would again be com-ing around. Could she once again receive it without opening the door all the way? Would this not signal that something was wrong? Julen decided to drag Bina into the next room and so launched into the task. The sleeping servant did not resist but uttered dream induced mumbling, "Over here, no over there, perfect!" Even in her dreams, Bina was in charge.

Julen was very strong for her slender size and had no trouble sliding Bina along the floor into the bedroom. She placed some pillows under her head and left her, closing the door. They would awake to find each other and no doubt start the whole wailing, screaming tirade again.

No sooner had this been accomplished than ringing again signaled a visitor. It wasn't quite time for the meal, but Julen, having removed the one obvious clue to the debacle, could open the door with increased confidence.

On the other side of the great door, Julen could see through the small window that it was Coldstone herself jingling her iron keys.

Oh, help, help! What will I say, she worried as the door opened up to the ice-blue stare of the head housekeeper.

"Is everything in order?" she asked looking around Julen to get a glimpse of the sitting room. There was nothing to see but the divan minus a few cushions. Julen tried to control her panic and replied, "Why yes, Ma'am. Mistress Chiselstone is taking a nap. She will wake soon and eat, thank you."

"I should like to speak with her," she continued with wrinkled brow.

"I am so sorry. That won't be possible. She is sleeping. Once she awakes it will take time to ready herself for visitors."

"Well then. Let her know that I request an audience with her when she is ready, will you please?" came the icy conclusion to their interchange. Taking a deep breath, Julen closed the window again to wait for lunch.

Julen enjoyed the lunch as much as she had the breakfast, hoping that the mistress would feel too ill when she awoke to eat. Sometime in the late afternoon, both women began to stir. Bracing herself for the next unavoidable disturbance, she looked around at how she might be more prepared. There was no way to ward off what was now about to happen.

CHAPTER 11

Preparation for a Journey

The fresh breeze blew in Damon's face as he made his way down the winding streets that led to the sea port below. The rain was clearing and the afternoon would be bright once again. He could have walked on such a day but decided at the last minute to ride his horse and avoid the drizzling rain. The distance was significant and the walk back up the hill would be difficult after a long day of working on his father's ship, the Mirage. A fine vessel it was. Once the men of the crew had made it ready for sailing, his adventure would begin.

He rejoiced at the thought of the voyage, though he knew he had a lot to learn. Hoping that the men would come to respect him for his efforts to learn the ropes, he anticipated that before long, he would be on deck with them pulling his weight.

Damon was a business man through and through. His father had inherited a small company that crafted knives for hunting. Master Chiselstone had shrewdly built it into a booming business, now producing not just knives but also swords, as well as many other implements of war. Their blades were so sharp and true that a single swing would take off the head of any enemy, even one in full armor. War was always a profitable business and the frequency of conflicts in and around Bellicosa had made the Chiselstones very wealthy.

But his father had let his other interests draw him away, his gambling habit being one. Damon was shocked that his father would take such risks and then let the business slide as he had done when there were still great things to be accomplished. He saw that his own ability and vision could take the stumbling business and again go forward to make it the greatest venture in the kingdom. Up and down the coast in every kingdom, within months of travel distance, all needed what Chiselstone blades had to offer—the means to compete in the game of war. What lay between that plan and the present was a few seafaring lessons and a great journey into the unknown. For so long, he had dreamed of sailing away from the town of Bellicosa in the land of Graystone, and it would come true at last.

Arriving at the docks, he dismounted and handed his horse off to a port servant in his father's employ.

"Eh, Captain, will ye be able to make a seaman out of the likes of him?" shouted a seaman noting Damon's odd attire. The young master had not heard the question but realized with a start that he felt out of place. The crew were dressed in rough woven shirts under a variety of dark colored vests. Damon removed his coat with its polished buttons, placed it out of harm's way, and pushed up his sleeves. His riding breeches, he could see, were a bad choice as well. There was little he could do about the outfit, so he presented himself to Captain Fairway for duty as he was.

"I know this is my father's ship and I am your master on this voyage. However, I wish to learn more about sailing. Will you please allow me to do that, Captain?" asked Damon. Fairway bore a look a suppressed amusement as he turned to the crew, "Master Chiselstone wishes to learn the sailing business. You do well to help him in this endeavor. Do I have your full cooperation?" Knowing this gentleman had their future in his hands, they agreed, even if they doubted there was much hope of his becoming tough enough to stand up to the rigors demanded.

"Right. You can start by hauling up that rope with the others here. We are still loading metal on board and it is mighty heavy," barked Fairway.

Damon jumped into action and pulled with all his might. After several loads were stowed, he could feel the muscles of his arms aching miserably. The crew joked and laughed with each other, but were careful not to offend the master. He took their lack of criticism as affirmation that he was improving in his skills.

Feeling elated by his small victory, Damon asked, "When do you think she will be ready to sail, Captain Fairway?" The Captain admired his pluck and said, "Oh, I think it will be before the hot weather begins, perhaps a few days. We should have good winds for the first few weeks, after that some calm. We must be on our way home by the end of summer. Can you do your business in that time, Sir?"

"We will do our business before then," said Damon with determination to become the master of his own ship.

CHAPTER 12

Tortured Souls

Julen slipped into the room where Dismalia had awakened and lay still in her bed. Tears slid down her cheek as the memory of the morning returned to her.

"Mistress, can I be of any help to you?"

"You wouldn't understand. I have to have that powder. It is the only way I can keep from losing my mind—what I have to endure! What will I do? How will I get more? It is very difficult."

"Pardon my asking, Mistress, but where did you get it before?" asked Julen without realizing the impudence of the question. Dismalia put her hands over her eyes and pressed against her temple.

"You are a slave, Julen. You do not know, nor should you know of these things. I have a connection. But I have to be careful. It is so hard to know who to trust." The mistress looked into Julen's face and saw that she was genuinely sympathetic, and was irritated.

"Where is Bina? She always knows what to do." Julen pointed to the floor where Bina was beginning to stir. Dismalia saw the sleeping form but could not understand why she was lying on the floor.

"Why is she asleep?" Julen did not want to be the one to tell the mistress that Bina had taken the rest of the drink for herself.

"Bina! Get up! What is the matter with you?" shouted the mistress. Bina looked up out of a hazy fog of sleep and tried to focus her eyes. Realizing that she was the center of unwanted attention, she tried to get up and resume a normal posture. Julen said nothing as Bina attempted to straighten her uniform and the body inside it.

Dismalia stared at Bina, putting the pieces of the puzzle together in her head. There was only one reason why Bina would be sleeping and all three knew what it was. "Bina? Who took my koma powder?"

"Mistress, I swear to you. I only used a little. I don't know who stole the rest!"

"Julen, was it you?"

"Mistress, I did not know about the powder until after it was gone."

Dismalia's shoulders slumped in despair realizing that the mystery remained.

"I will send a letter to my connection but he must not know that my powder has been stolen or we are all in danger of losing our heads." confessed Dismalia.

Jip staggered home along the crowded streets. The last hill was the worst, but he managed to open his door. As he did so, he looked down and saw the bent twig at his feet. He picked it up and realized what it had been used for. He shoved open the door and again searched the room. After assuring himself that he had missed nothing, he sat down in too much pain to move. He put his head down on the table and cried. Anger boiled up inside him and he slammed his fist down hard, and then immediately felt regret. Who could have done this? Had he imagined that he had a bag of coins and the powder? Someone had come in while he slept the sleep of the dead and stolen his long sought after prize. All the planning and cunning, all in vain. Perhaps someone had seen him enter the garden or the mistress' chamber. But who?

Tortured by the pain and by the burning questions in his brain, he did not sleep that night. There was no comfortable position in which to arrange his limbs, and his body craved the comfort of the substance he had discovered. His mind raced. There was only one solution to his whole miserable life.

CHAPTER 13
Ralda's Gift

Julen ran back to her room, exhausted after Dismalia's eyelids had finally given way and she had drifted into the fitful night's sleep. As she entered the dark room carrying her lamp to the bedside, she could see that Ralda's head was bowed and she looked pale and still. For a moment, Julen thought she had been too late. She knelt down beside the bed, thinking about the family below and about Bina. No one seemed to care.

Earlier in the day, she had seen Alumina and Nichola running up and down corridors squealing while Violencia played fairy godmother extraordinaire. Damon paid no attention, as his interest was the Mirage. Master Chiselstone watched for every chance to chat with Violencia, the two of them smiling and laughing.

Julen and Bina had gone about their duties to the very anxious mistress who would not dare come out of her rooms. She was terrified that they would see a change in her and know that something was amiss. Someone in the house knew about her secret and the mystery had unnerved her. Bina had been anxious all day, making mistakes and forgetting instructions, being mean and critical.

Julen held the cold leathery hands in hers and called her name. "Ralda, Ralda." A head jerked up slightly and her weak eyes opened. "My dear, you have come. I'm so glad. It is time. I'm sorry but I must go now and leave you," Ralda confessed.

Tears flowed from Julen's eyes and she buried her head on the old woman's shallow chest. "No, no, you can't. I won't let you go."

"My dear child, do not waste any time. I must tell you my secret now before it is too late. Remember I tried to tell you before?"

"Don't use your energy up on such things, Ralda."

"Nonsense, Child," came the rasping voice in the semi-dark. "For one, I must tell you the name Ralda is short for my real name. My name was... is Emerald. Yes, after the precious green jewel—very rare in these parts."

"Ralda...Emerald...what are you talking about?" asked Julen, thinking the old woman had lost her mind at the end of her life.

"Long ago, my child, before you came to the house, my life was different, not what you see now. I couldn't bare it. I escaped. Yes, I did. You wouldn't know it to see me now, would you?" She paused to catch her breath and then continued. "I won't bore you with the whole sad tale. It was fear, Julen. That is why I was caught and returned here. But there is one important part I have to tell you. Before that, I made it to the other side of the mountain. There I found a hiding place under the cleft in a huge rock. No one could see me. I didn't find it by myself, Julen. I had help," she gasped and stopped.

"Who helped you, Ralda?" asked the amazed Julen, as she tried to understand what her friend was talking about. Her ramblings seemed to make no sense. "Did someone escape with you?" Julen asked.

"No, Dear, it was him—him who rescues." The old servant was losing her strength and could not go on for some time. Julen waited patiently to hear the rest of the story, hoping that she would not go to sleep until the mystery was revealed. Julen thought that perhaps someone lived up there over the mountain, who helped people in distress who were traveling away from Bellicosa.

Emerald opened her eyes once more and tried to continue. "My time is coming. So sorry, Julen. Find my gift to you. It is here. Call out to him. He will...." She fell silent again.

"Who?" Julen puzzled. The curious writing in the closet jumped into her thoughts. What had it said? "Cry out to THE ONE," or something like that. Could this have been the one who lived up there? He must be a hermit. Perhaps he was known to the writer of the strange message in the mistress' closet as well as to Ralda. He must be very old, or dead, by this time. "Was it—'The One'?" asked Julen. Opening her eyes once again, Emerald looked at Julen and smiled. She then turned her gaze away, staring straight ahead, as if looking at something beyond her. Her smile broadened as she raised a shaky arm and reached out. Julen looked behind her and saw nothing. What did her friend see that she couldn't?

Her hand fell back to the bed and her eyes remained fixed. Emerald's head fell back to the side and she was gone. All was still for a moment until the weight of this precious woman's death was realized. Julen broke into loud sobs that shook her whole body.

"Please don't go. You are all I have. Please, please. I love you, Ralda!"

It was too late. Julen continued to weep until there seemed to be no more tears left in her. Her death was one thing, not unexpected, but Julen wondered why she had to die in such a state of confusion. *What was all that talk about at the end? Why was she trying to tell me to call out to someone for help? Was Ralda trying to encourage me to escape,* she asked herself.

Julen rested both of Ralda's hands over her chest and pulled the frayed quilt up over her face. It was too hard to look at the frail body lying there and to realize how empty her life would be now that there was no one who loved her and who she could love in return.

"Emerald...I shall remember you as Emerald, just as you told me. I know you must have been someone strong and brave long ago."

Julen stayed by the body of her friend for a long time, thinking over all the times they had together. She looked over the room and saw that there was little to remember her by. What was the gift she referred to? Julen began to move things around, searching for whatever it was. Under the bed, she found a small chest made from rough wood. It looked to have no value but, Julen thought, *perhaps it holds some memento of Emerald.*

The clasp was very old, thinly worked metal and broke off in her hand. She lifted the lid and made an alarming discovery. It was a broken wristband of bright copper metal, ornately decorated. It was the kind reserved for slaves of very high rank. It had been snapped and bent as if it had been torn off. Julen reached over and checked Emerald's arm but found no mark of her slavery. Why had she never noticed this before? She had helped her dress hundreds of times and not seen what was now obvious. Had this been Ralda's wristband once? That would mean that she had been a very important slave. Julen had seen such slaves from a distance, serving the king. *Poor Emerald*, she thought. When she ran away, she must have been punished by being demoted to her lowly position, alone and forgotten. What a sad thing to remember her by—the symbol of bondage, hardship, and cruelty. Hardly a great gift. In the back of her mind, Julen wondered why her master had not locked another band on the recaptured slave.

One thing more remained in the chest. Whatever it was, it had been wrapped in an old, dirty rag and tied with string. Julen began to unwrap the small parcel, unwinding and unwinding until a thin necklace was visible. Its chain was dark and dirty but rubbing it seemed to show a yellow metal. There was a large stone hanging at the center now encrusted with grime. Was this the gift—a necklace that Julen could never wear? The stone may be rare indeed but what purpose would it serve?

Julen wondered how Ralda, even in another life with a different name, could have come by this treasure. Had she stolen it before she ran away? Had she somehow kept the secret and concealed the necklace from those who returned her to Bellicosa?

In the end, Julen decided to keep it, for it was a gift from her one true friend. For that, she would save it forever. Carefully wrapping and retying the string, Julen hid the necklace again and both gifts went into her apron pocket. It would not be good for the master to remove her friend's things and find this small treasure—useless to one in her position. Thinking they might find it odd to see an empty chest, Julen put a few small things from the room inside and closed the lid, placing it under the bed once more. Taking a last look around, Julen saw the small book she had taken from the closet study room and placed it alongside her other treasures. If found by the servants, she would be questioned until she admitted finding the room, and then she would be punished. For one standing on the edge of a cliff there was no reason to let anyone push her over.

Something had to be done. The housekeeper must be told. It was difficult to tear herself away, but she had to go. It was very late. After a while, she made her way down the back stairs, two floors to the main level where Obdura Coldstone had her office and quarters. She rapped one knuckle on the door. The sullen woman came to the door in her nightdress, "What now at this hour of the night?" Coldstone could see the swollen eyes of the servant standing before her.

"Very sorry to bother you, Ma'am," choked Julen. "Ralda, the old servant, has died and I came to let you know."

"Is that all?" she snapped. "I'll have the body removed in the morning. Heavens, I have to get my sleep. Don't touch her belongings. Anything she owned now belongs to the master of the house, do you understand?"

"Yes, Ma'am." Julen was afraid to put her hands near her apron pocket lest the observant Coldstone suspect she had taken something belonging to Ralda. Just the same, who in the house would ever think that the old servant had anything of value to leave after death?

It was a miserable night with little sleep. Julen lay awake remembering all the good talks she had with Ralda, such sweet memories. In the morning, Julen looked over at the quilt draped figure that lay so still and silent. She cried again, but had to report to work knowing she would return to an empty room. No kind words would be spoken over her old friend, as a slave did not deserve a funeral.

When Julen returned that evening Emerald's body was gone, she knew not where. All her things had been removed as well, the little chest included. She reached down and touched the lump in her apron pocket. Emerald's gift was safe. Julen crawled into bed without the ritual of caring for her friend. She wept into her pillow until she fell asleep.

CHAPTER 14
The Festival of the Moon

A new day dawned warm and bright. It was the day of the Festival of the Moon, a very important occasion by Bellicosian accounts. The workday began and the old slave was left to her cold repose—her burial was but one more chore for other servants. Julen would not be there to say goodbye.

As Julen passed with Bina through the Great Hall, servants were running up and down stairs. Orders were issued by one or the other of the three people who were most affected by the coming event. Violencia and the twin objects of her attention fussed about primping and deciding on final touches to their new gowns.

Nichola, the tall slender of the two, had chosen a daring brown dress that looked like strips of tree bark sewn together in tight panels. The knot holes were in conspicuous well-placed locations while still being modest.

Alumina has argued for layers and layers of soft fluffy gauze-like material, but Violencia had wisely pointed out that she would look like a dried up dandelion about to blow away in the wind. A more subdued green layer over a yellow under gown was purchased that had more the look of a cob of corn on the stalk.

"Here, Nichola, my sweet, try this," she urged as she smudged a bit of charcoal like powder above the younger lady's eyes, giving them a deep sunken appearance.

"Splendid, and so mysterious," cried the artisan of female decoration.

"Should I wear the sash over one shoulder like this?" asked Alumina.

"Oh, yes, my dear. The corn has ripened—let its silk overflow!" responded Violencia admiring them both and tidying a few stray curls of Alumina's blonde hair.

"Don't you wish mother was coming?" Nichola asked the two.

"You waste your time worrying about her," Violencia replied in a flat voice. "She is not fit any longer to represent the House of Arcana." Her tone brightened, and she said with great conviction, "You will be its crowning glory tonight."

Both girls trembled with joy at the thought.

Arriving in the chamber of Mistress Dismalia Chiselstone again, Julen knew that a decision was at hand. The previous day, the two women had stewed and argued about a plan.

"You both will go the festival ball and at midnight you will hand this letter to my contact. His name is Legerdemain. You will know him by his black cloak and hat," said the mistress, holding out the missive in her hand. Julen didn't say anything, but she thought she had seen such a man visiting the house. He was a friend of the master as well.

Bina was a few steps ahead of the mistress and had already seen the danger in the plan. "What will people think when they see two slaves enter the ball and look for a man in a black cape? Wouldn't you think that looks a bit suspicious? We have no right to be there and everyone would notice right away."

Dismalia's face fell as she saw the problem. What now? Bina did not waste time in speaking up with the solution. "You must be the one to go. You have many fine dresses and could just stay for a short time. Smile and greet people, look like you are having a good time, and then do the job and leave."

The mistress saw the sense of it but was terrified to go out in public. She had once been a bright participant in such festivals but that was so long ago. The need was great, and after more urging, she agreed that Bina's plan was better.

"Help me get ready then. I don't know what to wear or how to look," she said with panic in her voice. Julen, who knew her closet by heart, said, "I'll find your very best and we will fix you up like a queen!"

She rushed to the closet and searched the back for a particular dress she knew would be right for the occasion. Bringing it out into the light she saw that it was dusty so gave it a shake. Little stones flew off in every direction as the threads holding the tiny decorations had perished from age. Noting that it still looked good without a few of the stones, she brought it to Dismalia. She went again and retrieved slippers, a sash, and hair ornaments. With the help of Bina, they soon had her looking regal enough to make her surprise appearance.

"You can do this! Remember to spend enough time greeting people, laugh at jokes, listen to gossip, and admire some dresses. That should do it," instructed the older servant, who had witnessed many such events with envy. Dismalia tottered a bit in the tight-fitting gown and shoes. After some practice, she was ready. By this time it was late and almost time for everyone to find their way to the king's castle, not far away from Arcana.

She began her walk down long corridors until she reached the Great Hall where everyone awaited the carriages. Staring eyes met her with shock. There was silence throughout the hall until Alumina said, "Mother! You look wonderful."

Violencia's shock was the greatest. It did not take long for her to notice the missing stones, tiny broken threads and just a hint of dust. She put her handkerchief to her nose and was speechless.

Master Chiselstone was the last to descend the staircase and as he came, he sensed something was wrong. Then he saw the tall, dark figure of his wife walking toward the front door. Genuinely surprised at her sudden appearance, he hardly knew how to react.

"My dear, you are…well…going to the festivities, I see," he said as he passed her and headed for the younger ladies.

The transportation arrived and everyone at last found themselves before the dazzling castle of king Ironfist. There was a grand display of entertainment, with quarry dancers demonstrating their ability to leap over one another while juggling an assortment of rocks, and blade tossers throwing spinning knives high in the air and catching them in their teeth. There was a hilarious puppet show, where slave drivers comically ran after slave workers thrashing about trying to hit them with clubs—always an amusement to the wealthy.

"Mother, come see the Dragon chase!" urged Nichola. Dismalia obeyed trying to look like she was enjoying the sights.

The annual Dragon chase was the highlight of the whole celebration in which a long, narrow, reptilian-colored canvas with life-like head attached draped over a line of runners and went round and round in a serpentine pattern chasing another group that was disguised as a large yellow moon. Everyone knew that each year the dragon would not quite manage to devour the moon but always hoped that the next year things might change.

"Wasn't that thrilling?" asked Alumina, hoping her mother would join in the excitement. "Yes, dear," Dismalia tried to sound enthusiastic. Both girls saw that their mother was distracted and nervous and assumed it was because she was out in public after such a long time of secluding herself. Nichola grabbed her arm and pulled toward a street vendor. "Come. Let's buy paper moons like we did when we were children." Dismalia remembered well the spats of years past when the girls argued over who got the brightest yellow circle attached to a wooden stick. The daughters waved the moons in the air and wondered what else would amuse them.

Two young men stepped between the mother and daughters and presented shining gifts. Small polished metal disks hung from chains and each had a name engraved upon it. The girls giggled and squealed in ear-splitting gales and thought of their mother no more, in favor of the male company. Dismalia was left standing alone in the crowd.

Five long brass horns trumpeted the call to those who were privileged to be invited to the Grand Ball. The mistress' heart skipped a beat. This was the moment she would enter the castle. She wondered if anyone would be suspicious of her unusual appearance. The only servants there were the ones attending the dazzling ladies of the neighboring gentry, which gave Dismalia a small degree of affirmation. At least Rubina was right that it would have been very suspicious to send her maids to the event.

Spotting her husband, she made her way toward him and walked a few paces behind as they mounted the steps to the castle. Violencia was in front of him flashing her long dark eyelashes over distant acquaintances.

Before long, dancers whirled about the room to the music of harp and drum, sending up a veritable dust storm that made it hard to breath in the towering room. Mistress Chiselstone forced herself to greet, listen, and smile, though she felt miserable. It did not take long before the corners of her mouth were fatigued. She could no longer force the muscles to contract.

It seemed like an eternity before she spotted the man she sought. He had come in late but he had caught her eye. She made her way going left and right, greeting people until she reached him. With a greeting she hoped did not sound unnatural, she said, "Ah, Chief Legerdemain. It is good to see you. How I have missed your company of late."

The man in black knew why she was there. She shook his hand and passed a small note, which he received with a discreet swing of his arm, putting it in his breast pocket.

"My mistress, it is a pleasure to see you once again. Have you been ill? I see you so seldom," he said opening the conversation for further information from her.

"I have indeed been ill, Sir, and I am hoping that I will find the cure very soon. Do you have any suggestions?"

"My dear, you know I never let you down."

"The truth is, right now I am feeling a bit faint. I may go outside, and perhaps the cool air will help. Good evening to you, Chief," she managed to say, despite her growing discomfort at this very open interchange.

Attempting to stroll without drawing attention was difficult, but the task had been accomplished and it was time to retreat. She felt a twinge of elation in the pit of her stomach knowing she had done something so daring for the first time in a long while, and right under the noses of all those snobs she used to call friends! She held her head high as she turned to take a last look before descending the stairs from the ballroom. It was then that the pain in her feet from the tight shoes overcame her senses.

Across the room, Violencia's eyes met those of the man in black. He nodded his head in her direction and both smiled with a secret pleasure.

Dismalia limped to the nearest coachman, who was willing to take her home when she explained she was not feeling well. He plainly saw her disability. No one else had noticed her departure, which left her with mixed feelings. Once back in her chamber, she would collapse with nerves and be wakeful the whole night. Her thoughts would be consumed, wondering when she would hear from her friend Legerdemain. How would he deliver what she desperately wanted from him?

Entering the Great Hall of Arcana, she was met by the curious Obdura Coldstone. "Mistress, you are back early. Are you ill?" she asked as if she had expected that to be the case. Dismalia wrapped her cloak around her shoulders defensively.

"I am ill. I shall return to my rooms."

"Yes, Mistress. Your servants await you in your chamber." The thin brows above Coldstone's eyes moved closer together into a lined, suspicious frown.

"Wake up!"

Bina and Julen raised sleepy heads at their mistress' command. Both had fallen asleep on the circular divan.

"I did it!" shouted the mistress. Bina arose and immediately began questioning Dismalia to determine if the mission had indeed been successful. Finding nothing to raise an alarm, she settled back down onto pillows.

"When will he deliver the powder?" asked Bina, always the one for planning.

"I don't know, but soon, I'm sure. I have the utmost trust in Chief Legerdemain." Dismalia laughed for the first time in years.

Two days later, an anonymous letter for the mistress arrived. She tore it open and read aloud to Bina and Julen,

Send your servants to the Old Slave Market late in the afternoon today. They will receive what is expected.

Your humble servant,

L

Julen heard the words and knew what they meant. Both servants would have to go on this errand.

CHAPTER 15

The Stowaway

The Rock Rat Inn had always been a popular place for men to gather after their day of labor was over. Those who did not have families were even more attracted to what it had to offer—a safe haven for haven for grumblers and complainers.

Jip's life would have been even more difficult if it were not for the fact that his few friends shared his laborious place in Bellicosian society. It was not the life of those who made much money and, therefore, had few options for any time spared from work.

Men like Jip gravitated to the inn to talk and forget the heat of the day, the bruises of the task masters, and the meaninglessness of their labors. Their common society provided at least some opportunity to compete with each other when things were going well, and to console one another when things were tough.

The evening after the festival found Jip and his co-workers again engaged in exaggerated complaints about the extreme difficulty of their lives. But this night would be different. Jip motioned for his three closest friends to join him at a private table in the back of the room. Tonight he was determined to find a way to end their agonizing labor.

"I have to get out of here. There is a way. Anyone interested?" asked Jip, who then tipped his tankard and emptied the contents down his parched throat.

"Hey. I'm in. What do you have in mind?"

"There is a ship leaving tomorrow and I plan to be on it," answered Jip. He paused as a serving girl cleared the empty cups.

"How do you figure you won't be arrested, and how are you going to convince that fancy son of the owner and master, Damon that you are better than shark bait?" whispered his companion. They all looked around to make sure no one listened to their conversation.

"Here is my plan," said Jip, hunched over like an animal about to strike.

A stealthy shadow glided across the yard, followed closely by two others. The figures crept along like prowling cats. Jip was in the lead moving ever closer toward his goal, which lay at the end of the long, stone jetty.

Dodging crates, piles of nets, ropes and sail, all three made their way, ducking in and out of hidden spaces, to the Mirage, which was bound to a wooden wharf. Going the first distance had been easy, as the jetty was not guarded or illuminated. The last section of wharf would be much trickier.

It was a night with no moonlight. The light from three dim lamps near the edge of the pier created eerie shadows. Two guards faced each other sitting on large crates that would be loaded aboard the next day. They stared at the lamp between them. Nondescript bugs and fluttery moths flew in frantic circles around the light, hypnotizing the two into a stupor—just what Jip wanted to see.

"Hoooooooaaaa," moaned Jip in a gravel, ghostly tone. Two heads popped up at once. The men shifted back and forth in their seats as they tried to find

86

the source of the sound in the pitch black. "Hooooooaaaaa," came the sound again a bit louder.

Both guards grabbed their swords from behind the wooden crates, made a quick turn, and faced the darkness in a defensive position, heads going this way and that.

"Huuuooooaaaaa," Jip again howled from the dark and began backing up away from the ship. Just as he planned, the two guards advanced toward him one little step at a time. In the blackness, Jip's two friends had gone, one to the left and one to the right, working their way around the edges. Jip could see them both coming in around behind the guards and then slipping up the gangplank. He laughed to himself at how well his plan was working.

Once the men were on board, Jip slipped back farther, making no more sounds. The guards retrieved the lamp, holding it out in front as they began to search the area. Jip was making his way around as his friends had done, unseen by the two guards. Keeping his eyes fixed on them, he advanced in a circle, waiting for them to turn away before making each move.

A tiny movement caught his eye. It was the faces of his friends who peeked out from behind railings on the ship. They were signaling him when to advance. Just as he focused on and understood their hand gestures, he let out an "Ugh" as he tripped over a stack of poles laid out in rows on the deck of the pier.

The guards changed direction and ran toward him in the dark. Jip regained his footing and leaped over the edge of the pier, disappearing into the water below. He swam under the pier, grabbed a piling, and waited to see if they would pursue him.

Soon Jip heard more voices and cursed under his breath. They had called for help. He let go of the piling and began to swim alongside the ship looking for a way to get aboard. Then he found it. A rope was dangling over the side of the ship. He gave it a tug and began to pull himself up, hand over hand. He was strong and well-muscled, but his hands were wet so it was difficult to grasp the rough hemp rope.

He was about to reach the top; he had to figure out how to get over the side without making any noise. He thought of his two friends and hoped they had found the hold and a secluded place in which to stow away. He would find them in the dark and together they would lay low until the ship was a day out to sea. Once they had achieved that goal, they would decide what to do next.

As Jip reached at last for the railing, he had just enough reserves to hoist himself up and over to drop onto the deck of the ship. He stayed crouched down and cautiously raised his head up to see where he was. In front of him stood three sailors waiting in silence for him to compose himself after the long climb. Panic seized Jip and he rose to leap overboard again. The three, expecting that very move, were ready for him and grabbed flailing arms, holding him fast.

"I ask you, Frag, how stupid do we look?" asked one sailor of the other.

"I think this fellow will have to admit we are pretty clever. It works every time. They can't resist that rope hanging over the side," laughed another sailor.

"What do we do with him now? I guess we hold him until morning when the captain comes," said another.

"No, we turn him over to the chief. That's the orders he left with us."

Jip knew he was in trouble again. He would get another beating for this.

"Good evening, men. What a night it is!" came a voice from a tall figure dressed in black. "And what have we here? A slave from the iron works, trying to steal the master's property and make off with it?"

"No, Sir. Me and my friends, we were just trying to go for a little ride," Jip replied, as if he thought someone might believe this story.

"You and your friends, you say?" continued the man in black. "Where are your friends now?" Jip realized at once that he had given them away, but it was too late. From the other side of the ship a faint splash was heard, and then another.

The Stowaway

"That, I take it, was your friends?" asked the chief, admiring his own genius. He snapped his fingers and sailors rushed to the far side to sight the other trespassers. Nothing could be seen below on the dark side of the ship.

"If I am not mistaken, this man has another crime to answer for this evening," he said, as the he brought from his cape a small bag of coins and an envelope. "Do you recognize these?" Jip fought to escape, but he was held fast. What would happen to him now was not something he wanted to think about.

Chapter 16

The Spider's Web

The doorbell jingled. Julen rose and crossed the room to see who was there. Damon stood outside and looked into Julen's eyes as she peered through the tiny window in the door. Inside Julen's cheeks flushed and she lowered her gaze. She had been crying and she knew she looked miserable.

"I wish to see my mother."

Julen turned to the anxious mother, who nodded her approval to his entrance. Dismalia stood to meet her son as he came in the door. She longed to embrace him but checked herself. He was grown up now and such affection seemed improper. He walked forward and kissed her cheek.

"Mother, I am about to leave on my sea journey, so I wanted to say goodbye." Damon searched his mother's face for any sign of emotion. She softened and replied, "Yes, Damon. I know that you must go. It is important to you. I send my blessing with you. May the great sea and the wind send you on your way and bring you back safe and sound."

"Thank you," returned Damon with a hint of sorrow that etched his otherwise confident stance. "I will return and, no matter what man or beast tries to stop me, you will see me again before the winter storms." Mistress Chiselstone looked into his face and thought she saw something in his expression. Fearing some interference from her husband, she asked, "Has someone caused you trouble, my son?"

"Nothing at all. Some men tried to board the Mirage in the middle of the night—just common stowaways. When they caught the leader, it turns out he was some kind of wanted criminal, so I am grateful to the crew for stopping them. He will be off to prison by now. We are not anticipating any further trouble or delays and will sail at dawn tomorrow."

Julen and Bina stood in the background and heard the report, but nothing in Damon's words triggered alarm for them. Bina retained the information as a part of her large accumulation of facts—facts that made her the keen strategist that she was.

Julen heard the soft voice of a son who cared for his mother, though there was a strange gulf fixed between them that she did not understand. Why was the mistress so incapable of embracing him and crying at his departure? Just thinking about it made Julen's eyes fill. She would miss him, despite the lingering shame of their recent collision, as his occasional presence brought a bright place to her days of servitude.

Damon, as well, was aware that the one he had injured so callously was standing behind him. Trying to relieve the tension, Damon quipped, "I hear you went to the ball last night, mother. I hope you had a good time. You should get out more, you know."

The mistress smiled and shook her head, "I tried, Damon, but those occasions are just not for me."

Damon kissed his mother again, took her hands in his, looked into her eyes, and said, "I will be well and I shall miss you. Perhaps someday you will find a sea voyage just the thing you need."

The Spider's Web

Mistress Chiselstone smiled and replied, "That will be a wonderful day, won't it? Off with you now!"

He turned and left the room, the sound of his footfalls fading down the corridor until he was gone. Mistress Dismalia gulped in air and looked as if she would break down and cry. She closed her eyes and held her breath until the emotion passed. For a few minutes, she was quiet.

"We must get you ready for your errand," she blurted and turned to walk back to her bedroom chamber. "Julen, bring me two long capes from the closet. We will go about our day as usual and, when it is afternoon, you will leave by the back garden gate." She rummaged through some keys in a small chest by her bed.

The old gate swung open, but not without loud protest from the rusty hinges. The mistress pushed them through the door and waved them away. Bina's face was hard with determination and she was anxious to meet the challenge of whatever must come. Julen felt a cold numbness mixed with the heat of past pain.

Their journey would end at the Slave Market—that hated place. Still fresh in her mind was the clatter of hooves against cobblestone pavement, the smell of musty straw, and the rumble and bump of the wooden wagon in which she was carried as it found its way through the crowded streets. Wide-eyed and shaking, Julen remembered peering over the rails at a strange and frightening world from the tentative security of an old, shabby blanket.

"Clear off! Move aside!" the driver had yelled at the throng who paid no attention to his demands. Slowly the tired horse pushed against the resisting mass, sensing from habit the end of the journey.

To those who passed them, the dirty figures in the cart did not stir any interest. They were sad, colorless creatures who knew no hope or cheer. Only the eyes of the child, shining with fresh tears, searched the faces and begged to meet the eyes of one who was familiar or would offer rescue. Julen felt the tears welling up again remembering the helpless child that she had been.

Dragged from the wagon and handed off to a rough slave trader, she had stood trembling before the throng of noisy brutes gathered to gawk at the new merchandise. It was then that she had seen his face. A boy dressed in fine clothes tugged at his mother's sleeve, his eyes locked to Julen's in dreadful fascination.

"Mother! Look. Who is that?" he had asked the mistress. His mother raised her gaze with hesitation, as she knew what she would see. They had been shopping on a market day and come upon the Old Slave Market after making a wrong turn. Instead of the jeweler, there now before them was a platform where people were bought and sold. Julen shivered remembering the cold and the man whose evil grin revealed red and brown stained teeth.

She had been clothed only in a nightdress with neatly hand-worked patterns decorating the neckline. It had been white but had become smeared with brown dirt, something she found very distressing. Soiled hands wiped through tears had smeared her clean olive complexion. Her thick, black, wavy hair lay in tangles around her shoulders.

"What am I bid for this fine child? She will grow up to be a strong worker, and who knows what else?" the grizzled trader yelled and heard from the crowd the laughter and course jokes he expected. He spied Dismalia's sympathetic response to his Netherian prize and shouted, "Mistress. I see you are interested. Bring your coppers here and we will make a deal!"

"Mother, why are they selling a child?"

Julen had seen Dismalia impulsively pull her servant to herself and implore, "Bina, go and see how much they will take for her. Surely she could scrub floors or wash clothes. She can sleep with one of the servants."

Twelve years had passed since Bina had obediently bargained for her life—twelve years of carrying buckets of water, scouring tiles, and shivering in the cold and baking in the heat of the dormer room alongside her only friend, Ralda. Now that friend was gone, like her father and her past. Whatever lay ahead would only be as bad as what had come before. Julen began to sob quietly.

"What are you sniveling about? It's been years since you were there. Surely you have forgotten all that by now. You think you are the only one who has had to endure hardship? You know nothing!"

"It's more than that, Bina. I have such a horrible feeling about going there again. Something awful is going to happen."

"Whatever it is, we are stuck now. We had no choice, you realize. Don't carry on like a child. Everything will be fine."

Arriving in the town square, they looked around to understand their location. Bina knew every street and shop. Looking now for a particular building, she followed a street to the left, down a slight incline, and there it was.

The Old Slave Market consisted of two long, rundown buildings without windows, and a raised platform between them in a wide open space. Each building had one large door that slid on a rail fastened to the top. Both were in a state of disrepair, despite the lucrative business that took place beside them. The wooden sides showed loose, weather-beaten boards that were in need of paint. Cobwebs hung between posts and trash was strewn randomly about. Not a soul stirred.

Julen did not want to look up at the platform. She kept her head down and followed the knowledgeable Bina, who scanned the street for the promised contact. Thinking she saw something close to the male slave building, she moved in that direction. From around the back, the dark figure of Chief Legerdemain appeared like a spider delighted that his prey has found its way into his web. His black cloak was wrapped around his body, giving him a bat-like appearance.

Julen looked at him and felt a chill. Bina, assuming he hid the koma powder within the dark folds, concentrated on his hands and impatiently waited for the conclusion of the deal.

"Good afternoon, Chief. We are here for Mistress Dismalia," Bina said while pulling a small bag of coins from her cape. Legerdemain smirked and also reached into his garment. He brought out a bag of powder and held it before Bina. As she reached for the bag, the chief drew it away again without warning.

"The money first, good servants." Bina handed over the bag and reached once again. The chief grinned.

"Bina! Yes. I know your name. I know everything about you. It is my job… remember? Bina jolted in shock. "You think yourself clever—scheming and planning, working and groping for what you will never get. And you Julen, isn't this where you began your career of bondage? Now you will end it here as well."

The two stared at Legerdemain's face trying to see what he meant. Having stunned his prey, he continued to wind the threads.

"Ah, this victory is so delicious. I love this part of my work."

Being half bound in the chief's words, Bina stood paralyzed and unable to answer. "You have flown into my trap like two small flies," he said, unable to suppress laughter that now turned venomous.

"You are under arrest and will both be hanged for this outrage of breaking the law of the king." He turned to Bina, "You and that rebellious son of yours, who I already have secured in my prison."

Both women were frozen with fear. From the shadows, armed men appeared, waiting to arrest them. They began to step backward, but there was nowhere to go. The men moved in closer, surrounding them.

"Take them away," commanded Chief Legerdemain, as he turned and walked away. Surrounded as they were, they had no choice but to walk in the direction the swords now pointed them. "You three, back to the barracks," and the chief waved them away. "You two, remove this scum to the prison."

Julen and Bina walked slowly toward the prison, each with the point of a sword at her back. Julen neared hysteria. "I knew it. This place is evil."

"That's enough of that," shouted a guard and poked Julen's back.

As they passed a dark alleyway, Bina's mind was racing. She grabbed Julen's arm, ripped off the two cloaks, threw them in the faces of the guards, and bolted down the alley in a flash that defied her bulk and short stature. She would not go to prison and would rather die by the sword than spend the rest of her life in that stinking, wretched place. There was just a chance that, while the men struggled with the capes, the two could find a hiding place.

Sprinting down the narrow alley, they saw that it led to another street filled with late afternoon sellers of baskets, fruit, dried fish, smoked bobbit, and trinkets of every kind, and their prospective buyers standing around bargaining. They headed into the crowd dressed in gray and melted into the masses of people.

It took the soldiers several seconds to gain composure. They darted after the women, overturning baskets and carts as they tried to keep visual contact with the escaping offenders. Darting in and out of vendors, Bina headed down yet another street and found they were heading back toward the slave market. "We can't go that way," yelled Julen. "Yes, we can. They won't think to look for us there." They ducked low, scrambled back, and dove behind the slave block just as the soldiers appeared behind them. Struggling to catch her breath, Bina signaled to Julen to run for the shelter of the nearest building. No sooner had they risen than the points of two swords pinned them to the wooden planks. This time the soldiers were in no mood for games. One soldier stepped back, raised his long blade, and prepared to strike both women with a single blow, removing both heads at once.

Julen and Bina both squeezed their eyes shut and turned their heads away waiting for the final blow before death.

"Help, help, help, please!" muttered Julen in a low voice.

They heard the swing of the blade cutting through the air, then perceived through closed eyes that it became darker, then a sickening groan and a thud. Being still alive and untouched, the two opened their eyes and beheld a shocking sight. A man lay crumpled up at their feet with blood flowing from a wound to his head. He was dead.

How had this happened? The two soldiers stood in shock and disbelief, frozen to their position with eyes wide open staring at the man on the ground. Where had he come from? Why did he jump in front of the swinging sword? No answers came.

Quick-witted Bina once again grabbed Julen's arm pulling her past the immobile guards and into the street. They ran as fast as they could and did not stop for anything, taking one street then another for the next half hour.

Exhausted, they stopped at an open door in a deserted lane, dashing inside and into a dark corner to stay until sundown. Inside the Rock Rat, men were talking in low voices, but loud enough to be understood by the two fugitives.

"Did you hear about those thieves who escaped from the king's soldiers?"

"What happened?"

"The soldiers just let them go, can you believe it? They had some story about a man who stepped in front of their swords as they tried to dispatch these two. They say they killed him. But when the others arrived, guess what? No such dead man."

"How did they think they would get away with that, I wonder."

"It takes real intelligence to come out with a story like that one," laughed a silly grinning man at a nearby table.

"Do you think it was that mystery man they used to talk about, The One?" he asked with mockery in his voice. They all broke into laughter shaking their heads. "Nah."

CHAPTER 17

Trapped

Mistress Dismalia paced back and forth from sitting room to bedroom trying to occupy her mind with anything but what was becoming more and more obvious. The sun had been gone for hours and there was still no return of her two maids. She hoped they were taking extra precaution to avoid being seen as they wound their way back up the hill to the house. Her ears were alert for any sound that might come from the direction of the back garden.

A different sound met her ears than what she expected. It was the tinkling bell at the main entrance to her chamber. There was no servant to see who it was, so Dismalia approached the door with apprehension. What would they think if she answered? How would she explain the absence of her servants? Panic was pressing to overtake her emotions, but she stifled the fear and opened the door. To her surprise, it was Violencia. *What could she want at this late hour?* This was most uncalled for.

"My dear, Mistress Chiselstone, may I come in?" she cooed as she swept past the shocked mistress who held the door. "Why, Violencia, how surprised I am to see you," said Dismalia in icy, fearful tones. "Is there something wrong?"

"I should be asking you, my dear. Have your servants gone to bed and left you to get yourself off to sleep?" asked Violencia in her own cunning way. "Or have they gone on some errand and left you all alone with no help?"

"Why, yes," stammered Dismalia, "they have gone to fetch me something I needed."

"And what would that be, my dear? Was there no one else to send, or was this particular errand a secret?"

"I don't see that it is any of your concern. They will return when they have completed what I requested of them," continued Dismalia.

"Are you sure of that? I could have sworn someone this evening reported that two women had been arrested in the Old Slave Market this afternoon. And would you believe, they were trying to purchase koma powder? Everyone knows that is punishable by death, or imprisonment at the least."

Dismalia could no longer conceal her shock and horror at this revelation. She gasped and drew her hands up to her mouth, too late to stop the sound.

"Could these two women have been your trusted servants?" Violencia asked with a smug smile. "Ah, yes. I see it is so. Who could have sent them on such an errand, my dear? Certainly not yourself, who knows the punishment for such things."

"Get out of here this minute! I don't want to hear any more of this talk!" shouted the terror-struck mistress.

"I'm afraid it is too late. You have chosen a slippery path and avoided a fall by pushing others on ahead. Now you will topple on their bodies and plunge into the same fate. Do you understand?" asked Violencia. "If not, I will tell you. Your servants will die and so may you. Leniency will mean, at the least, prison for a very long time. No more servants, no more comforts, but plenty of isolation, if that makes you feel any better."

Dismalia began to weep and sunk down onto her cushioned divan. What was to become of her now? There was silence between the two for several minutes before Violencia again spoke.

"I do see one possible solution for you. Are you interested in what I have to offer?" said the unwelcome visitor.

"How can there be a solution?" cried Dismalia.

"Your husband is a man of great influence and power. He has but to speak for you and the king may see yet another punishment," said Violencia.

"Why would Master Chiselstone do that for me? You should know better than that!" Dismalia spat out the words in disgust.

"There is one thing you could offer him in exchange for his favor. I have here a document that, once signed, releases Harrasster from his vow of marriage to you. In light of your high crimes, he would be merciful to let you go in this manner. Because of that mercy, he would allow you to live unmolested in this apartment, without servants of course, for the rest of your life," said Violencia in a flat voice.

"What? What are you saying? And then what comes after that? You married to Master Chiselstone? You did this, didn't you? You planned the whole thing to usurp me!" screamed Dismalia.

"My dear, think what you are saying. No one planned for you to become dependent on koma powder. You did that all by yourself."

Dismalia thought back to the first time she tasted the powder. Her friend Chief Legerdemain offered her a small sample for a headache and she had taken it with gratitude. And he was so willing to continue supplying it to her. How did they find out if it wasn't Chief Legerdemain himself? Did they plan this, together, the three of them, to overthrow her position as mistress of the house?

Her mind reeled in regret and sorrow at what had now transpired. Her two trusted servants caught in the same trap and now doomed along with her, but reaping a much more severe punishment than her. She wept again for them and what they must now be facing. Dismalia did not want to think such horrible thoughts. They were just slaves after all. She agonized at the thought of having no one to help her ever again.

She wept for her son who would find out about this and be ashamed of her, perhaps never want to see her again. It was too late now to do anything else but comply.

"Give me the document!"

Violencia handed her the paper and a pen to sign. From the corridor, two magistrates appeared and witnessed the signature. Violencia had thought of everything well ahead of time.

The lonely figure, who was now stripped of her title of mistress of the house, saw it all, but too late. Flames of anger burned into her soul where they were dowsed by floods of grief. She had become a prisoner of the house.

CHAPTER 18

Escape over the Mountain

In the dark where Bina and Julen were hiding, they conferred with each other about what to do next.

"Bina, I'm scared! What are we doing?" asked Julen, keeping her voice low but squirming with anxiety.

"We are escaping. That is what we are doing. Get used to it. This is not going to be easy so quit whining and pay attention," said the older woman. She surveyed the room, gathering strategic information. Where they could see into the Inn, there were about fifteen patrons sitting at tables drinking and laughing, unaware of any activity in the corners where no light shone.

Bina spied a cloak rack near the door. She pointed one small finger and formed the words, "Over there," with her mouth. Julen trembled and wanted to cry. She kept looking at Bina to follow her lead.

They waited until the men in the room had drunk plenty. Two men got up and staggered toward the door. "Good night to you all, my good friends.

It is home to my bed now," and they wove their way to the cloak rack, picked off two and departed. At long last, two remained, but they were too drunk to know much.

"Come on, you two, its time you were out of here. I have to close up for the night," said the innkeeper who was by now tired and irritable. "Ohhh, yah. Gotta be going," said one with slurred speech. He stood up and stumbled to the floor. His friend stood and raised the drunk man to his feet. Together they staggered toward the door looking toward the rack for their cloaks.

"What? I was sure we brought our cloaks with us, didn't we Clog? Or did we forget to bring them?"

"Whaah d'ya say? Whas a cloap?"

"Ah, forget it, you two. Out you go. You must have forgotten to bring your cloaks and now you deserve to get cold. Get on with you!" prodded the innkeeper, as he shoved them through the doorway and pushed the heavy door shut behind them.

"I was sure I had a Clog, didn't I, Cloap?"

Bina and Julen wrapped themselves in their newly acquired garments, more for the camouflage than the chill, and crept in and out of dark empty streets. Neither of them knew where the best exit from the town was, though they could see that above the town were barren mountains.

Bina took the lead, pulling the whimpering Julen behind her.

"Hold on to your senses, worthless child!"

"I'm sorry, Bina. I...I...where are we? What will we do now?"

"We go up, and out of this town. That's what."

After passing building after building and then house after house, the structures of civilization grew thinner and farther apart. They had climbed quite a distance but were still in the town. Where was the end of it?

They approached a short decorative metal fence and followed it until an ornate gate was within sight. It screeched open and they peered inside, finding a graveyard.

"I've been here before," huffed Bina breathless from exertion. "There are servants buried here, and on the high side, there is no fence. This is where the trail to the high mountains begins." Julen wondered in the moment if Emerald had been buried here. Near the railing there were heavy stones marking the graves that were chiseled with names and dates. As they neared the back of the graveyard, wooden stakes with no discernible markings replaced the stone. She spied a new grave with dirt piled high over the top and no marker. Was this the final resting place of her beloved friend? She would never know, as they had to keep up a rapid pace to leave the city behind them before the light of day.

I still have your gift to me, Emerald, thought Julen, as they hurried past the grave.

Without warning, Bina stopped and bent over double, taking large gasps of air. Julen bent down and asked, "What's wrong? Are you ill?"

"I've got to stop. I'm winded. Wait."

"Bina, we have to keep going!" cried Julen. Hesitating, but then moving forward, Bina was determined that the younger woman would not show her up. She stood up and lunged into the dark, putting all her strength into their escape.

The terrain was rough, with stones of all sizes strewn over the side of the mountain. Scrubby small trees and shrubs sprouted from here and there but did not offer much as obstacles. They knew they should continue up and up as long as their legs would carry them. They also were aware that time was running out. Darkness had turned to a dusky light. The sun would be coming up and they would stand out like two black dots on the side of the mountain.

"Stop." commanded Bina. "We need...to get rid," and she struggled for breath, "of these cloaks. They will...give us away. Someone...looking up the mountain...will see us. Gray won't stand out...as much." Taking off the cloaks and hiding them under a large rock bought Bina a short time to recover from exhaustion.

"What about these aprons? They are so light-colored, surely they would show up as well when the sun is up." Julen shed hers and added it to the cache. Bina saw her remove some items from the pocket before burying her apron and asked, "What are those?" Julen removed her waist sash, flattened it out, and wrapped the items up as best she could before retying it. The small book was harder to hide so she wedged it in the front. "Just a few things that Ralda gave me before she died," explained Julen.

"Looks like a book. Ralda owned a book?" Julen did not answer.

"Aren't you going to leave your apron?" asked Julen, noticing Bina tucking hers away under her dress. "Not a chance. It's the only one I have now. You have your keepsakes, and I have mine."

The women finished piling stones on the hidden items and continued their slow painful walk up the mountain. Bina grew weaker and weaker but kept on moving. At one point, she stopped to heave from thirst and exhaustion. She felt her body temperature rising and wondered at Julen, who appeared to be taking the extra exertion in stride. *Disgusting youth!* Bina thought to herself as she pushed her weary body forward and upward.

The sun was beginning to rise, and far below Julen could see right down to the bay where ships were dotted about in the blue-green water. In one of those ships was Damon, setting sail for his journey—Damon, whom she would never see again. But what did that matter in light of the current urgency? Unless they crossed the mountain soon, Damon was not all she would never see again.

CHAPTER 19
Close Call

The sun rose bright and clear. Damon, having slept on the ship the night before and risen before dawn, looked out to sea and felt a surge of exhilaration. They would soon be setting sail. The last of the preparations had been made and the ship had checked out in all its rigging and equipment. Nothing could go wrong on a morning like the one before him.

Captain Fairway, who stood nearby, felt the light breeze and smiled, knowing that it would be a good day for sailing once they left the harbor. Below the quarterdeck where he stood, there was a buzzing of deck hands moving about briskly, cheered by the coming voyage.

A messenger arrived and was cleared to go up to speak to the Captain. There was a quiet conference held with the messenger before he turned and left.

"Master Damon, a message has come from Arcana that may interest you, though I see no cause for alarm at this time."

"Yes, Captain, what is it?" replied Damon as he stared out to sea.

"It seems that the fellow we had here the other night trying to board the ship has a mother who was in on his deed. She tried to purchase the same illegal powder that her son was found to have stolen earlier," the Captain continued. "I am sorry to have to tell you this, but the very same woman was the servant of your mother." Damon turned in surprise.

"She has two servants, a tall one and a short one. It must be the older, short one. I think she has a son, if I'm not mistaken. What an atrocious thing for my mother. But what of the other servant?" asked Damon. The Captain told him the rest of what the messenger had said. "The other servant was in on the plot as well, and both have been arrested and put in prison. All three may hang for conspiring against the king's law."

Damon was shocked and concerned for his mother who would now have no servants. But that could be remedied well enough with the help of his father and Coldstone. This was not welcome news to his family, but they would cope with it somehow. Perhaps his mother would have to interact more with the rest of the household as a result of this new deprivation. Again, the haunting eyes of Julen pierced Damon as he imagined her hanging for her crime. *Why should I care about servants?* He let the matter go and again faced the sea with great anticipation.

At the Captain's orders, the last gangway was pulled away from the ship. The anchor was weighed, the large ropes holding the ship to the wharf were unwound and hauled away, and before long, the ship was being pulled out of the harbor by the heaving of heavy oars in two smaller boats. As they neared the open sea, the ship began to roll with the waves and the order was given to hoist the sails. Damon's stomach lurched and he steadied himself for the adventure ahead.

"Bina," gasped Julen as they continued their climb. Bina could not reply but just stood, breathless. "Ralda, the old servant who died, told me about a place of refuge over the mountain. If we can just find it, we may be safe for a while."

Bina shook her head in disbelief, "Are you going to believe that daft old woman?" She found herself replying, despite her resolve not to use any energy for this purpose.

"She described it to me. I think I'll know it if I see it," said Julen as they continued.

They were nearing the top of what looked like the summit. They were sadly disappointed to find another summit beyond them. They could no longer be seen from below, but they were far from safe. Each step became torturous for both women. Their footwear was not designed for rough rocks and gravel paths. Aching feet slowed them down as much as lack of rest.

At last, they reached the summit of a pass between mountain peaks and looked with relief at a slow descent on the other side. What lay in front of them were huge boulders scattered across the horizon as far as the eye could see until the ground dropped out of sight beyond. Julen was dismayed at the sight of so many boulders. She had pictured Ralda's description as a lone rock, easy to spot. But what had she said? She had not found it by herself. Someone was there to help her. So where was this person? Did he live close by and should she call out to him?

She raised her hands to her mouth, "Hello!" she yelled.

"What do you think you are doing?" gasped Bina.

"There is supposed to be someone here to help us find shelter."

"Stop it this minute! We are wanted criminals. If there is anyone here we don't want to be found, is that clear?" Bina dropped in a heap on the ground.

"I can't go much farther. We have to find some place to hide until we can rest. Doesn't look like a very good place to find water," Bina choked out, as if resigned to crawl into a hole and die. She began to drag herself to the nearest large boulder, vainly looking for shade. The sun was directly overhead, bearing down with heat. "Let's at least sit behind this rock so that if anyone does come, we won't be seen."

The two women found a spot behind a boulder that offered a very small amount of shade, but neither cared as long as they could lie down and rest. Julen laid her head on the ground facing Bina, wondering what they would do now and how they would find any shelter or water. The place looked about as desolate as a place could be.

She had closed her eyes and was drifting into the numbness of sleep when a rumbling pounded in her ears. She lifted her head and listened— nothing. She lowered her head to the ground again and heard the sound. Was someone coming to look for them? If that was true, they had just seconds before discovery.

Julen closed her eyes shut and screamed out a whisper, "Please help us! Please help us!" She gave Bina a shove, "Wake up. Horses coming. Soldiers!"

Julen spied a large boulder with a cleft underneath. If they could just make it over there, it could be a hiding place. How much time was there before the horses came upon them? Was there enough time to get under the cleft? Was it deep enough? *Too many questions. Must act now*, she thought to herself.

She grabbed Bina and hauled her out from behind the rock, pushing her ahead to the cleft. Stuffing Bina under, Julen crawled in beside her just as the horses appeared in a cloud of dust. Julen kept pushing and shoving Bina, and withdrawing her own limbs in behind her in hopes that they might not be seen. Looking out toward the path, Julen's eyes fell upon a sight that made her heart beat twice as fast. Her book lay just out of her reach at the edge of the rock.

The hooves of six horses halted a short distance away from the trembling women.

"I saw something," cried a voice. Another rider came forward and spoke with the first. "Where did they go?" came the second voice. "I think they ran and hid under this rock," shouted the soldier. Hearing this, both women stiffened. The second voice answered, "Search under every stone. The sun is bright and you may not see them at first. They must be here somewhere. They haven't had time to go farther than this."

Close Call

Julen held her breath and knew that they would be found. There was not enough room under the rock to squeeze in any further. She shook with terror thinking what would happen to them once dragged from under the rock.

A fierce looking soldier bent down and looked directly at Julen as she braced herself into her hiding place. Their eyes met. The soldier continued his search turning to the left and then to the right.

"Nothing under here, Chief," reported the soldier. "Nothing here," reported one after the other until all had been accounted for. "Shall we give up the search?"

"No, indeed. The king has a special interest in these two. They must be beyond. This is as far as most runaways get before we find them," Legerdemain lamented. "Ride on!"

Clouds of dust choked the two as the horses galloped down the hill. The rumbling sound ceased and all was quiet.

"What was that about?" asked Bina. "Didn't he look right in here? Why didn't he see us?"

"I don't know," confessed Julen who was just as bewildered, but nonetheless relieved. She squeezed out of the hole and caught up her book before Bina could see it.

"It might have been the brightness of the sun." She felt confused but in the back of her mind were the words of Ralda. *She talked about someone helping, but we have seen no one. What did she mean? This must be the magic cleft that she referred to, a place where one cannot be seen by their enemies.*

"I think it was magic," Julen said to Bina.

"What do you know about magic? You, girl with no brains, girl who knows nothing at all except the tales of an old, senile woman. We were lucky this time. The sun was too bright and we are safe for a few more hours. But how long?" Bina emerged from the cleft, shook off the dust and continued, "Come on, we have to find a REAL place to hide before they decide to come back looking for us."

Julen thought about the sun, but she knew there was no way they could missed seeing the book lying at the edge of the stone boulder.

111

CHAPTER 20

Hard Labor

Dank, foul smells radiating from the walls and floor of Jip's solitary cell invaded his nostrils and beat up on his stomach. He wretched with nausea but could not win the fight against them. The prison odors had joined forces with the human enemies outside his miserable confinement to render him senseless.

It was painful to remember the last thirty hours since his arrest. The guards, waiting for the prison to open, had tied him up and left him lying in a heap until it was morning. Untied and shoved into this cell, he waited now, for what he did not know.

An entire day had gone by with no indication of what was to come. He was ravenously hungry and thirsty and the increasing heat was making things worse. The floor was damp earth and had been used no doubt as a latrine for other prisoners who had no choice. If they had brought food, he wasn't sure he could eat it.

Through the small, barred window high over his head, he could hear the faint sound of men yelling and snapping whips, a forced labor crew beginning the day of work. Could it get any worse than it had been working at the iron works? Wasn't it just exchanging one form of slavery for another? Anger swept over Jip and he squirmed like a startled earthworm. He could do nothing but wait. Perhaps they were going to starve him to death.

The sound of men's voices increased in volume until Jip was sure someone was headed toward his cell. Opening a small window from the outside of the cell, someone peered in and stared. Metal scraping sounds in the hollow room warned that the lock was being turned. The grimy door opened and there stood a heavyset guard dressed in leather leggings and an apron over rough woven tunic. He looked like a meat butcher, lacking his clever to make the picture complete. Next to him was the man in black who had been at the jetty when Jip was arrested. He bore the manners of an aristocrat, standing tall and dignified, in sharp contrast to the present company. Making sure his attire did not become soiled in the filthy prison, he sidestepped piles of questionable debris on the floor.

"I don't think we were introduced the other night," he said as he stepped forward into the cell. "The name is Legerdemain, and I take a personal interest in Master Chiselstone's affairs." Jip said nothing, but sat on the dirt looking sullen.

"Guard, help this man to his feet. He has forgotten his manners in the presence of a superior." Legerdemain's anger flared.

The leather-clad guard pushed his husky frame into the cell, grabbed Jip, and hauled him to his feet. "You are a rebellious young man and those kind don't fare well here in the prison. Will you allow me to advise you on this matter? I suggest you find a different attitude or things will not go well for you. You have committed more than one offense worthy of severe punishment." Again, Jip cringed at the thought that somehow this man had known about the theft in the house.

"Now I must inform you that your deeds have reaped an even greater punishment than you anticipated. Your mother's involvement has been uncovered. She and her fellow servant have been arrested and will come to a bitter end, just as you will."

The chief stared hard into Jip's eyes to detect pain at the news of his mother, but saw none. Jip knew what the man was trying to do. He would show no softening, no emotion. They must think that hurting his mother would not affect him at all, though he inwardly stormed against the crushing knowledge of having caused his own flesh and blood such a fate. Jip hoped that Legerdemain did not see him gulp and hold his breath.

"Perhaps that news does not alarm you. But then again, you look like a tough fellow. We could torture her in the next cell and that wouldn't bother you at all, would it? Hard labor for this one," commanded Legerdemain, and he turned to leave.

As the chief retreated, the guard pulled him aside and whispered, "Pardon Master Chief, but I thought his mother and that other one got away."

"No, no, no. It is a rumor. Those idiots I sent to escort the two to prison have come up with some kind of strange tale to account for their stupidity. Everything is under control." Legerdemain brushed him aside and left.

Jip was then driven to the center hallway where bands of steel were fastened to his ankles and wrists. He was thrown back in his cell and a bucket of gray mush was kicked inside the clanging door as it was being shut in his face. Despite the awful taste and smell, Jip surprised himself by wolfing down the mush, licking his fingers, and leaving the bucket wiped clear. There may not be more for some time and he had the day's labor to look forward to.

Somewhere inside Jip, the thought of his mother came back to him. What would they do to her? They were not close. Vivid memories of her constant nagging and anger at everything he did or said could not be forgotten. She even seemed to know what he was thinking and scolded him for that as well. *It wasn't my fault that she had gotten involved with the mistress' drug habit. It would have been found out sooner or later, and she would have been punished just the same. It isn't my problem after all—maybe just the reverse. If she hadn't been involved*, Jip reasoned, *I wouldn't have been tempted to help myself to her cache. It was her fault! And that stuck up Julen. Did she think she was better now than those who worked with their hands? She deserved to get caught in the web. She was just as bad as my mother—always bowing and scraping for favors, always sniveling about some lost past.*

There was no more time to contemplate his misfortune, as the clanking sound again diverted him and signaled the next stage of his imprisonment—chained to other prisoners and forced into hard labor.

"Up and at 'em, scum," the guard ordered. His job was rounding them up, chaining them, and sending them out to their duties for the day. Jip would be digging for metals in the mountainside under the watchful eye of a whip master. There would be no lagging behind or laziness on his watch.

"Come on, move it out. And don't worry about that mama of yours. They done her in already, chopped her head clean off, is what I heard." teased the laughing guard.

CHAPTER 21

Wandering in the Wasteland

The sun was strong and heat radiated up from rocks and sand bringing a glare that made scouting out the area difficult. Bina lay on the ground groaning, "I'm sick, and tired, and thirsty, and hungry," she complained, knowing it would not help their situation, but somehow she felt better to say it out loud.

"Better get out of the sun then," advised Julen who was scanning the terrain for some hint of shelter. Bina wanted to ignore the girl's admonition but knew better and moved into what little shade was available.

"I can't walk. You are going to have to see what you can find for shelter," said Bina looking at her shredded sandals. Julen shuddered. The glaring face of the soldier who had almost found them left an indelible picture in her memory.

"I'll get lost!" Julen cried. Bina tossed a small stone to the frightened girl. "Take that stone and put it on top of this boulder. When you get a ways off, make sure you can still see it," instructed Bina. Julen obeyed, though found it difficult to put the rock on top, and tossed it up instead. Satisfied that it could be seen, she started off.

Wandering this way and that, Julen kept looking back to make sure she could still locate the marker. Loud groans assured her that Bina would not be difficult to find.

The surrounding area proved to be just as monotonous and unchanging as the place they had topped the mountain pass. Walking on, she found that the ground fell away and went down into a ravine. Knowing that she could lose her way, Julen marked another boulder nearest the ravine before she climbed down into it.

Descending into the shade, the cooler temperature gave instant relief and she knew she must bring Bina. She was about to return up and out when she heard a familiar sound down between two rocks. Bending down, she leaned over and found a trickle of water making its way down a narrow hidden stream, which then disappeared again under other stones. She struggled to reach down and could feel the cool water flowing over her hand as she formed a cup with her fingers; she attempted to raise as much up to her mouth as she could. It took many repeated motions to slake her thirst, but at last, she felt cooled and refreshed. She lay back on a rock and rested for a few moments before beginning the ascent. Following her stone markers, she was soon back at Bina's side with the good news.

"Water, Bina, I found it," she laughed and began to pull the exhausted woman to her feet. Julen walked her over to the ravine. "Down there," she said, pointing with her chin.

"Ah! Ouch! Oooh!" cried Bina, as she took each painful step down. Slowly they descended into the cool shade and smooth stones. Bina could hear the sound now and thrust her hand down into the cleft to retrieve the water. Finding her hand insufficient, Julen raised water to her companion's mouth with her own cupped, long, slender fingers.

The afternoon wore on and soon the shadows were long. A wind came up with a chill that sent both women seeking each other for warmth. They huddled together in the rocks but could not find any comfortable position. The silence grew just as uncomfortable while both thought about all that had taken place in the last hours.

"Bina, what Chief Legerdemain said about Jip, I'm very sorry." Weary beyond words, Bina waved away the thought with her hand and closed her eyes.

"I know he has lived away from Arcana, but it is still a horrible thing to think that...to know that he may be," Julen hesitated before saying, "gone."

"What would you know about such things? You've never born a child," came the stinging reply. "What is done is done." Bina spoke no more but clutched her wadded apron to her chest.

They fell into deep sleep. Waking to sore muscles and intense hunger, Bina scanned the clear sky overhead. The morning was cool, but both knew that the temperature would soon grow hot once the sun had fully risen. Julen looked at Bina, who was deep in thought rubbing the fabric of her apron between grimy fingers. "Bina, are we still Netherians if we escape?"

"How should I know? I have never escaped before. What we will be is dead!"

Julen rubbed her hands over her aching leg muscles and wondered if Bina was right. "We can't go back the way we came, and not the way the horse riders went down into the desert. Perhaps we should follow the ridge parallel to the sea coast and see if it leads down to some forest or plain. We dare not risk being found by the soldiers." At this point, Bina did not care where they went, as she was worried about her ability to move at all more than anything else.

With sighs and much effort, the two rose out of their shelter and walked wearily along the top of the ridge until it began to drop off, as Julen had thought it might. On and on they walked past escarpments of jagged stone pointing to the sky far out to sea, and climbing over broken chunks that had long ago fallen down.

The going was rough and hot, and seemed never ending. Julen looked ahead and could see that the ridge kept going for a long way in the distance.

Should they now head down into the valley and hopefully find water and something to eat? But there was no valley that promised water and food. There was only miles of desert below them; no plants or trees could be seen.

Bina began to faint and dropped to her knees. "Let me die," she moaned. Julen put her arms under Bina's and walked her down the hill. Going down at this point seemed to make sense, and they could not go up or over any longer. Closer and closer the desert drew them, and Julen realized the hopelessness of their situation.

Julen's arms ached from holding up the heavy little woman, but she kept going, in the end carrying her on her back to the bottom of the mountain. Lowering her burden to the ground, Julen searched the horizon for any kind of shelter but saw none. It would be night soon and their prospects looked grim. Julen closed her eyes against the discouraging sight. Perspiration trickled down her forehead, neck, and back.

Walking along the edge of the desert at the base of the mountain, she didn't care now if she lost sight of Bina, who was beyond even noticing her absence. It wouldn't be difficult to find the way back, but what difference did that make since they were hopelessly lost? *Death will come soon*, she thought, *so there is nothing to lose.*

Strolling along, keeping the flat plain to her right and the mountain to her left, she came upon a deep hollow between two ridges that ran down into the desert. Julen turned to her left and followed the hollow back to its source. It held some potential as a shelter, if nothing else. Further back, it looked like a small cave was formed by the fallen rocks piled on top of one another. She thought for a moment that creatures might have found this place first, but looking around, there was not much to attract even wild life. She decided to bring Bina to this place, for lack of any better plan as to how to pass the time before the sun set again and brought with it the evening chill.

Bina was not happy about being moved, nor was Julen at having to carry the dead weight as she made her way back to the cave. Again, Bina fell in a heap.

"Leave me. Let me die in peace," sobbed Bina, as Julen tried to prod her on.

"I don't fancy the idea of having your dead body picked clean by vultures so come on. You have to come with me." Bina dragged onward.

Julen stared hard into the back of the cave and knew that she must climb between the rocks and see how far they could move inside to find shelter. Gingerly picking her way over and around boulders, the space widened and proved to be bigger than she first had suspected. It was a cave. Going back, she convinced Bina to make the effort and together they positioned themselves inside the opening. Bina was asleep in an instant and began to snore loudly.

Julen surveyed the bleak surroundings. They were lost with no idea of what to do next. Was there any hope of finding a land where people were kind, where she could find a home? Was it even possible that a person who had been a slave could be free? Did she not have the wretched band on her wrist that would give away to anyone that she was a runaway slave? She and Bina would be returned and face certain death.

Julen untied her sash, as the objects folded within and the book were pressing uncomfortably into her side. She laid them out before the fading light, remembering her friend and the strange things she had said before she died. Where was the man she said would help them? There had been no help, only near capture as they hid under the rock, starvation, thirst, and grueling exertion to get this far.

Hoping to distract her mind from her aching hunger, Julen untied the soiled rag wrapping and looked intently at the green stone in the necklace. She had never seen such a stone before and wondered if it was valuable. Emerald had said she was named for it. *It was an Emerald then,* she thought to herself. With tender care, she began to rub the dirt from the surface of the jewel observing that underneath it was bright and colorful. She leaned to the side and lay down on the hard ground with the stone in hand. *Tomorrow,* she thought, *tomorrow I will see if I can clean it and see how beautiful it is.*

CHAPTER 22

Stranger in the Desert

The night was black and deep. Julen found herself walking away into the unseen desert, walking aimlessly with no purpose. Stars overhead were bright, but their light did not reach the ground to allow the perception of more than vague outlines. She knew that the landscape was barren and dead, and felt no loss at being unable to see anything in her path. She had no energy to worry about tomorrow or how she would continue to walk on the uneven ground with aching, blistered feet. Even they felt numb, like her head—there was no feeling, just exhaustion and emptiness.

In the sterile stillness of the desert, not even night creatures stirred. The silence was complete. Then a faint sound reached her ears. She stopped and listened. Was it the sound of someone's labored breathing, maybe even groaning? Had Bina found her out here in the darkness? The thought dismayed her as she anticipated the stress of caring for her needs. Julen stood immobilized by the curious sound. The tone was deep and carried with it an anguish that made Julen want to weep as the sound drew nearer and nearer. Whoever it was walked toward her. She was not afraid. Still there was an urge to run away and not face a strange emotion that moved closer and closer.

A figure drew near just to her left side and came up beside her, shoulder to shoulder, still breathing heavily as if with grief and sorrow. Without any warning he—for she perceived that it was a man—stood before her, very large, and silent, so close that his garment almost touched her. Julen wanted to look into his face but he was standing too close. She looked up but could see nothing.

Neither of them spoke a word. Without any warning, a warm, thick liquid flowed over the top of her head, down her face and onto her dress. She drew in her breath in shock, knowing that it was blood, his blood. *What? Why?* The initial surprise and abhorrence passed as the balm soaked into her skin and an invigorating sensation of cleansing washed over her whole body.

"Who are you?" asked Julen of the stranger in a hoarse whisper.

"I am HE, the one you have been looking for," replied the man in a soft inaudible reply, not heard with the ears but with the heart.

"The blood, is it your blood?"

Julen remembered the strange man who appeared and stepped in front of the soldier's slash of the sword. "Were you the one who took the blow of the sword for me?" she asked in the same inaudible voice of the heart and knew that it was he. "I thought you were dead," she continued. She knew that he had been dead, but was now here, like a ghost come back to comfort her in her hour of need.

Heavy darkness still covered the land but in her heart she heard him say, "Yes, my precious one. I gave my life so that you could go free. My blood has bought you back and washed you clean. Now you are my precious Jewel."

Julen realized he was talking about her name when he said my precious Jewel. He was calling her Jewel, just like Ralda who was really Emerald. This must be the same man she had met long in the past. How could that be?

"What would you have me do? I am lost and alone. I seek a home and family and safety," Julen begged.

"I will give you a home. Come!" the stranger said softly. He raised his enormous arms and held them outstretched before her as she stood there pondering the promise. In an instant, the arms were together enveloping her within a powerful embrace, pulling her into another world of warm glowing light that flashed with brilliant radiance. Inside, she floated in mid-air as currents of love washed over her in peaceful circles spiraling higher and higher. She felt new and bright, as if she was dressed in the finest gown in the land, with waves of shimmering light flowing from her movements. He spoke words to her:

Forgiven,

Safe,

Accepted,

Treasured

A new wave of wonder and gratitude followed the first and Jewel began to cry, sobbing uncontrollably in a release of fear, guilt, sorrow, and pain. They flew away from her as vultures, waved off by a powerful force. Was this real or was it a dream?

A bright bubble of luminescence surrounded her and the stranger. She was not standing in front of him any longer, but seemed to be inside him. He was no longer a figure standing before her, but a huge presence of light. She stood in the middle with her arms, now bare of the iron symbol of her enslavement, raised up as if to return the embrace.

The presence grew larger and larger and the light spread. The feelings of warmth and love continued to fill her.

"Oh, stay, please stay," she begged. "Don't ever leave me!"

"I am here," the words came to her. "Look!"

Around her neck was Emerald's gold necklace with its wondrous stone, but now it was clean and bright. She held it in her hand, looked into the stone and saw sparkling lights shining from within the jewel. The words she had just heard were locked inside and beaming their truth to her mind and heart. The ground glittered with jeweled light beams forming a pathway that led off into the distance, across the desert into the hazy beyond that she could not see well. Through the haze, a tiny dome of yellow light sent beams out in rays that covered the whole of the starry sky. "Follow me," he said again, raising an arm in the direction of the wasteland ahead, "and I will lead you home."

"Where is your home? What is it called?"

"The Kingdom of Light," came the voice fading in the darkness.

Wet tears lay upon her face as she opened her eyes, letting in the first light of the coming dawn. Julen's back ached and she was cold. The dream world was gone, replaced with a sense of ordinary humanness that was flat and gray. The awe remained. She willed her mind to return and feel the incredible sensation of being drawn up into pure love and goodness. She savored every remembrance, going over and over every detail, trying to relive the ecstasy while she could.

"Don't leave," she whispered into empty air. "Don't leave!" she said louder.

Bina stirred, turned over, and opened her swollen eyes, staring in disbelief at Julen. "Am I seeing things?" she blinked and rubbed her eyes, staring again. "I've lost my mind or you have something around your neck from another world. Oh, my eyes! I'm going blind."

Julen raised her hand to her neck, felt the jeweled necklace and a chill went through her entire body. *Maybe it wasn't a dream, but it had to be,* she thought, still lost in the whole experience. When she had gone to sleep, the necklace was in her hand, dull and grimy. Now it was bright and clean and sparkled like the reflection of the sun on the sea.

"Bina, I had a strange dream. It was too amazing to tell about it," her voice husky with the lingering emotion. Words would not come to her mind to describe the feelings that she had never felt before, or come even close. It WAS something from another world, another life. It had to mean something. It could not have been a dream.

"Oh? And I had a dream too. I had a drink of water, but as you see it was only a dream and I am dying of thirst instead!" Bina shot back sarcastically as she tried to move but found her limbs too stiff . She lay there moaning.

"I dreamed…" Julen paused to try to find words, "that someone gave me this jeweled necklace and you see it is here." She knew that Emerald had given her the necklace, but it had not looked like this until now. There was so much, how would she convey it? Maybe it was impossible. Julen felt she was looking down from a high mountain, down on her life, a place where thirst and hunger waited for her, but she did not want to descend to meet it. Where she had been was beyond this life.

She moved her tongue around the inside of her mouth and found that Bina's concern was real. Julen willed herself to return to the desperation of the moment. "Maybe there is water in our future as well."

Bina turned to stare at the wall of the cave burbling garbled speech, "HUH! Starvation has clouded your mind and given you brain fever."

Julen felt the necklace again looked down into the depths of her jewel, remembering the words of the stranger, "I am here!" She stood amid throbbing pain, faced the desert with raised hands, and loudly implored, "Help us please. We need water and food," then paused before adding, "Thank you!"

Bina put her hands over her ears and said, "I can't believe this. Stop! Are you a raving lunatic?" She continued to stare at Julen and for the first time noticed that her companion's wristband was gone. Choking with additional shock, she closed her eyes and pretended she was seeing things.

"This can't be happening. This can't be happening."

Julen turned around and walked to the back of the cave. With a bit of effort she began to move a pile of stones.

"What now?" shouted Bina, afraid to find out the answer.

"I have a feeling we missed something last night, that's all," remarked Julen. Bina hummed a disjointed tune and shook her head. She shut her eyes tight against the reality that her young assistant had contracted a brain fever. But how did that explain the necklace AND the band.

Before long, the gurgling sound of water reached Bina's ears, despite her efforts to block out the sound. The spark in her attention was immediate.

"What should I call you now? Miracle Girl?" she scowled as she emphasized the name and crawled toward the sound.

"No, Bina. Call me Jewel, for that will be my name," said Jewel with a look of serenity that frightened the disheveled Bina.

"Do my ears lie to me, your highness? I thought I had run off with a puny, witless slave. Now you're going to tell me your new carnival trinket, probably found lying close by, no doubt lost by some phony traveling circus magician, has altered your mind to the point you think you are someone ELSE? And I actually thought back there in Bellicosa that you had potential!" she said coldly, reaching out her hand to let the water run over her fingers.

"Did you really think I had potential? You have never said so in the past."

"Just give me that water. I know I will die soon without a drink," Bina insisted, ignoring the younger woman's question.

"Didn't you just ask someone out there for some food as well? Where is it, Oh, bejeweled one? Rub your green glass and see if a magical spirit appears! I'm starving."

Jewel could not explain to Bina why she felt confident that help was there. She had been full of fear and doubt until her dream. The stranger had promised that she would be provided for. Looking out to the desert, there was nothing that offered any hope. Looking into the green jewel, she was comforted. A strange peace settled over her like a warm blanket calming her spirit with the knowledge that someone was there making sure they would not starve. There would be a way out of the desert.

"Bina, I am going to look for food. I'll be back soon." Bina looked at her with disbelief. "You are going to leave me here? Alone? And just walk off? What if you are seen? Think of the danger!" Bina yelled after her, but it was no use.

Making her way carefully over the rough stones, Jewel left the cave and walked out of sight of Bina. She reflected on how differently their situation looked. She could still remember the feeling of being wrapped in light and held secure in the love and forgiveness of the stranger. He would not have them die, but survive, and live to follow him to the home he promised. Out there somewhere was something to eat and she was determined to find it and show Bina. Surely, she would believe someone was helping them when she saw the proof of food.

Hours went by and Bina began to weigh the consequences of Jewel's failure to return. Death would be slow by starvation. Perhaps she had teased too much. All they had was each other, even if one of them had lost her mind.

As the noon sun shone directly overhead, Jewel returned carrying some strange looking flowering plants. "I found these along the edge of the desert. The leaves and stems aren't much, but the flowers are great—kind of sticky, but sweet." She sat down crossed-legged and leaned against the cave wall.

"You eat it first. I would rather die of hunger than in agony of being poisoned," said Bina. Jewel gathered a bunch of flowers in her hand, plucked them from the stems and carefully inserted them into her mouth taking care to look as pleased with the taste as she could. "Hmmm. HmMMmm!" she made exaggerated sounds to make her point. Bina waited a few minutes, watching closely, and then pounced on the remaining plants in Jewel's lap. Ripping and tearing and shoving the buds into her mouth, she agreed loudly, "MMMmmmm! Yes, mmmMMMmm. Oh, where can we get more? Let's go now!"

"Not unless you listen to my story," Jewel insisted with complete seriousness.

"Anything you say, I'm with you! But food first. Go now. Food!" said the wide-eyed Bina as she pushed Jewel out of the cave.

CHAPTER 23

New Routine

Far out to sea, Damon stood on the upper deck trying to make himself useful. He hadn't been very good at it as yet, but he was improving, of that he was sure. As the ship had weighed anchor and was pulled out of the protection of the harbor, he had felt a thrill of excitement and adventure. Out on the open sea under full sail, it was another matter, as the rolling of the ship over gentle, but substantial, waves brought to bear the battle going on in his stomach and gave him second thoughts. He swallowed hard and was determined that he would not allow himself to be sick. All the crew, he felt, were looking at him, and he very much desired to have their good opinion.

"Here, Master, let me tie that knot," a sailor had suggested to Damon the first day. "No, no, I can do this," he quickly replied, as he twisted and turned a stubborn line. He kept tying and untying it until he got it almost right. Satisfied with himself, he went to the next task, while the sailor who had not gone far away quietly re-secured the rope. Damon wondered if the crew was protecting him or if he was really being given the responsibilities of a seaman. He was not afraid to take a few knocks if necessary. *The men just have to see that I won't break with the first fall, that's all,* he thought. Even a future master and owner can learn the skills of seamanship.

One of the first things he realized was that being dressed in his land clothes was not a good idea. The work on board the ship was rough and required loosely fitting garments that were not too heavy. At night, it was cool; but during the day, swabbing decks and hauling on ropes, he worked up enough heat to tempt him to jump overboard just to cool off. Of course, he did not seriously consider such an action as the ship was traveling at a good clip and he would soon be lost if he had been so foolish.

As far as the eye could see, which didn't seem very far, there was only blue water dotted with caps of glistening white tossing constantly up and down in a hypnotizing rhythm. The common sailors who worked steadily around him saw the greenish tinge in his face, looked at one another with knowing glances and smirks, but always took care that the young gentleman's back was turned.

Captain Fairway saw that Damon was given a tunic and trousers befitting a sailor, and once donned, only his sandy colored hair, clean and groomed, kept him from blending in perfectly.

Damon's favorite pastime, when he permitted himself, was to watch over the side; he had already been rewarded with a close up view of a school of smiling porpoises leaping alongside as the ship sailed in the northwesterly breeze. Captain Fairway had told him that they were likely to see more, so he kept checking in case those or other sea creatures made an appearance.

The very next day he had seen the spray of a spouting whale in the distance, with the rising hump of the back and a tail fin large and distinct against the blue sky—such powerful creatures, majestic and free to wander their seemingly limitless home. Damon was aware that he too was wandering far and wide seeking the freedom to find his own way, free from the constraints and cares of family, free from the emptiness of a life that came fully prescribed before he was born. Was there more somewhere out there in the great beyond? He longed to know.

In the next few days, they would reach their first port. Chiselstone blades would be delivered and payment taken before setting sail once more. He would take out his fine clothes again, transform himself back into the shrewd businessman, and impress those on land with his knowledge of cutlery and weapons of all kinds. *Ah, what would it be like in a different town with different people?* he wondered.

The Bellicosa Prison, built against the vertical cliffs on the west side of the bay at the edge of town, limited the likelihood of escape. With a sheer cliff at the back, the other three sides were well guarded stone walls that closed in the hapless prisoners and closed out sunlight. An iron grating opposite the cliff rose two stories high at a gap between the walls, with a gate at the bottom. It looked like an enormous fort with battlements around the top, but the weapons wielded by the guards were aimed inside rather than outside the structure.

Inside the prison were four levels. The ground level housed a common room for the guards and soldiers in which they ate and exchanged news. Those who entered or exited could not avoid going through this room, which gave an added element of security. Stairs led up and down. The upstairs area held cells for those whose trials were pending. Sentences would be either death or incarceration. After a judgment in favor of the latter, the other stairway only led down and down until the vilest were put away in the dungeon and rarely seen again.

Jip and the other prisoners condemned to hard labor were on the first level below the common room. Each day they were rounded up and driven out through the large room in view of the guards whose only enjoyment of the day was jeering and insulting the prisoners.

Out the gate they went each day to accomplish their assigned task, then were herded back in again at night, always guarded heavily. Day after miserable day saw Jip's strength ebbing. He had been muscular and fit but the foul tasting gruel he ate each day did not provide what a hard working young man needed to keep his strength up. He became more and more aware that to stay there meant certain slow and miserable death. Consequently, his mind churned with the desperate desire to escape, though he had heard that no one had successfully done so in the past. He would die trying. To stay was worse than death.

With this in mind, the only thing to look forward to each day was the formation of another plan. Carefully, he watched every move of the guards, trying to discover a pattern that would be useful to him. *How much longer can I take this kind of life?* he asked himself over and over.

CHAPTER 24
The One

Jewel led the way along a path formed by the level plain of the desert on the right and the base of the mountain on the left. Going in a direction beyond where they had slept the night, a slow two hours passed as Bina annoyed Jewel by impatiently asking, "Where is this place?

The afternoon sun beat down on the sand and reflected back scorching radiant waves. They both regretted that they had no means of carrying water.

As they continued, Bina spied a tiny plant growing out of the sand just in front of them and sighed audibly in her disappointment that it was too young to bear flowers. After another five minutes of walking, the plants were bigger and more mature. Bina grabbed the flowers as they passed and yelled at Jewel, "Slow down! I can hardly pick them if you are walking so fast."

Up ahead the path curved to the left heading into another ravine. As the two made the turn, a whole hillside of plants was revealed, growing thicker toward the center of the groove between two smaller ridges coming down from the mountain. Jewel turned to Bina and said at last, "There! Is that enough for you?" Bina stood with eyes wide with happy surprise then broke into a hobbled run. Both women gathered until they were exhausted, then sat down to eat.

"Bina, if there are plants here, maybe there is water somewhere as well. How else could they grow?"

"I don't know, but one thing is sure. This stuff gives you a terrible thirst—and sticky hands!"

Jewel rose and looked around trying to decide in which direction they were most likely to find water. As she leaned forward to get up, her necklace swung forward gleaming in the last rays of sun before it dipped behind the mountains. She was reminded of the help she had gotten that morning and Bina's sarcasm about her jewel. She knew the stranger was not a magical spirit, but perhaps rubbing the emerald was an idea worth trying. She picked up the large green stone, rubbing it between her fingers, and held it up to the light of the sun. As it moved around in her hand, rays of light shot out this way and that. One of the rays found a shiny surface and reflected a beam back into Jewel's eyes. She blinked and looked again more carefully. The light came from ahead of them in the center of the ravine. Walking over to the place where she had seen the light, she found a small trickle of water running down the face of the rock wall. It was barely enough to make the rock look wet, but it was enough to catch the reflection of the sun from her necklace.

"Bina, I think we have water here."

Bina could not believe Jewel's good luck. How was she doing this? Two days in a row, she had been able to find water and then food as well. She was too tired and frustrated by the whole experience to want to think about it so she decided just to ignore it. Telling this ignorant girl she had done something important would just encourage her to think she had had some kind of vision. It had to have been hunger and exhaustion that put those funny ideas into her head. Perhaps the koma tree grew nearby and Jewel had secretly been imbibing its magical properties. Bina knew that Jewel could not keep this up, and before the day was out, it would be clear who really had the brains of the two.

Jewel pulled away stones at the bottom of the flow and found a small pool. They took turns bending low on hands and knees to drink, then washed their sticky fingers.

"Bina, you promised you would listen to my story," said Jewel once they were resting after their meal. "Right…story…wake me if I snore. I'm feeling mighty sleepy."

Jewel began telling her about her dream, beginning with the walk in the dark. She got to the part about hearing a strange sound when another sound arose, now coming rhythmically from Bina's throat. *This isn't the right time,* Jewel thought. *Maybe later she will hear me out.*

The sun had passed the edge of the mountain and was sinking in the west. Shadows grew out into the desert sands, cooling the day at last. Jewel looked at the hillside and noticed that they had pretty much stripped the plants of all their flowers. What would they eat the next day? Should they sleep in the ravine, which was very rocky, or look for shelter for the night elsewhere? She closed her eyes and tried to shut out the questions and bring back the vision of glowing light and warmth. Except for Bina's snoring, it was perfectly quiet where they rested.

Sounds of laughter in the distance disturbed her reverie. She stiffened as she recognized the male voices and imagined the soldiers coming upon them. For once, she was grateful to be dressed to match the stones of the hillside, now with the added dust and dirt from sleeping on the ground. Retreating back, she abruptly woke Bina and warned her of possible danger. They both crouched low at the back of the gorge, afraid to move a muscle.

The sounds got louder and soon they could see a party of soldiers heading back toward the direction of their previous day's escape. The black-caped man was no longer with them, but they were searching nonetheless. They knew the women had to be out in the desert somewhere and they were determined to find them. The men rode by very close and glanced toward the shady ravine.

"Could they have come this far and we not find them? Perhaps they went along the top of the mountain before descending," said a red-haired, bearded soldier. Jewel gulped as she spied what looked like the capes and apron the two women had shed on their way up the mountain being carried by one of the men.

"We have gone the whole way around the desert and not seen any sign of them," said another. "We had better head back as it will be dark before we arrive in Bellicosa."

As they rode out of sight, Jewel breathed a loud sigh. "They haven't given up. Why are they so worried about two lowly slaves? What is important about us?"

"And how do we get out of this desert?" asked Bina.

Jewel stared out into the desert and remembered the stranger pointing in that direction and promising to show her the way. "I think we are supposed to go into the desert," she said knowing what Bina's reply would be.

"You will walk out into the desert sun over my cold, stiff body!" Bina cried adamantly. "An imbecile could predict what will happen to the one who ventures into the deadly wastes with no food or water, and no promise of respite in sight." The exhausted woman looked up with dread and resolve in the opposite direction to the mountains behind them. "We have no choice. It would be suicide going any way but up. Believe me. Whatever you think we are *supposed* to do is crazy. Once we are up on the mountain, we will be able to see the lay of the land."

Jewel was silent in the knowledge that this made the most sense. "I'm sure he told me to go into the desert," she said softly. "Look," Bina interrupted, "we put you in charge of food and water and, see! You did your part. Now I am in charge of choosing the direction. And I say we are going up! Is that clear?"

Looking up the side of the mountain, they both imagined how hard it would be to climb out of the dry valley. Jewel had no notion either of the terrain or contours of what lay in any direction. Her only experience had been in Bellicosa with its rocks and dry, barren mountains.

Jewel and Bina slept on the mountainside among the plants that night. As they lay trying to arrange their bodies to fit the rise and fall of the ground, Jewel asked, "Did you wonder who the man was who was killed back in Bellicosa?"

"Some unfortunate passerby, I suppose. I am sorry for him but it did come at a good time for us."

"It was not an accident, Bina. He did it on purpose."

"Don't tell me you saw that in your dream as well."

"I did. It was The One."

"What on earth, or I should say, who on earth is that?"

"The day you were sleeping in the mistress' room, I went back in her closet, into a secret room. On the wall, I saw that someone had written a saying about calling on The One. It was him, I'm sure."

"You did what? Oh, it all makes sense now." Bina could endure no more. "Better get some sleep," Bina said, hoping to bring an end to the bizarre conversation. "But try not to have any more dreams, alright?" She rolled her eyes with a look of complete incomprehension.

"It isn't just a dream, Bina. It is real!" said Jewel.

"And I'm the Queen of Bellicosa. Listen, I only believe in what I can see, and I can't see any ONE. Goodnight."

CHAPTER 25
The Goddess Remora

It was not a comfortable night's sleep. Morning arrived with a gradual yellow dawn and then a cool, fresh sunrise over the eastern horizon. With the light, came a surprise to both women. Delicate pale blue flowers surrounded them. The plants had flowered again overnight, drowning them in such pleasant fragrance that their waking thoughts were of another world. And there was plenty to eat for breakfast.

After making their best attempt at washing accessible skin areas that were, by this time very dusty, they gathered their last sustenance before the hike almost straight up the mountain.

"These sandals are ruined," observed Bina as she looked at her blistered, scraped feet.

"If we are leaving what's left of them behind, we had better bury the remains," warned Jewel. They piled rocks on the shredded shoes. Jewel ripped the bottom of her dress around the hem and took the strips to bind her feet. Watching with measured scorn, Bina finally did the same.

Jewel found it easy to step up to the next foothold, but it was not so for short-legged Bina. Each upward movement was difficult and strained her ageing muscles.

Approaching a short precipice, Jewel slipped when a rock she had stood upon gave way under her foot. Her shin scraped against sharp edges. She sat down and held it, watching the blood surface and run down her hands. Bina sighed again as if tending a naughty child and said, "Whose dress this time?" Jewel could see that she had more length to work with so tore her own to bind the leg. After a rest, they trudged on.

By mid-day they had reached a summit. It did not afford much of a view, and it was another hour going in and out of hills until they finally saw for the first time a valley on the other side of the mountain. A river ran through the center of the valley and met the sea in a wide delta. Back from the river, they could trace the lines of streams that fed the main waterway. One such stream was fed by the runoff from the mountain on which they stood. The two continued in the direction they both hoped would lead to the head of a spring.

As they descended, they began to pass small trees and shrubs. Soon there were larger trees and then a full forest. It was cool and green and a great relief to have shade after being in the sun for hours.

A trickling of water caught their attention and they followed the sound. A tiny spring percolated from the ground and grew as it moved down the mountain. They stopped to refresh themselves and then continued, hoping to find a place to bathe.

Stumbling with tiredness, they walked into what looked like a clearing made for gaining access to the water. The sound of water falling from a higher ledge of rocks and into a quiet pool contrasted sharply with the dry and dusty mountain quietness. Grass as green as Jewel's emerald was neatly trimmed, and ornate wooden benches were constructed on all sides of the pool. They sat down and looked around in wonder.

"What is this place?" asked Bina in amazement.

"It is so beautiful. I wonder what it is for?" added Jewel.

"What is that white thing behind the waterfall? It looks like a small cave and someone is standing there in the opening." Bina tensed and realized that they may have come upon someone bathing and looked away. Jewel walked closer and tried to peer into the stream of water. The form was very pale and still.

"I think it is a statue of some kind—a woman perhaps, carved from marble. She is beautiful with long flowing hair," said Jewel. Bina looked closer, noting the similarity of the statue's features to those of her companion.

"How strange," remarked Bina.

"What is it?" asked Jewel. "This statue looks very familiar." Jewel stepped closer to have a look. The water spray falling on her felt delightful after the heat of the barren mountains.

Just then, a young girl appeared through the woods and was startled to see Jewel looking as if she had just stepped out of the waterfall. She stopped and stared. Jewel realized she was frightened so she said, "Hello. This is a lovely place. Do you live around here?"

The child's mouth dropped open in surprise. She turned and ran as fast as she could back the way she had come.

"I don't like the look of this," said Bina. Jewel did not know what to think.

"Maybe we should leave. It looks like we scared her. After all, look at us, dirty, bruised, torn, not to mention our clothing being a bit brief!" Both women bent over the pool to see their reflection and busied themselves trying to wash off the grime from the day's hike.

"We'll have to find some new clothes somewhere so we look like the locals," suggested Bina, who was wondering what was in fashion in this part of the world. "Come on, we have some spying to do."

With that, she moved off back into the woods until the clearing was no longer in sight. She slowly picked her way through bushes and dead trees until they had descended into the valley. In the distance, they could see the village more clearly. At the outskirts was a house, and at the back stood an older woman bending slightly and listening to a child as she waved her arms around and pointed up the hill. "Looks like our little darling is telling mama quite a tale," said Bina. "That food would have tasted so good that we probably won't get now."

"They may be friendly and want to help us. I don't think they are slave owners. I think they will feel sorry for us escaping from Bellicosa," said Jewel.

At this time, the woman and the child went inside the house. "I don't think so. No. Looks to me like she went to fetch a weapon or find someone else to help catch the runaways."

The woman came out of the house and hastened up the path followed by a bevy of children of all ages.

"I think she is friendly, Bina." The two retreated back to the clearing. It wasn't long before the group breathlessly arrived at the waterfall.

"Quiet children; it's all right." She bowed self-consciously and said to Bina and Jewel, "It is an honor to meet you. You have come down from the sacred waterfall." The woman hesitated again, as if trying to remember her manners. "I know who you are," she gulped and bowed again. "We welcome you to our...I mean, welcome to Credulos, Oh Great One."

They all bowed deeply to the ground and did not get up. Bina and Jewel looked at one another in amazement and wondered what was happening. Bina spoke up making a quick decision to go along as the scene played out.

"You may rise."

Jewel shot her a look that asked, *WHAT?*

"Tell us, who do you think we are?" asked Bina. The humble woman rose and said with tears in her eyes, "You are Remora our awaited leader and her servant Onusia. We have not forgotten you in all these years."

"Can you take us to your home please? We are hungry," said Jewel, shrugging her shoulders and turning to Bina, hoping she might have something to add.

"Yes!" added Bina. "That's right. We are hungry and we wish to go to your home to eat." They both smiled and waited for the next clues.

The mother and children dashed back down the path toward their house, laughing and skipping gaily, as the mother scolded them for their lack of reverence.

"Did she say we came out of the waterfall?" asked Jewel incredulously. "Did she call us Great Ones?" Bina continued baffled but encouraged.

They reached the house and the woman turned to them again and said nervously, "Please wait here. My home is so humble. I will be right back with someone who is greater than I." They waited for a few minutes and an old woman came from inside the house. She was bent over with snowy white hair pulled up in a small bun on top of her head.

"Greetings, Oh Great Ones. You are most welcome in our town," and she bowed low.

Bina spoke, "Yes, I am Remora and this is my servant...eh, Asonsia." The old woman laughed hesitantly and replied in a raspy voice, "I didn't know Goddesses had a sense of humor, or perhaps you test us to see if we know the legend well enough. Of course, you are the servant Onusia. And this is the most honored one, Remora of the Waterfall," she said pointing to Jewel. "You even wear the green stone of Mount Cupidity. Honor to you, Blessed One!"

Bina's mouth dropped open as she realized the mistaken identity. Willing to go along with the charade, she jumped into the part she would play as servant to Jewel. This definitely had taken a turn for the worse, but right then food was most important, so she decided to swallow her pride and play along.

A small contingency of towns people was headed their way. Bina and Jewel braced themselves to see how the misunderstanding of who they were would continue. An older man stepped forward and bowed at the waist. He looked to be around sixty years old judging by the lines on his face and his graying hair. He was tall and straight with a large protruding belly. Formally dressed for his position of authority, he wore a dark green coat with tails hanging almost to the ground over knee length breeches of a woody brown color.

"Profoundest greetings. We are honored, Great Ones. I am Paramount Torpid Harbinger." He rose from his bow to inspect the two. The two women curtsied clumsily wondering how a goddess is supposed to act.

"You have come to us to test our faithfulness and we wish to prove to be your humble followers. We were expecting you to come dressed in fine clothing, but now we see you are in rags. Whatever it is that you need we will supply from our finest."

Jewel stepped forward and spoke again, "Thank you. We are on our way to a great city known as the Kingdom of Light. Can you tell us the way?" Bina blinked in shock. She had not heard this from Jewel before, and knew it was not the time to be making such revelations.

At this, all the people cried in alarm, "Please, no. Remora, do not leave us again! We will do anything you say." Paramount Harbinger lost his balance and his mouth gaped open.

"Well, I didn't mean right now," Jewel corrected herself. Everyone collectively sighed in relief. Bina whispered, "Let ME do that talking."

Playing the part, Bina fell in ten paces behind the great Remora as they walked along the road to the paramount's home. Jewel tried to look like a dignified lady, though it made her feel very uncomfortable. Was it really right to let them believe she was a goddess? Surely, the people could see that they were only runaway slaves.

The citizens had been caught unprepared, but they did their best to bring out what food they had. The bread was a bit stale and green around the edges, and the fish had an odor that turned their stomachs. Julen and Bina were seated at the table next to the town dignitaries who went to great lengths to make them comfortable. However, the sun was shining in Jewels eyes so she squinted and squirmed to adjust to the brilliant light. As she did, the rays of light caused the green jewel at her neck to sparkle. Reflected light bounced around and shone in the eyes of those in attendance.

"Look!" cried an old woman hunched over the table. "The jewel has turned the food into a feast fit for a king."

"Yes!" cried another, "I see it! The bread is dripping in fresh butter, and there is fruit sauce, pies, and cakes better than any country fair could produce!"

Bina was shocked. Jewel was even more shocked as they both stared at the food, which had not altered from its stale and odorous state.

"It is a miracle!" shouted one, then another. "The Goddess Remora has brought us prosperity once again!" and they all cheered loudly eating and drinking the spoiled food as if it were nectar from the gods.

Word spread of the Miracle of the Leftovers, and the next two days were like heaven for both Jewel and Bina. Despite the fact that it was galling for Bina to bow to the great Remora, and the fact that they took her apron away to burn, she could not believe their good fortune to have come upon the town of Credulos.

They bathed in perfumed suds and had their hair dressed in the fashion of women of high status. Banquets of food were laid before them, along with the finest wine in the region. Servants came and offered an array of new dresses for Jewel and a lesser quality to Bina; they had only to pick what they wanted.

Jewel chose a green gown embroidered with colorful flowers and designs. Seamstresses attended her to make sure that the fit was perfect.

"Well isn't it amazing what a baggy, gray dress can hide?" commented Bina when she saw Jewel's curves in the new outfit.

A shining red tunic that fitted her shape better was offered to Bina and she consented to wear it. Putting on the new clothes for the first time made tears come to Jewel's eyes. She looked in the looking glass and saw her reflection. The green of the dress made her brown skin look iridescent. Even Bina couldn't believe what a good job they had done cleaning up this one who was not long ago lower than a scullery brat. And the jeweled necklace—like nothing anyone had seen ever before in the town of Credulos—continued to sparkle and reflect blinding rays of light.

Paramount Harbinger approached and bowed. "We know the legend well and will honor you accordingly. We will have a splendid promenade in your honor, Great One. The man that you choose to marry will become a leader among us."

At this, Jewel gulped and held her tongue. *Marry!* Oh, no, what had they gotten into? Bina's eyes were wide open though she did not register any other emotions on her face. They both turned away and Jewel whispered intensely, "What? Bina, what are we doing this for? A few clothes and some food?" The fast thinking Bina came back, "Hold it. This could be good. You could wind up living like a queen, with me your servant living alongside you with, of course, special privileges. Why go looking for some Kingdom of Light when all you want is here? Wouldn't you rather be a goddess here than a slave anywhere else? Think about it!"

Jewel turned again, imagining that this could have been what the stranger in the desert meant when he promised to lead her to a home. She replied to the group, "Why thank you. Yes...may the legend be honored."

The next several weeks saw both Jewel and Bina showered with gifts. They were given their own apartment in the house of the paramount. Word was sent around the entire region that single men of high rank should present themselves to the Great Remora at the Mid-Summer Ball the following week.

Each day, visitors came to ask for a blessing or to merely bask in the presence of the Great One. Some older ones sought to explain local history and customs.

"How many years has it been since the legend began, you ask?" replied old Mistress Roundbush when Jewel asked about local history. "Well you yourself should know of all people...I mean...Goddess. When you came the first time, I was a child. You can see that I am now old and you are still young. How I would love to know the secret of that accomplishment," she added as an offhand comment.

"I'll grant you some forgetfulness...I'm pretty forgetful myself these days, but I haven't forgotten your story. Oh, no. Remember how you ruled Credulos with wisdom, and cunning, I might add. And you always were a beauty." Jewel blushed and smiled. "And that emerald necklace, I remember that too. Sparkle, it did, and it had power. The story went that if anyone else touched it, they would turn to dust."

So far so good, thought Bina as she watched carefully.

"The trouble started when you asked us to find you a suitable husband. He had to be the handsomest, most intelligent and talented man in the kingdom, but that was easier said than done. A search was made far and wide and one man met the criteria who was then presented before you, Great Remora. You remember now, don't you?" she asked nodding her head.

"On the evening of the presentation, you were not pleased with the one chosen. I was too young, of course, but they say that the night of the wedding, you and your handmaiden walked up into the sacred waterfall and were never seen again. For months afterward, it didn't rain and the crops grew very poorly. That was naughty of you," she said light-heartedly so as not to sound offensive. "We have learned from our mistake, Oh Great One, if ever you returned, we determined that you would choose your own husband. And we will all live happily thereafter." She finished her account with a hopeful smile.

Jewel tried to absorb all the implications of what Mistress Roundbush had said. Playing this part was dangerous. Surely, someone would see that they did not match the legendary figures. How could she live up to the expectations put upon her as a leader of the people? Perhaps if she did find a handsome and intelligent man, he could do the leading and she could enjoy the life of a wife. *What are the chances of this really working?*

Others who came for an audience had another agenda in mind. One woman proclaimed, "Oh, Great One, I would like to tell you about my son. He is very handsome and intelligent. And talent? He can balance ten spinning plates on top of his head while riding a wild horse! He has even leaped from the roof of a house and flown to the nearest tree!" The proud mother was pleased when Jewel responded, "What noble skills your son has, madam." The mothers especially liked it when she called them "madam."

CHAPTER 26
Mister Perfect

The time for the Promenade and ball arrived, and It was rumored that several men had come to seek the favor of the Great One. Remora was dressed in her green creation that would become her wedding gown when she finally chose her mate. Her massive hair had been braided with colorful ribbons and fresh flowers, then piled up on her head like a crown and pinned in place. She stood tall and elegant, despite her nervousness, and walked slowly and with great dignity into the hall. At the sight of her and her magnificent sparkling green jewel, the lines of towns people bowed and spoke reverently, "Long live Remora!" Bina, in red, came along behind her blowing kisses to the crowd and strutting proudly.

The Promenade started as a long walk around the Hall with two boys carrying a banner between them proclaiming the Great Remora had come at last. Paramount and Paramountess Harbinger, followed by Credulosian officials and their spouses, walked behind dressed in their finest. Local citizens threw butterfly wings and colorful, chopped zorbot leaves. The pageantry was stunning.

A drum of low timbre thudded out a steady beat then several flutes and pipes picked up the tune. Lively music with a haunting melody had begun, and made everyone want to dance and enjoy themselves. Jewel stood at the front of the large room presiding over the festivities.

The first suitor of the evening approached her and bowed asking for the dance. He was quite a bit shorter than Jewel and the lamp light reflected off the top of his bald head. He had a rich smile and a merry step as he whirled Jewel around the floor. She had never danced before and found it difficult not to trip over his fast moving feet. He was a good sport about being trampled, but at the end of the dance, he bowed low and disappeared into the crowd.

A second man was waiting for the next reel. He had watched the first dance partner and quickly realized the Great One's lack of greatness on the dance floor. He did not want this to be a distraction so they proceeded at a slower pace, in fact at about half the speed of the first dancer. Jewel's impression of this man was much better. He was good-looking and had a lovely smile. As soon as they began the dance, he opened his mouth to speak, and did not finish with his presentation of himself until the music stopped. It was a blast of information on his accomplishments and good qualities that left Jewel's head spinning.

Several more men tried their hand at impressing Remora, all with little success. The more she saw, the more tired she grew, and finally, she could not remember one from the other. One more man remained to be evaluated, but by this time, Jewel was so weary she could hardly stand.

The young man bowed, kissed her hand, and introduced himself, "Remora, I hope you do not mind me calling you by your name. If we are to be married then we should by-pass formality. Don't you agree?" Jewel dumbly nodded. "I am Master Derrick Karakul. You may call me Derrick. I see that you are weary of this game. Shall we sit?"

"What a wonderful idea," returned Jewel. She raised her hand and he led her to a soft couch on the podium. Jewel tried to focus her attention on this last man. Perhaps he would stick in her fatigued mind. She hadn't said much during the evening, as everyone assumed she had nothing to say. Hadn't she been in some kind of suspended goddess state up there in the waterfall?

Most of the candidates had spent their time boasting of their credentials and accomplishments. Feeling quite overwhelmed with all the information, Jewel was incapable of making a decision about a future spouse.

Master Karakul was charming and thoughtful. Bringing her a drink of cool wine, he asked her how she was feeling and gave her all his attention.

"This is a difficult task. My future is at stake, but I do not have any notion of one of these gentlemen being better than any of the others," she told him honestly. He looked softly into her eyes and said, "Remora, my sweet. Do not make a decision tonight under this kind of pressure. Tell the paramount that you wish to think about it for a few days. In the meantime, I wish to show you the wonders of life in our humble kingdom. I have an estate not far away and you may visit my home. I will be honest with you. I hope you will decide that I can care for you lovingly for the rest of your life. And your servant will perhaps want to be the head of my household staff." He continued to smile now holding her hand in his.

Jewel was hypnotized by his warm words and charming ways. How fatherly and affectionate he was, so honest and true. Perhaps he was right. She would tell the paramount Harbinger her decision to make the choice in three days, and spend more time with Derrick. What a wonderful plan!

"Sir Paramount," she said with a certain air, "I wish to announce my decision in three days. I will spend more time re-acquainting myself with your town so I may make the best decision."

Everyone was disappointed that there would be no announcement that night. Occasions like this brought many people out because they wanted to see the romance and ceremony of it all. Now they would simply hear of a match and be invited to the wedding later. The crowd broke up and drifted away into the night.

Jewel and Bina went back to their quarters and talked about the evening. "Well, did you find Sir Perfect, Oh Great One?" Bina asked sarcastically.

"I'm not sure. I was so tired. But I did meet Master Derrick Karakul who, besides wanting to make me his wife, mentioned that he had an opening for a person to head his household staff. That's a big step up for both of us," said Jewel hoping to at least interest Bina in the proposition.

"Head of the household staff…hmmm…let me think about that. It beats being YOUR servant, Oh Tall Skinny One," Bina mocked as she continued to poke fun at the exalted names Jewel was accruing.

Jewel fell asleep thinking about the change in her circumstances that had all come about so quickly. How had it happened? The stranger was right! She was finding a home and love and family all in one fell swoop. Never did she think she would have so much in this life, but here it was about to be hers.

The next day, Jewel woke with suffocating nightmares again. Would they ever go away? She gathered herself together and put a smile on her face. Today she would visit the House of Karakul and the master himself would treat her like a fine lady, spoiling her with anything her heart desired. She rose and chose to wear her shimmering green dress once again. She felt like a queen as servants prepared her hair and rubbed the pleasant smelling cockleshell oil on her skin to make it soft. Such luxury raised her to new heights of exhilaration.

"I suppose you should go too, Bina, if you are to look at this future household you might be managing," said Jewel, knowing that Bina would be hard to convince to stay behind on such an occasion. Bina was two steps ahead of Jewel, having already readied herself, and was about to walk out the door.

A carriage called for the two at mid-morning. Inside, the handsome Derrick reached a hand out and welcomed the goddess and her servant. A footman helped them in and they were off to the master's estate.

The countryside was beautiful in the late summer. Perfume from flowering trees and the soft music from songbirds lulled Jewel into a peaceful trance.

The lane was lined with stone walls, behind which were fields of hay and grazing sheep. As they neared the great house, Jewel's heart beat faster and faster. Then she saw it, graceful and massive, much like Arcana, except a less severe appearance due to the light brown plaster that covered the exterior walls. The windows were large, and multi-paned glass allowing light to enter the many rooms. Ivy grew up the front of the building surrounding the front entrance in green.

As they drove up to the front doors, they opened wide as if automatic, and servants in tight fitting blue and white uniforms came out and stood at attention. The carriage stopped and Jewel could hardly believe the wealth of Derrick and his family.

As Jewel and Bina were being helped down to the driveway, an elderly couple came out of the house and stood with arms spread in a welcoming gesture. Mistress Karakul was a well-kept woman whose life-long wealth showed through her smooth skin and exquisite gown. She smiled graciously, as if they could hardly wait to meet their potential daughter-in-law. The master's thinning hair did not take away from his still handsome face. With lips oozing charm and reverence, he kissed Remora's hand.

"Oh, Great One! We are so glad you have come to honor us with a visit to our humble home. Please do come in and make yourself comfortable," said the older Master Karakul. Turning to his wife, she added bowing, "Indeed, we are so glad to meet you at last."

"I am honored to meet you," said Jewel exuberantly. She was overcome with joy and excitement.

"Remora, dear, these are my parents, the older Master and Mistress Karakul. I, of course, will inherit the title sometime in the future," assured the younger man.

"Yes, yes, indeed. He will be the master someday," added the father.

"Father, Mother, this is the Great One, Remora of Old. You may call her Remora," he said and turned to her to explain, "It's much easier don't you think?" Before she could answer, they had taken her by each arm and ushered her through the doors into the Great Hall. Jewel was stunned by the opulence and stood speechless staring up at the grand staircase winding its way up to the upper floor. Suits of armor stood at guard at the bottom of the stairs and lush tapestries hung from the walls along with the prominent coat of arms of the House of Karakul.

"I see you admire our family crest," said Master Karakul, proudly realizing that Jewel was staring at the green and purple shield that hung on the wall. "It is Shallowdra, the great dragon. They say she lives still in the mountains and keeps watch over us day and night. You might have seen her up there." Jewel recognized the central symbol as being similar to that of the Bellicosan reptile. It was a version of the same green dragon, though it was oddly different. Instead of the fierce threatening mouth and eyes, it bore a silly grin, which made it look more like a pet.

"Yes, I do recognize her. I think I have seen her before, but last I heard she was living in the sea."

Derrick laughed, "What nonsense!"

They moved on and Jewel, followed by the subservient Bina, was given a tour of the whole house, the gardens, stables, and the lake. It was all thoroughly impressive and Jewel believed this was the greatest display she had ever seen. How could anyone not say yes to a handsome Master-to-be AND all of this in the offer? She was swept off her feet by the courteous and thoughtful parents, the charming Derrick, dogs, cats, birds, beauty, wealth, and love.

Other tours took place after that one, but none made that kind of impression on her. At the end of the three days, she could hardly wait to say "yes" to Derrick and his family, secretly giving thanks to the One for such a provision.

The town was overjoyed when the announcement was made. One week from that day was the date set for the wedding. There was not much time to prepare, but Jewel and Bina did not have to do anything. The wedding dress was made even more beautiful by adding stitches of golden thread here and there. The Karakul family presented Jewel with a pair of earrings to wear for the wedding that went back in their family for many generations.

"My sweet Remora," said the older Mistress, "why not leave your emerald necklace at the house and wear these fine jewels of our family instead. They will match your dress so much better."

Jewel considered this momentarily, reaching up to her neck. The necklace had become part of her and she would miss it now. But it was heavy and did attract too much attention, and possibly took away from the fine things that the people of Credulos had given her.

"You are right," replied Jewel. "Before the wedding I will put it in your care."

The wedding was to be held on the green in front of the town hall. Inside the building, Jewel was being prepared to look her best. The two women stood gazing at one another admiring every item symbolizing the generosity of Credulos.

The groom and his family were in another room also preparing. They planned to come together at the door and go down an isle formed by pots of flowers contributed by the Karakuls, and become goddess and husband.

Jewel grew increasingly nervous. The time had arrived for her to remove her necklace and give it to Derrick's mother. Bina unfastened it for her from behind and carefully wrapped it up in a soft cloth. Taking a last uncertain look, she placed it in a leather draw string bag provided to her by the family. How thoughtful they had been in everything. There was no more fortunate girl in the whole world.

Walking softly out the door of her assigned room, Jewel slipped down the hall to the room where she knew the Karakuls were dressing. She was about to knock on their door when she overheard the older Master speaking inside the room. "We are so proud of you, Derrick. You have managed the best move of your career. Tonight you will be married to the so-called Great One," he said sarcastically, "and your family will become the most powerful in the country."

Then the mother added, "Oh, my, I have to laugh to think that this little imposter has managed to fool everyone into thinking she is the Great Remora from the old legend. What a gullible bunch they are! They don't remember the legend as well as they think they do. Everyone used to know that it was an Alexandrite that the real Remora had, and it was not a necklace but a ring on her hand. It was famous in the land for changing to all colors of the rainbow. How could they have forgotten that?"

"Mother, Father, I too am proud. My charm has convinced her to become my bride. I am quite the young man, eh?" Derrick joked as he winked at his mother.

"You are my dear," added the mistress. "Once I get my hands on that necklace, I don't care what you do with the two of them. I am certain that stone is magical and I know someone who will pay a very big sum for it. You can ship them back to Bellicosa if you wish for I am almost certain that is where they have come from. Who else would be wearing the gray tunic of a slave?"

"Do you think she will simply give you the necklace, mother?" asked Derrick.

"I do, for I convinced the simple girl to let me keep it for her until after the wedding. After the wedding, indeed. She will never see that trinket again!" and the three laughed heartily at the humor in it all.

Jewel ran as lightly and as quickly as she could down the hall to her room. Once inside with the door closed she whimpered softly to Bina, "We must leave at once!"

"What are you talking about?" asked Bina admiring herself in the looking glass.

"I mean we have been found out. They know I am not Remora. All they want is my necklace, not me, not you!" she cried. "We have to leave before they find out we know."

"How do we leave all this?" returned Bina who just could not believe they would walk out on all of it.

"I'm sorry. I had thought that this was the home that the One promised. It looked too miraculous to be anything else. But I was wrong. Oh, I should have known," lamented Jewel as she tried to face her sorrow and disappointment.

"Where shall we go? Back up into the mountain?" asked Jewel.

"No, that is the first place they would expect…you know, the legend and all. We have to find a way out that they will not look for us." replied Bina.

They searched the room for what they would take with them and realized that it would all have to stay. She and Bina both grabbed their cloaks and put a few things in the pockets, including Jewel's necklace and her book. Bina pulled a tattered apron from her things and stuffed it in her pocket.

"Where did you find that?" asked Jewel, surprised that Bina still wanted such a rag.

"I found it. I've had it too long to lose it now," the other replied.

Hearing nothing in the hallway, they cracked the door open and peered out. They snuck softy to the entrance and waited until they were sure no one was there. Opening the door, they eased their way out into the dark and darted across the green to a small shed that had been built close to the trees bordering the grounds. The two crept inside. It was totally black. Bina had seen workers come and go wearing their everyday clothes but appearing for work in garments more fit for the outdoor labors maintaining the center of town.

"There are work clothes in here somewhere. Let's change so we won't be recognized." Feeling around the building, they both located the grungy clothing and managed a quick change. "We can't just leave these dresses behind. They will know what we are wearing once these are found and that will hamper our escape," said the experienced Bina. She carefully rolled up her dress and fitted it into a deep pocket in her cloak. Jewel did the same though hers was bulkier and harder to squeeze into the space.

"Which way?" asked Jewel as they tip-toed out the door. Since they had seen most of the town while touring, Bina took Jewel by the hand and pulled her in the direction opposite to the way they had entered the town. Jewel followed. The two were careful to go around the edge rather than directly through the middle of town.

They had hardly gone far when they heard an uproar coming from the hall. Their disappearance had been discovered and a search party would soon be launched. Certainly, the people of Credulos would not take the disappearance lightly. Hanging in the balance was the economic success of the whole regions, and all would not be lost on account of a moody goddess. The lights of torches could be seen on the path heading up the mountain toward the waterfall.

"Please, Great One, don't do this to us again!" the shattered citizens looking to the sky implored. "Once again, we are doomed to the cycle of the legend."

CHAPTER 27

The Key

Consciousness began to return to Jip and he was aware only of darkness and pain. He lay in a heap on damp earth trying to move his limbs, but found them heavy with chains. He moved his arm and attempted to check parts of his body for damage. Caked matter, he took to be blood mixed with dirt, covered his face and hands. Straining to hear any sounds, he lay still but heard only an incessant, hypnotic dripping of water.

His mind was still trying to comprehend his situation and, with difficulty and regret, he remembered his last actions before ending up in the lowest and worst place in the prison—the dungeon. How had he made such a rash decision to risk sinking to this low level of existence? *Why didn't I believe them when they said no one had ever escaped from here before?* He had hoped that it was just a rumor to keep the prisoners from attempting an escape. *I hoped I would not survive and they would kill me and get it over with. I won't last long in this place. I'll die a slow, painful death here.*

Jip tried to remember exactly what had happened. After eating the daily mush and drinking as much acrid water as he could manage to get from the guard, he and the other prisoners had been herded together to be chained to a central line and marched to the quarry. On the way to the place where they would spend the day swinging picks and heaving heavy stones, he knew there was a brief period when they were on a public road. He had planned to overpower the guard, grab the key, unlock his chain, and set himself free. It was a foolish plan; he could see that now. What else was there?

The timing was critical. On the way to work that day, there had been no opportunity to put the plan into action, but he looked forward to the journey home when it was nearly dark. That would give him an advantage, so he worked and waited. As the men were being driven along on their way back to the prison, a guard passed right by Jip. The opportunity came and he knocked the guard unconscious, who fell to the ground at Jip's feet. Hastily, Jip took the key from his belt and unlocked his chain. In a few moments, he would be free. He rose and was about to flee when a second guard saw what he had done and yelled the alarm. Others came running and, just as Jip had anticipated, they beat him until he knew no more.

This is what he got for that moment of glory—excruciating pain and probably broken bones, cuts, bruises. He was glad it was so dark because, if he had seen his condition in the full light, he would have felt even sorrier for himself.

Jip tried to straighten one leg but found it too painful, so he stayed in his twisted position, unable to help himself in even the smallest way. The guards would probably bring some kind of food. Jip decided he would not eat. He would starve and end this suffering. His throat was parched and the sound of water dripping was causing him to hallucinate about the liquid falling onto his tongue. Between thirst and hunger, Jip wondered how long it would be before his body would give up and let him find release from all his cares.

A stirring in his cell woke Jip. He had dozed off and the jerk of waking up wracked his body with spasms. He breathed heavily for some seconds before the pain subsided. He listened to the noise close to his head on the ground. There was a squeaking and scurrying. It sounded like rats, probably having a fight over which one would take the first bite of the new hunk of meat they had been thrown. Jip grimaced at the thought of being eaten alive by rats and realized that things could actually be worse than merely lying there in pain unable to move. Gathering every bit of energy and strength he could muster, he raised himself up to a sitting position, and hoped they would not start to dine on something still living. He was afraid to go back to sleep lest they gather and begin their meal.

Little by little, he moved this muscle and that until he determined that he had no broken bones. His ribs hurt terribly; he must have taken some powerful kicks in his sides. His head was the other part of his body that had taken the most beating. Passing his fingers over his head, he could feel bumps and cuts, but his brains were still intact so maybe he would recover—that is, if there was any point in recovering, which there was not.

Each ankle was encircled with an iron band that was held securely with a heavy chain anchored to the wall. If he were able to stand up, he could walk no more than a few steps without stumbling. His hands were not chained, but the iron bands that had been locked on his wrists when he entered the prison were still there.

Hour after lonely hour went by with still no sound of another human being. Jip believed he had been put away to die, forgotten and alone. No one would come to feed him or give him water. He was meant to suffer the final defeat of rotting in this dark dungeon and being eaten by vermin. The horrid smell in the air was likely the corpses of other rebellious prisoners who had come to the same fate.

A surge of anger rose up in Jip and he raged against his life. How did he come to this end? Was there no one who cared? Was his life so worthless that he would be dumped and forgotten like a piece of trash? He had always been a man who enjoyed taking risks and playing on the dangerous side, breaking rules, sneaking, hiding, getting the things he wanted. Now he was paying with his life and he wondered at last if it had been worth it. He thought of what he might have had if he had been like many of his Netherian companions. Would he have had a family, perhaps? But all that responsibility? No way. A better job? What was the likelihood of that when your mother is a slave and your father is unknown?

Anger was followed by sorrow and regret, and then misery. Jip wept in the dark, tears mingling with the blood and dirt. He hadn't cried much since he was a small child, particularly in front of others. If felt good to cry and weep and let out all the pent up anger and hurt and sorrow of his short meaningless life. As the intensity of his sorrow reached a peak, he let his reserve go and screamed out, "NO! NO!" and wept even more. The effort it took to breathe heavily with weeping and to raise his voice to this extent caused a sharp stabbing pain in his ribs. He stopped himself, despite the fact that he felt he hadn't yet expressed all his anguish. One more time he cried out, "Help me! Someone help me get out of here!" and he slumped back and fainted.

Jip awoke again after hours, minutes...he was not sure. He stared into the dark, shaking and tense. *Was that a dream?* Only moments before he had been surrounded by a wall of flames. Everywhere he looked, circling him on all sides, there was only hot yellow and orange fire hemming him in. He had tried to move, but the circle of fire would not allow him to escape. He beat against the fire and cried out, "I want to be free! I want to be free!" But it was no use.

This seemed to go on for a long time until he found he was able to peer through the flames and could see a fleeting shadow of what was on the other side. He was horrified to see flashes of ghoulish faces, claws, and fangs of beasts with gaping mouths intent on tearing him apart, if only they could get through the fire.

Jip remembered the strangest part of the dream. He had looked down through the fire and seen an object lying on the ground. It was a golden key. It sparkled with brilliant light as if it has been made of fire. At the end of the key was a stone that shone with an intense blue light. In the dream, he picked it up and, as he did, the circle of fire began to become smaller, the flames coming nearer and nearer. Expecting to be burned up by the heat of the flames, he was surprised to find that he was engulfed by the fire and together with it became a pillar of light. Inside the flame, he saw a man standing near him who held out his hands and said "Gem! Be free and shine!"

He was awake. The pillar of fire had disappeared and the black, dank cell was back. He sat leaning against the cell wall in drowsy astonishment as the last words penetrated his waking thoughts. *Gem? What was that about? My name's not Gem. And how can I be free and shine in a place like this? Dreams are such hogwash.*

Contrary to Jip's expectations, he felt relieved. No rats were eating his flesh yet. His head was aching; his throat was still dry as dust. Nothing had changed in his situation except for a sense of resignation. Jip wondered if crying and screaming had sent some poison out of his body. Something was different. He sat for a long time thinking about it, and about the dream.

A clank of the iron lock in the cell door got Jip's immediate attention. The door swung open on squeaking hinges. A dim light from the corridor outside shone in and he could see for the first time his swollen and bruised limbs. A grimy, bearded face peered in attached to a hand that held a small lantern.

"Well, boy, if you haven't gotten yourself in a fix!" said the old man. He was hunched over and dressed in rags. His streaked hair, the color of dead leaves in autumn, was long, hanging in matted ropes, and his beard, uncut for many years, was grayish black from filth.

"Who are you?" asked Jip.

"Who am I? What a good question," he said with a laugh. "I ask myself that often, lad. When I was a man, I was known as Canape Grubstacker, head cook in the king's kitchen no less—call me Canny—but it has been many a year now since I was that man." he informed Jip.

"What are you then if you are not a man?"

"I am one who can keep a young rascal like you alive if you follow my advice," warned Canny, trying to make a stern face as he placed the bowl of brown mush on the floor of the cell.

"I was like you long ago, thinking that youth would never end, that everything needed to be tried once, that I would never be caught. But alas, that day ended for me, as it has for you. Now only one thing is left, and that is, follow the rules. You see, I followed the rules, kept my nose clean, did what they wanted, and now look. I am in charge of bringing this food and water to your door daily," he added putting down another bowl of green water. "I have come up in the world wouldn't you say?" asked Canny.

Jip asked him, "You mean you are not locked up in a cell?"

"Right, my boy! You are learning. I am locked into this dungeon, but I have the freedom to walk up and down this corridor. Perhaps someday, I'll be promoted to feed prisoners up in the world of windows and see the sun again. What do you think about that?"

"Doesn't sound all that promising if you ask me," replied Jip.

"Oh, but you are wrong," he corrected. "I can see you have a lot to learn yet. I had better be about my duties. See you tomorrow," he concluded smiling and pulled the door shut with a thud and the click of the turning lock.

Freedom. Freedom to walk the dismal corridor and carry slop to miserable souls, to lock and unlock the doors, and to see them decaying day by day. Somehow, that did not seem like freedom to Jip. Maybe after he had sat in the cell for years, this demeaning task would seem like heaven itself.

Jip reached over and felt for the food and water. It smelled sour, but he had to either eat it or die. It was so tempting to choose the latter. In the end, he ate and drank. After hours of sitting with nothing to do or hear, Jip decided to explore his immediate surroundings, just in case there was something there. Moving his limbs was difficult. He reached out with his hand to the earthen floor. It had a muddy texture. There were his thick chains that felt as if they were rusty and old, loose stones of various sizes, bits of grass or hay, and an old rag. As he moved, he heard scurrying some distance away and realized the rats could see him, though he couldn't see them. Were there other creatures in the room as well? If he got hungry enough…he banished the thought for the time being.

The Key

His hand continued to move over the surface of the floor until he thought he had found something. It was half buried in the soil so he scratched until he could get hold of it. He lifted it out and held the object in his hands, fingering its shape from one end to the other. It felt like a key. No one would allow a key to be inside a prisoner's cell. He picked at bits of dirt and rubbed it between his fingertips to clean it off. It was a key, not very large, but it had all the important marks. At the head of the key, it felt like a stone embedded where he would have expected to find a hole for stringing on a key ring.

I'm in another dream. But if I am dreaming, why is it still so awful in here? Jip continued to finger the object in his hand, picking away at dirt and polishing it against his shirt. Was it really a key? Hours went by with no further diversions except the rustling of rodents. *It is too big to fit into the locks of my chains,* he reasoned. *It is too small to fit into the lock on the door.What could it fit?*

There was nothing else to do, so he decided to try the key in the iron bands around his ankles. He held on to the key with one hand for fear of losing it and, feeling with his free hand, he bent over to find the place on the band where a lock had been fastened. It was difficult to do because of the pain in his ribs and back. Gradually, he was able to bend in half to get to the lock, feel for a keyhole, and put the key in.

Shock registered through his whole body when he found that the key went into the hole and seemed to fit perfectly. He was afraid to turn it. The disappointment would be devastating if nothing happened. He was too excited to wait long. He wrenched the key and, to his amazement, the lock fell off, and the band was lying on the ground. The surprise was so intense that he could not move. How was this possible? He reached for the other ankle and the pain of the movement convinced him that it was not a dream. In just a few moments, his legs were free. He tried his wristbands, and the key worked again.

He crawled from where he had been sitting; his companions squeaked loudly as they ran off. Jip stood for the first time with hands outstretched to find the walls of the cell. As he walked around the room, he came to an ancient wooden door. The grain was rough to his fingertips as he felt its entire construction—hinged with curved iron and nailed with large round-headed spikes. His hand continued to move over the surface until he found a metal plate with a center hole. The chances that his key would fit this lock as well were very slim, he knew. But shouldn't he try? The hole was much larger than that of the ankle bands. He pulled out the key again and carefully placed it in the hole. It was too small and barely made contact metal to metal. He turned it nonetheless and to his surprise, something inside the mechanism gave a loud, clear click.

He stood again not knowing what to do. There was no handle on the inside. He moved his hand up and down the doorframe, trying to find out how the door opened. He pushed on it and unexpectedly it sprung toward him, ajar just enough for him to get his hand through to pull it open all the way.

Outside the cell, dim light from a lantern hanging on the wall cast eerie shadows behind him. In the other direction, there was only darkness. He crept painfully toward the light and heard Canny shuffling along the corridor around the corner to the left. Not far from there was a flight of narrow stone steps leading up into more darkness. From somewhere up there in the dark stairwell came the muffled sounds of men laughing and the low murmur of talk. Jip backed away and wondered which way to go. He stared at the key in his hand and saw that the polished yellow metal did have a jewel in the end, dark colored but cut expertly like a jewel from a king's crown. *How did something of such great value end up in a prison cell? Does Canny know about it?* Nothing made any sense. *Is this a cruel joke to trap me? Are the guards waiting up there to kill me? Maybe this is how they entertain themselves during a boring shift!*

The noise of talking seemed to get louder. Were the men coming down the stairs? He panicked and hobbled back in the direction he had come from. Seeing his cell door was still open, he quietly pushed it closed. *It will be at least another day before I am missed,* and continued down the dark corridor in hopes of finding a temporary hiding place. He felt his way along the wall until it ended. Iron bars met his fingers. Determining that he had come to a barred gate, Jip feared he was only going deeper into the bowels of the prison and was loathe to try his key again. But what other choice did he have? The whole adventure was so absurd. Why should any of these locks respond to his key? It must have been magic. He tried the key and the gate swung open away from him. Jip stepped through and slowly pushed it shut behind him. He turned the key once more locking himself in to whatever space this was.

A long flight of stairs went down in front of him. He could see nothing but continued going down and holding onto the sides of what must have been a cave. The stairs ended and the tunnel continued. He walked on and on groping his way along, hoping that if he came to a hole in the floor, he could catch himself in time before plunging to his death. He thought to himself, *how impossible and foolish*, like so many other things he had done in his life. But here he was, one minute back there screaming for help, then listening to a raving old man, and now walking down a tunnel into blackness.

Jip slowed his pace and continued to feel along the wall with his hands and along the floor with his feet. A sudden whooshing sound rushed past his head. Several more followed as he clung to the cave wall. As quickly as the creatures had come, they had disappeared into thin air. High over his head he thought he heard tiny squeaks and rustling wings of bats as they settled on the roof.

"Hello." he said softly and perceived that the echo of his voice went into a higher cavern. A gentle breeze blew past his face wafting high into blackness. He kept going.

After what seemed like a long time, he began to see some of his surroundings. The light was not like that of a lamp or even a torch, but the light of day, getting brighter and brighter as he went. Jip stopped and thought about where he might be. His sense of direction and space was better than most, and it did not take long to conclude that he was in a cave. Somewhere in the past, men had deepened it until it joined the deep parts of the dungeon. Breaking out into full sunlight, he saw the sea from a low cliff and realized that he was west of Bellicosa, out of sight of the town. Off to his left, he could not see the harbor or any ships. The opening in the cliff was small and ships seldom would travel close enough to the shore to see it. *I wonder if Legerdemain knows about this exit,* Jip pondered to himself.

Back in the dark corridor of the dungeon, Canny, having heard an unnatural grinding of hinges, held out his lantern to inspect the doors of each cell. Everything looked to be in order, but the new man in number six was a hothead. The old prisoner intended to unlock the door and see for himself. He pulled it open, holding the lantern inside. In silence and shock, he saw only the beady, red eyes of rats staring back at him in the darkness. Canny gulped hard and spoke softly to himself, "Grubstacker, you are in serious trouble here. If they find out you let a prisoner escape you will be sleeping in this cell tonight, if they let you live at all." As he backed out into the shadowy corridor, he made a plan. He looked both ways, his face hardening into a decisive glare. *No one checks these cells but me. The boy would rot here for years with no one to know whether he is alive or dead. For now, he is alive and he is in the cell, just as he is supposed to be.* And he walked back to his post as if nothing had happened.

Jip looked down at the pounding surf and wondered how he could proceed. For the moment, he realized he was very tired, so sat down and leaned against the wall of the tunnel. Before long, he was asleep.

He awoke to blackness, but this time the black of night. His eyes began to adjust, and soon he was able to make out the edge of the cliff and the sea below in the faint moonlight. The noise of the raging waves below had quieted and Jip realized that the tide was out. If he could manage to climb down the short distance to the rocks below, he could walk along the shore and find a way to escape. Of course, if the cliffs continued for a long ways, he may be trapped by the rising tide and be dashed to pieces on the rocks. It was a risk he would take. He had seen some footholds in the rocks while it was still light. The short distance to the beach would not normally be a challenge to Jip. Pain made the descent more difficult.

The Key

He had no safe place in his clothing for his key so he tore a piece of his tunic off, tied a secure knot around the yellow metal and tied the band around his neck, freeing his hands for the climb.

It was painstaking work as he felt along for each step, but finally he made it down to the rocks. There was some sand visible, which made the going easier, the light color reflecting the moonlight and showing a path for him to take. His head was aching and his ribs were burning with pain, but he had to keep going.

As he continued his journey, the wind began to pick up, clouds covered the moon, and it became very dark. The wind grew stronger and rain began to fall, light at first, but then it came down in torrents. The waves were rolling up and licking his feet, a sign that it would not be long before the tide came back in. He was chilled to the bone as the wind beat against his side. The worst of the storm raged, but eventually passed. A steady rain fell. Jip was drenched and cold. The water was getting deeper around his ankles and he knew the tide was coming in. He had only a short time to find his way around the cliffs.

CHAPTER 28

The Storm

The sea was a brilliant blue when the new day began. After a crisp, clear sunrise, the sun shone intensely as it rose high into the cloudless sky. With the advancement of the day, the wind began to pick up and clouds appeared. Damon stood on the deck enjoying the cool, clean breeze blowing in his face. He was glad to have the liberty to take such breaks without worry of any task master, for he knew that he was the real master of the ship. Perhaps this meant he had not fully embraced the life of a sailor, but that was all right. He had the best of both worlds right under his feet. He stroked the Chiselstone sword at his side and pondered its success as a weapon of choice. He had no need to wear it on deck, but this day it was a symbol of all he stood for and he wore it proudly. His business venture had been very successful. *What will my father say now?* he asked himself, knowing that regardless of his father's reaction, he knew he had done well.

Slowly, the world under his feet began to change and the now familiar sea sickness was coming back. He would not let it conquer him; he stood firm, willing it away. The wind blew stronger and stronger as he—Damon, the merchant hero—sailed east, east and back home to Bellicosa. The thought was exhilarating as he imagined his triumphant arrival—Damon, master of land and sea!

The daylight was fading when shouts from above reached Damon's ears. "Storm Ho!" All the men began to muster and move more quickly about the ship. He looked out to sea and saw a dark gray line across the horizon. With each passing moment, it grew larger and seemed to chase the light from the sky.

The captain gave the order to lower the sails and batten down the hatches. *How bad will it be?* wondered Damon, as he watched the men prepare the ship for the storm. Two more days and they would be back home, if only the storm would hold off. But it was not to be so.

As night descended, the black storm front was upon them. It blew sideways with a terrible force that whipped the sea into frothing mountains of water. Damon had never seen such waves. The rain hit them horizontally; the large drops stung and saturated everything in their reach instantly.

"Go below, Master Chiselstone! You'll be blown overboard!" came the yell of the second mate, who scrambled to stay on his feet. Damon thought to himself, *if they can do this, so can I*. He fought his way to the poop deck and was determined to stand beside the captain and see the storm through like a man. As he climbed the ladder, he could barely hold his stance. He pushed against the wind with all his might until he grasped the rails of the upper deck.

"Get below, Master!" commanded Captain Fairway. Damon leaned into the wind and yelled, "I'll be all right, Captain."

"Well, at least take off that ridiculous sword. It will only slow you down and get in the way!" Damon nodded and felt embarrassed that he hadn't thought of that himself.

The Storm

Returning the way he had come, he lowered himself down the ladder and struggled to stay on his feet on the deck. The waves were over his head and the ship tossed wildly from high to low and high again. Just as he tilted one direction to maintain balance, the ship rushed down the side of another wave sending him crashing to the boards in a slippery heap. Again, he groped for a way to stand, but as soon as he had managed some kind of stability, he was being shoved in the other direction unable to grab hold of anything around him.

The terror of the moment finally dawned on him and something inside broke loose. He panicked. Any bravado he had tried to trump up was gone. The truth was blasting his face; he was not a sailor. The storm threw him from one end of the deck to the other and he was powerless to do anything to prevent being washed overboard.

With eyes burning from the salt water and the dismay at his helplessness, he looked up and nearly fainted in horror. Above his head, the wild shades of black and green swirled together in the wind to form a picture he could not deny. Two eyes glared down at him accompanied by a ferocious grin with bared fangs. A flash of lightning sent laser beams of light through the eyes, which now met those of the paralyzed sailor. The head rose and fell and seemed to dive back into the depths, then reared again closer and closer.

Damon blinked to make it go away. When he opened his eyes, the apparition was still there rearing back to strike him as he grabbed onto the railing and rode the storm. It was Leviathan, preparing to clench its jaws around his body and bear him away to the bottom of the sea. Damon screamed and clutched his sword. He drew it out of its sheath and waved it wildly in hopes of scaring the dragon. Realizing how small and pitiful his efforts were, his courage dissolved and the sword dropped harmlessly into the sea. Closing his eyes, he screamed again to anyone who could deliver him from his sure fate, "Help me! Help me!"

Up on the deck the Captain and other sailors could see him but did not hear his cry for help, so loud was the wind. Just then, ropes snapped. A boom tore loose and swung swiftly toward Damon's head with killing force.

It struck him hard on the back of his head and sent him flying overboard into the savage waves. A flashing light burst in Damon's head and he felt his body break the surface of the water. Sinking deeper and deeper, the light faded as he cried out in his spirit, "Help me, please!" Then all was quiet and black.

Chapter 29
Man with No Name

The waves grew stronger and each one reached higher on his ankles. Light was growing, so Jip stopped and surveyed the cliffs above him. They were not as high as when he first began his journey. He looked for a way to climb up and found just enough protruding rocks to gain the elevation he needed. He pulled himself higher and higher until at last he reached a small plateau. He was safe for the present, despite hunger, thirst, and pain. From this vantage point, Jip could take in more of the scenery, especially the westerly direction away from Bellicosa. Beyond the cliffs, all he could see was the sea.

Jip wondered how much higher it was to the top of the cliff. He studied the rocks to see what might be possible. He began to climb again, and this time was surprised that the going was easier. Before long, he arrived at the top of the cliff and saw that, not far beyond him to the west, the land sloped down and down until it came to a barren sandy beach. It was a long ways off.

Jip surveyed the beach, squinting to focus on a dark object lying on the sand just at the shore line. Studying the surrounding terrain, he at last spied a way to get down to the beach. He stumbled along, despite his physical suffering, looking right and left to make sure there was no other human presence. The beach was deserted. Only the brown lump lying at the water's edge marred the perfect beauty of the scene.

As Jip approached, he recognized the form as human dressed in torn clothes, covered with sand and wound around with green and brown seaweed. He was lying on his back revealing a young face with a blonde beard, a mass of tangled hair, and debris from his wild ride in the waves. Jip watched as the wretch struggled to his side and vomited seawater, choking and coughing up the foul liquid in his lungs.

He rushed to the man's side and beat his back with his hands trying to help him get his breath. The man continued to struggle and gasp for air, then he lay very still. Jip watched the back of his coat rise and fall and saw that he was alive. He momentarily waited beside the quiet form seeing if he would regain consciousness. Shelter from the hot sun was the greatest need at hand. He spied overhanging tree branches away from the beach then pulled and tugged the inert body toward the spot. As the sand dried, he wiped it away from the man's face while studying the features more closely. He was about Jip's age and handsome, in a familiar sort of way. Had he seen this face before? He wasn't sure. He looked very much like Master Chiselstone of Arcana. *That's impossible. It couldn't be.*

Thoughts of Arcana and his mother rushed into his mind and brought a flood of grief. He leaned back to reflect on his recent past. A jab of searing pain came upon him as he imagined his mother hanging from a gallows because of him. He tried to focus on the sleeping man before him.

What if this is Chiselstone's only son and heir? Will he recognize the son of his mother's servant? Dressed as a torn up sailor, Jip decided that this could not be any but a poor victim of the storm, perhaps the only survivor of his ship. Jip looked at his own arms and legs and realized he was a mess of blood and dirt.

He quickly made his way to a small stream and tried to alter his alarming appearance.

"Where am I?" came the mumbled, barely audible words from the sailor's sand-caked lips. His voice was hoarse and dry. Jip leaned over and brushed more dried sand from the man's face as he tried to open his eyes.

"Don't open your eyes yet," demanded Jip. "You have sand all over your face and you will get it in your eyes. If you can make it to the stream over there, you can wash it off."

"Who are you? How did I get here?" the sailor asked in the weak voice. "Don't worry about that now. Be glad you're alive, man." Trying to rise to a sitting position, the sailor grabbed the back of his head and winced in pain. Jip inspected the site and found a lump with a gaping cut at its center. The blood had stopped, but the cut was full of sand.

"Woah, friend. You took quite a wallop there. Any idea what hit you?" asked Jip as he helped the man to his feet.

"I can't remember…." He paused as if trying to remember anything at all and found only emptiness where his memory had been.

"Well, one thing is for sure. You are a sailor and your ship must have wrecked in the storm. I see no other survivors so you must be the only one. A piece of the ship's debris must have hit you on the head."

"I don't know. I can't think. I only remember a flash of light and," he paused to form the right words, "someone pulled me up. That's all!" Jip tried to understand what he meant, as there were no other survivors who could have helped him.

"The good news is you are alive no matter how it happened. What is your name?" The sailor was still for a moment urging his mind to find the information, but to no avail. "I…I don't know," he cried, as he searched for an answer.

Jip helped him untangle the weeds and then walked the sailor to the stream. Seeing the belt and sheath buckled to the man's waist Jip realized it normally held a sword. The weapon was nowhere in sight. On the leather was clearly tooled an ornate letter "C" with a set of fangs inside. Instantly, he recognized the Chiselstone crest. The missing blade was of Bellicosan origin. The sailor had to be Damon, son of Master Chiselstone. But how could he be dressed as a common sailor? Did he steal the sword, or was it his own? It is so finely worked that it could belong to none other than the young master himself. Jip remembered the Mirage and for a moment was glad that his plan to stow away aboard her had failed, for it now appeared that the ship had been lost with all aboard.

Jip decided not to draw attention to this, realizing that the survivor had lost not only his ship but also his memory. Was it possible that Damon would not discover either his own or Jip's real identity. His hand went habitually to the metal band marking his slavery, thinking to make sure his tunic sleeve was pulled over to hide it. Jip was shocked to find it was not there. How was that possible? But it was true.

"You look like you've taken a beating yourself," said the sailor as he now focused on the man who had pulled him from the beach. "Oh, this?" Damon motioned to his bruises and cuts, "Yah, I got in a fight. There was this girl. You know what that's like. It's nothing serious," he replied as he continued to rub his wrist in wonder.

He was safe from scrutiny for the time. But how long would it be before Damon's lost memories returned?

CHAPTER 30

The Barn

Jewel and Bina walked for hours into the night, roughly following the river, which Jewel suspected led eventually to the sea she had seen from the top of the mountain.

"We had better stay off the roads and travel through the fields," suggested Jewel. Bina, who was trying to come to grips with the disappearance of a lovely hope, didn't answer, but numbly walked on without comment.

Jewel began to suspect that their route along the river was too predictable so, noticing a track that left the river path, directed Bina to head north. The underbrush was thick and promised to be a secure hiding place. Badly in need of rest for the night, they slipped through the bushes, pushed aside a bed of ferns, and attempted to get some rest.

The late summer sun was about to rise when Jewel awoke. A brisk breeze made the air chilly. She moved and found her limbs were stiff from a night on lumpy, damp bracken. An unfamiliar hunger and thirst assailed her for the first time in weeks. With the cover of underbrush, she did not feel any danger.

Jewel moved away gently from the still form next to her. Looking for a place of solitude, if for only a few minutes, she made her way to a gap in the bushes that afforded a view of the rising sun. Its first light cast a bright, yellow glow on everything. Jewel unwrapped the necklace and held it in her hand. It glowed with the joy of the morning. Jewel gazed into it once more, looking for hope and guidance. Her hands tingled. Her thoughts went back to the moment in the desert when the choice was made to go up the mountain. *I should have listened to the One who told me the way to the Kingdom of Light. We never should have gone to Credulos.* Jewel closed her eyes and tried to reach the one who promised not to leave her. *Show us the way to your Kingdom.*

"Do you see something about breakfast in your green glass? Jewel was startled to hear Bina's sarcastic voice behind her. She dropped the emerald and tried to think about the day before them.

Jewel laughed. "I don't know, but it sure isn't anywhere close by," she returned. "Let's get going and see if we can find someone who has never heard of the Goddess Remora." Jewel fastened her necklace in place and prepared to leave the site.

"Are you sure you want to wear that thing?" asked Bina.

Jewel simply replied, "Yes" and stepped out into the sunlit path.

"So what is The One telling you today?" Bina asked skeptically, after walking some distance in silence. Her tone continued to dismay Jewel, as she longed for her to understand that she was not making up her encounter with the stranger in the desert.

"He is telling me that I have a place I must go. It is called The Kingdom of Light. The stranger I spoke of is the son of the king of that kingdom and he bids me to join him there." Jewel heard her own words and knew they sounded like lunacy. What could she say? She knew he was real.

"Do you know the way to this kingdom?" asked Bina who instinctively knew they were lost.

"No. I don't know, Bina. I think we were supposed to go into the desert. But you said the mountain was better. See what happened?"

"Oh, it's my fault that we were treated like queens and had all the food we could ever eat?" Bina yelled.

"Did you forget how it ended? We would have been sent back to Bellicosa and hanged!"

They walked in silence, following no particular path. Finally, a road crossed their path and a choice had to be made—left or right. Jewel favored a right turn, which would take them north and closer to the kingdom she perceived was in that direction. Bina examined the road looking for some indication of human habitation. She brushed past a low shrub and saw that a signpost was hidden in its leaves. The both bent down to try to decipher it. Neither was skilled at reading, however, the arrow pointing left was obvious.

"That's that. We are following the arrow," snapped Bina, who headed down the lane.

Hours later, the forest began to thin and the two stood at the edge of a golden field of grain waving in the wind. As the breezes blew stronger, they could see the sky in the distance turning dark and threatening. Twittering birds were interrupted by the rumble of thunder, and bright flashes highlighted the approaching storm. The day was far spent and they would be drenched in rain if they did not find shelter.

In the distance beyond the grain field, they could see a thatched roof and suspected it was a farm building. They pushed against the blowing gale and arrived to see bits of grass fly off the roof; they hoped that it would hold up under such a powerful force.

They found a split door in the side of the building; the bottom half closed and the top half open. Inside it looked dark and dry, so they let themselves in. There was hay spread on the floor and several wooden pens for animals. Two black and white, wide-eyed cows peeked warily over the rails of their pen as the wind stirred rattles, bangs, creaks, and groans in the old building.

On a short stool beside the pen, there was a half loaf of bread and a glob of churned butter. A hunk of cheese and a knife made the meal almost complete. A tankard of fresh milk stood by the bread and cheese as if it had all been set out just for them.

Where was the farmer who left his supper? No doubt, the howling wind and threatening storm had drawn him away to other duties about the farm. Bina and Jewel looked at one another thinking the same thing. At once, they both made a decision and gobbled down the meal, passing back and forth the three components until every crumb had disappeared. The milk was the last to go. Bina drank her half and then Jewel finished it. A contented belch erupted from Bina finalizing the meal.

"I think this is where we will be staying until the storm has passed," advised Jewel with no argument from Bina. They crawled over the fence, wrapped up in their cloaks and laid down in the hay where they could not easily be seen and fell into a deep sleep as the storm raged outside.

Hours went by and, at last, the two woke to silence. It was early morning and the only sounds heard were the dripping of the rain as it drizzled its last drops. In the dim light of dawn, the farmer entered the barn and crept over to the cows.

"Oh, my dears...I am sorry to have neglected you. I've come to give you your well earned hay, and to eat my well earned bread and cheese."

Jewel held her breath as she pictured the old man finding the empty plate and cup. "What's this? Since when have you taken to eating a man's bread? And how neatly you have drunk my milk and eaten my cheese? 'Tis strange indeed. I'd almost swear that someone else had a hand in it, strangers who prefer not to be seen." Jewel scrunched up her shoulders as discovery was imminent.

"What have we here?" asked the alarmed farmer, leaning over the railing. The two looked up sheepishly. The farmer saw the grubby clothing and unwashed faces and did not know what to think.

"Good Farmer, please have mercy on us. We have traveled from a far country and are lost. Could you direct us to one who will help us make a new home?" Bina sniveled with great dramatic effect.

"Why, I...ah, who...where did you say you are from?" stammered the confused old man.

"We are daughters of a rich, though cruel, merchant, only disguised to look humble. See the fine jewel my sister wears. Please help us escape from our hard life and find a new one." Bina continued to spin her story, though Jewel wondered if the farmer would believe they were sisters.

"Huh, very strange indeed. You must be telling the truth. Where would the likes of you get that stone otherwise?" The farmer frowned, a tinge of skepticism showing in his narrowed brow. "I'll give you some advice. There is one you may go to. He is known by all as one who helps those in need."

Jewel's attention immediately picked up when the farmer said "one who helps." *Perhaps Bina had been right. We were meant to go in this direction. We will find The One after all.*

"We should be going," announced Bina. "Can you tell us how to find the man you are talking about?"

"When you get back to the road, follow it until you get to a tiny house. The mistress there will tell you what you need to know."

Wearily, the two thanked the farmer for his advice and his food and left, hoping and praying that their final destination would not be far.

CHAPTER 31

Gem and Diamond

Drinking the fresh water was a relief to the two men. Both had endured the lack of it for many hours. The strength of the shipwrecked sailor was returning and he moved about to get his limbs working again.

Jip was not sure how to proceed with a conversation, as to say too much might give away information he did not want known. Finally, the sailor broke the silence. "Thanks for the help. What did you say your name is?" Jip searched for a plausible name that would not awaken memory. Quickly, the name Gem came back to him from his dream. "Just call me...ah...Gem."

"Gem," Damon said to hear the sound of it from his own lips. "Gem, what is that tied around your neck? Is it some kind of good luck charm?"

"Oh, this? Yah, I found it buried in the ground. I figure it's gotten me out of a few scrapes already." He had forgotten about his key being tied to his neck and now wondered about finding a more inconspicuous place for it.

"And since we are asking questions here, what is that lump sticking out of your pocket?" returned the man with a new name. Damon had not noticed the lump yet but when he examined his pocket, he produced a small rock of what looked like translucent glass. "I hate to sound like I'm repeating myself, but would 'I don't know' work again?"

"Looks like a big hunk of diamond before it's cut," posited Gem, having heard of such things, but having never before seen anything like it. "Maybe you carry it because it looks like a diamond and so it's YOUR good luck charm. I'd find a better place to keep it, though. Maybe we could take that sheath of yours and make ourselves some charm holders, what do you think?" suggested Gem, hoping to get rid of the one bit of evidence that could link Damon to his past.

"I don't think I know how to do that. Go ahead if you want to. Without a sword, this sheath is worthless."

"Hey, think about this," said Gem. "You don't remember your name. I have to call you something so why not Diamond. Get it, Gem and Diamond."

"Diamond? Hardly a name, but why not? If that is what you want to call me, then do it. I hope I will soon remember my real name." Those words chilled Gem and he hoped it would be a while before that happened.

"I'm starving," Diamond said, looking around for a sign of civilization and seeing none. "Me too. It's been a while since I had a decent meal, believe me."

Diamond turned to Gem and added, "Maybe I shouldn't mention this, as you did help me, but your clothing and your state of health suggest that you have had a rough time of late. You say that that key has gotten you out of difficult circumstances. Would it be perhaps that you have escaped from some type of jail?" Gem was stunned at the perceptive ability of his companion and did not know what to say in return. He stood with mouth gaping.

"I thought so. I won't ask any more about it." Diamond gazed out to sea with all the dignity of a master.

I won't be able to fool him much, thought Gem. *He has run with another kind of mob!*

Loud yelling broke the silence and off in the distance away from the beach they could hear men's voices and the clanking of metal. Thuds and bangs of wood against wood, then groans and moans of victims met the ears of the two dumbfounded listeners.

"Someone is really going at it back there behind those trees," observed Gem who knew the sound of a fight when he heard it.

"Should we run away?" asked Diamond.

"Are you kidding? I gotta go see who's getting the worst of it. Come on. This will be fun." Diamond wasn't sure and held back as Gem limped clumsily as fast as he was able toward to noise.

Both men hid behind bushes and watched the two groups of men lunge at one another with homemade swords and spears. Some held only long sticks sharpened to points on the end, but stabbed and poked with just as much energy. Several lay on the ground holding superficial wounds and groaning in pain. All the participants were dressed in ragged tunics and trousers and it was impossible to tell which man belonged to which group except to see who each one attempted to kill.

Very soon, the number on the ground outnumbered the ones standing. The last fighters yelled rude epithets and growled curses at one another and parted going to the aid of their wounded. With shaking fists and violent gestures, each group stumbled back down opposite directions on the road upon which they had done battle.

"Whoah! What was that?" Gem scratched his head in astonishment. "Not exactly a friendly bunch. Wonder where they are headed now." Diamond was appalled but his reaction further amazed Gem. "They would have done better to use their swords to better advantage. What bumbling bumpkins!"

Gem laughed out loud. "Did I hear you right? You think they ought to have done a better job of killing each other?" Diamond listened to himself and laughed as well. "It just seems like the truth, doesn't it? Maybe in my lost life I was a sword fighter, well a sword-fighting sailor then."

At this, Gem wanted to change the subject, so asked, "Which direction should we go? Either way looks like we could get ourselves in trouble with some ugly roughnecks.

"Judging from their attire we will fit right in, wouldn't you say?" Diamond picked up a flat stone and spat on one side, "Dry side says go left, wet side says go right, agreed?"

"Agreed," and the stone was tossed.

"It's wet. We go right." and they turned onto the road and began their joint adventure.

CHAPTER 32

Back in Bellicosa

Ear-piercing caterwauls flooded the corridor and Great Hall. Servants ran scurrying like frightened mice up and down trying to regain control of the hysterical household. Master Damon was dead.

"I am very sorry to report this, Master Chiselstone, but your son Damon was lost at sea. There was nothing any of us could do—our deepest sympathies to you."

Captain Fairway had come himself to report to Master Chiselstone the unfortunate loss of his son and heir. When the news reached the quarters of Dismalia, the ex-wife-in-hiding, her heart was broken. She screeched in horror. No one had seen her respond in such a way her whole life and did not know what to do. Her only son, the one she loved the most, had been taken from her. She could not believe the depth of her loss. Now there was truly nothing to live for.

The wailing went on and on until Obdura Coldstone was ready to lock and bar her door. "Please, Master Chiselstone! Can you do something to calm her and let the house have some peace?"

Harrasster Chiselstone merely hardened his jaw and ground his teeth. His loss was great as well and he was unable to focus on what to do next. Violencia rushed to his side, "My dear Harrasster. This is a terrible thing. You must come to our apartment and take a calming drink. I have just the thing that will help your nerves. Come." He dumbly followed her up the grand staircase and down the hall, ignoring the chaos below stairs.

Behind the closed door of their rooms, Violencia quickly prepared and gave him a cup of liquid. He drank and lay down on the bed, a tear rolling down his cheek. "What will I do Lency? He's my only son."

"There, there, my dear. Do not even think about it. Haven't I always come up with a plan? Sleep. Sleep."

Hands falling to his side gave Violencia the indication she waited for. Master Chiselstone was asleep and delivered for the moment from his pain. Now she must think what her next move would be. *The heir is gone. This could not be working out any better if I had planned it,* she thought chuckling to herself.

High on the hill stood a house even more imposing than the Chiselstone's. It was the castle of the king of Bellicosa. In a small receiving room on the second floor, reserved for confidential gatherings, and secluded from normal foot traffic, Chief Legerdemain stood facing his sovereign, King Ironfist. The tall door overlaid with gilt was locked and the servants awaited his command from the other side.

The room was a miniature throne room with the king's chair of carved wood and soft velvet in the center. There were no other chairs, as it was expected that his subjects would kneel before him. On the wall behind the chair hung the ferocious, attacking, green dragon of Bellicosa captured in delicate needlework.

"My King, I bow before you in humble obedience. How may I serve you this day?" began Legerdemain, in a sniveling voice and bowed head. He did not know why he had been summoned, but instinctively felt that something of grave importance was at stake.

Ironfist did not wish to beat about the bush. "Legerdemain, rumor has reached me that two criminals you arrested actually escaped from you. Is this true?"

"My Great Sovereign, unfortunately you have heard correctly. I have been seeking to recapture the offenders these many weeks but they have evaded my men. We have searched everywhere and I fear they have died in the great desert as they are nowhere to be found." Legerdemain braced himself to find if this explanation would calm the king's obvious agitation.

The king, looking even more disturbed than before, rose and paced the richly-carpeted floor, throwing his royal robes behind him as he made each turn.

"There is more, Legerdemain," he barked. "Rumor has also reached me that when these two were arrested, an unknown accomplice came to their aid and assisted in the escape. Is this true?"

"Oh, King, may you reign supreme. This is greatly exaggerated to be sure. The guard who sought to recapture them only *thought* he saw a man help them. It was never proven, as he was not found. I fear the guard did not see anyone but only used it as a ruse to avoid greater punishment for his ineptitude. I have duly punished the slacker and removed him from your service."

"There is more!" At this, Chief Legerdemain shrunk to the floor prostrate before the king. "A story has reached my ears that the man who helped the felons escape was none other than the prince of the Kingdom of Light, the one who claims to help those who cry out, or some such rubbish. Do you recollect that person, Chief Legerdemain?" The man in black shrunk lower.

"Of course, you know who I mean! Imposter! Insurgent! Insurrectionist! Your orders were to stamp out these rumors completely and see that no memory of this fictional character remains! And now what do we have? Everyone on the street knows that he has struck again. What do you have to say for yourself?"

"Oh, my King. I am sure it is only a rumor. No such person exists. If he did, we would have found him." The flattened form in black slowly attempted to rise but the king stood directly over him.

"This is not good enough, Legerdemain. You must find the malefactors and make sure they and the rumor dies forever! Do you hear me? I will not have my people's allegiance stolen by some wandering, half-witted, imbecile calling himself a prince of Light!"

At the sound of the name, both men winced as if it was painful even to utter the words. "He won't get away with this will he, Legerdemain?"

Chief Legerdemain crawled to kiss the feet of the king, but as he aimed his lips at the fur-lined slippers, the bottom of a foot met his face and shoved him across the room, sending his black cape flying like the wings of a frightened bat.

"Take that from your beloved Sovereign. If you value your position as chief of intelligence, you will not let me down. There are greater things at stake here than you know. Now get out of my sight."

Legerdemain backed out the door and crawled down the grand hallway. Once in the clear, he rose and straightened his garments, held his head high, and proudly walked down the stairs to the entry hall. His face burned red with anger. Passing by the royal servants, he dared not look to one side or the other lest they see the hatred and violence in his evil eyes.

I will not fail, he determined, as he walked out into the sunlight and headed down the hill to the prison command post.

CHAPTER 33

Carpville

Warm, humid air rose from the muddy road as Gem and Diamond strolled under the shade of yellowing leaves. Neither knew that summer was near its end and soon the leaves would turn to shades of orange and brown. The two men marveled at the verdant countryside. Gem knew that they were only a mountain range away from the dry, dusty land of Bellicosa where such sights were unknown, and Diamond imagined that he had forgotten how beautiful a place could be. His conscious mind took in the sights, all the while searching for anything familiar that would lead him to discover who he was and more about his new friend.

"Where are you from, Gem? Do you have family who are missing you?"

"Missing me? No way. My mother is no longer living," he said with a catch in his throat that Diamond did not fail to notice. "I don't know who my father was. Mother never mentioned it." It was hard to keep the sarcasm and pain from his voice.

"I guess that makes two of us, at least the part about not knowing who my father is. Sorry, I don't mean to make light of your predicament. You didn't tell me, are you from around here?" Diamond continued to fish for clues.

"I am not from around here. My home is an awful place and I plan never to go back there again. I want to travel up the coast," and he pointed to the west.

At this, Diamond realized that Gem's home was most likely in the opposite direction. But not knowing that he himself was from the same place, he lost interest in pursuing the question.

"Do you have a trade?" asked Diamond still trying to make some connection. Gem knew that his only trade had been in the manufacture of the very sword that Damon lost at sea. "I work with metal. Making tools," Gem declared proudly, and then in a lower voice, "and blades." Diamond nodded in approval and tried to think of how to make conversation with someone with so many secrets. "I guess you have the advantage here, Gem, as I can't answer many questions you might have about me."

"Yah, you're right."

Changing the subject, Diamond suggested, "New clothes would be nice."

Gem added, "And how about a patch for the back of your head." Diamond lightly fingered the wound and agreed.

"You know," said Diamond. "I can't escape the feeling that someone pulled me out of that storm. It's a sensation I remember of yanking on my shoulders and going from the darkness of the deep sea to the light at the water's surface. Why can't I remember any more than that? I should have drowned before reaching the shore." Gem was not very interested. "Have you ever had an experience like that, Gem? Like being transported out of danger to safety?"

Gem's memory was pricked and he thought of the dream and the key in his cell. He wanted to share this memory, but thought better of it. "Yah, right," was all he could say.

Carpville

The journey eventually led to a quaint cluster of buildings, which formed a tiny village. A narrow street wound between a half dozen small business fronts with what looked like residences attached at the back, or on top, of each one. Most prominent on the left was a blacksmith and stable tucked neatly under an overhanging apartment. Under the brown reed roofs, latticed windows were open to the ones on the opposite side of the street. On the right side, a bakery beckoned. Delicious smells wafting out the split doors and over the breeze tantalized the hungry travelers. As the two men entered the town, the eyes of every citizen turned in their direction—the smith's hammer held in mid-air over his anvil, the stable boy leading a roan mare caught himself in mid step, and the grandmother whose coins lay in her hand stopped half way to the baker selling her a loaf over the counter.

Diamond waved and smiled a self-conscious grin as Gem lowered his head and sought to slink by unnoticed. It was no use. Their stomachs growled in response to the torture of delicious smells. Stern faces stared in deadly silence.

"Hello. The name is Diamond and this is Gem. We are friends...just passing through," Diamond said, nodding his head, hoping that others who stood motionless would respond.

"We don't take to strangers around here," came a voice from behind them. They wheeled around to see a short, pudgy, middle-aged man approaching, hands held at his side as if ready to draw a weapon from a hidden pocket on short notice. He looked hard into the eyes of the newcomers and finally asked the all important question, "You ain't Cavils are ye?"

Gem and Diamond looked at each other and then looked back and responded, "No, no. Certainly not Cavils. Who are Cavils?"

"I'm asking the questions around here, son. Tell me who your fathers are." They looked at each other again in disbelief and then Diamond spoke for the two with a laugh, "I know this is hard to believe, but we don't know who our fathers are."

"I knew it, Clam. They is Cavils for sure...lyin', stinkin' Cavils. And look how they're dressed," offered the smith.

"We don't know what a Cavil is, really!" Diamond insisted.

"A Cavil is a no good scoundrel," said a voice from the left.

"A Cavil is a cheatin', murderin' blackguard," came a voice from the right.

"We can explain the way we look," reasoned Diamond. "I am dressed as a sailor, you see. I washed up on the shore only this morning and have lost my memory. I don't know who I am and my poor companion here is in much the same state as I."

The pudgy man narrowed his gaze and contorted the muscles around his mouth, which pulled his long curled mustache in all directions like the tail of a cat about to strike. He was trying to understand why these Cavils hadn't taken the bait yet. Normally, calling them names made them insane with anger and ready to tear the town apart. Surrounded as these strangers were, it was going to be a pleasure for the locals to beat them to mush and send them packing back down the road to Cavilton. Maybe they weren't Cavils after all.

"There's a word for people who don't know who their fathers are and it ain't nice." At this, Gem clenched his fist.

"I'm sorry, sir, that we have taken your community by surprise. But we are who we say we are and not Cavils. We wish you no harm and only ask that you help us as we are bereft and at your mercy." Diamond bowed as he motioned for Gem to stand still.

"Ain't no Cavil can resist fightin' words. They much be zilch, nothin' at all! Right, Clam?" asked the voice from the left. Gem fumed at the charge but held his peace.

"We are lower than low, your honor," said Diamond trying to be diplomatic, perceiving that the mustached man was the authority in this village.

The baker stepped forward and handed them each a bun and added, "Long as you're not a Cavil, you are welcome here. If you stick around you can help us get them boys back for the damage they did to ours today." Gem's arm muscles flexed in response to the suggestion and he prepared himself for the challenge. Noting Gem's agreement, Clam slapped him on the back, "That's the spirit, my boy." Others piped in adding insulting comments about Cavils and waved fists in the air. The numbers grew until Gem and Diamond were the center of a noisy crowd.

"If we can be of any help in dealing with your enemies, we would be glad to try," offered Diamond while choking down the bun. "Do you have a little drink to go with this?" he asked on the side. Someone ran for water.

"You some kind of strategist? We need a good plan for getting the best of them Cavils."

"Yes, perhaps I am a strategist," replied Diamond. "Have you tried making peace with the Cavils?"

"PEACE! There ain't never goin' to be peace with those vile, verminous villains," said the baker.

The water arrived in a large bowl and both men drank freely, letting the drops fall to the ground that missed their mouths. "If you will help us with food, shelter and some better clothes, we will see what we can do," Diamond bargained.

Everyone cheered at the idea of finally making progress in their battle with their archenemies. "Help has come at last! We are going to get those scoundrels yet."

"You help me in my saddle shop and it's a deal," said the liveryman. Gem and Diamond followed the stable owner out of the crowd and into the barn at the back of his store front. He was young, strong, and covered with bruises, old and new. They wondered if he had been among those they had seen in the fight earlier in the day.

"The name's Raspy Gripe. You can call me Gripe. Sleep here in the barn until you prove you're worth. Back there, the missus will give you something to eat," and he pointed to the tiny thatched house behind the barn.

Mistress Hurla Gripe was polite and charming, though still suspicious. She brought out meat pies and wine made from her own grapes.

Neither traveler could speak as their mouths were full and their hearts were cheered by the windfall of hospitality. "Ma'am," said Gem, "I have never in all my life tasted anything so good!" The mistress blushed and went to find some new treat she could offer.

"Hey, Diamond. Remember I told you this key was my luck charm. Well now," said Gem, "I've changed my mind. YOU are."

CHAPTER 34
Happy Valley

Before Jewel and Bina had gone far they decided the time had come to change back into their gowns worn in Credulos. Their shabby working clothes were only arousing suspicions. Safely hidden in the bushes, each removed a rolled up dress from the deep pockets of their cloaks, put them on, and resumed the journey, feeling much more like themselves. Soon they saw a garden with neat rows of colorful vegetables. Peering through the thick trees, Jewel saw a fence, and behind, nestled snuggly among tidy shrubs, was a miniature cottage. The whole scene looked perfect and inviting.

Jewel and Bina walked carefully along the narrow cobblestone path lined with petunias, daisies, roses, and chrysanthemums. Jewel knocked softly at the small door and a very old, bent figure opened to them. The tiny woman's face was heavily wrinkled with thin lips painted like a large red heart. Her eyebrows were drawn in brown symmetrical arches over each eye. A scarf framed white hair curled into ringlets that hung around her shoulders.

Smiling, she greeted the strangers and bid them enter the miniature home. "How nice of you to come visit me," said the ancient woman. "I'm sorry but I can't remember your names. I'm so forgetful these days."

Jewel realized that she thought they were visiting neighbors and wasn't sure how to explain their presence. The size of the entrance made it difficult for the tall Jewel and the wide Bina to enter, but they managed. Inside, the small furniture and low ceiling made both feel oversized.

"My name is Jewel and this is Bina. We are new in the neighborhood."

"Yes, and we wanted to make sure you have enough food," added Bina hoping that this would prompt the woman to feed her guests.

"Oh, my dears, how kind of you. Then you must know that I am Fleecia Sweet. The road is actually named after me as I have been here so long. You have seen my wonderful garden, I suppose. Let me get something for you both. Please be seated."

"And hurry!" Bina formed the words with her lips and pled silently. Mistress Sweet soon returned with a tiny tray loaded with cakes and tea.

"I made these cakes with my own pumpkin," she said in her tiny voice. Both visitors wanted to eat them all quickly but tried to pace themselves so as not to appear greedy.

"These are delicious, Mistress Sweet. You are a wonderful cook." Jewel said. "That is right," Fleecia replied. "I am the best cook in Happy Valley. Everyone knows it." "Sounds like we found the right place," whispered Bina, "I'm ready for *Happy* anything."

The three conversed politely about the perfection of the mistress' house, garden, food, flowers, and furnishings until they were all bored with it. Jewel finally changed the subject switching to the one closest to her heart. "Mistress, we were told that you can help us find a man who is reputed to be "the one who helps people. Does he live close by?"

"Yes, of course. You must mean our wonderful Master Perphidius." Jewel was staring into Mistress Sweet's face trying to read the smiling expression that had not altered since they entered the house. *What an odd name. Could he be the stranger I long to see again?* Jewel's heart raced at the thought that she would soon be in the company of the one who had rescued them from death.

"Oh, he does help so many people. He is amazing. I will give you instructions to find his mansion. It is glorious, indeed. Such a place of light!" Jewel grew more elated with each new bit of information.

"Thank you. We are very grateful. You have been most helpful to us."

"I know, dears. It is my strong point."

Once back on the road, Jewel laughed out loud. "Bina. I think we have found the man I was telling you about. He is known as the one who helps people. It is just as I read in Mistress Dismalia's hidden room. I don't know how he gets around so well, being in one place at one time, then far away at another time. He must have a lot of magical powers."

Bina listened patiently, but had heard so many crazy things from her companion that this, as well, was dismissed without comment. What was the use? The girl would not listen to reason. Continuing down the lane, only the sounds of the gentle breeze in the trees and singing birds could be heard. Slowly, the strains of music reached their ears. It was raucous, yet merry sounding, and grew stronger as they rounded a curve in the road. The sun was still high in the sky behind them so that, when they first laid eyes on the source of the sounds, they were almost blinded by the flashes of light.

Jewel held up her hand as a shield and walked the last hundred paces to the entrance gate. Drums played a catchy background beat to the sound of flutes and horns. It made Jewel want to dance. She tried to move in time to the music but found the beat just irregular enough to make it impossible. *What a very strange place!* she thought.

The sun was suddenly obscured behind clouds and the blinding light disappeared. Jewel could see that the enormous house was covered with scraps of polished metal, all at different angles and fastened to the exterior. That would explain why Mistress Sweet had thought this was a house of light. Not only was the music out of rhythm, but the house was out of kilter. No windows or doors were on the same level and no two planes were parallel. Even the roof was slightly curved, and one end was higher than the other. Some windows were round and had small panes of glass. Others were oblong with leaded panes forming pictures of animals in unnatural poses.

Guards opened the gates and welcomed the travelers inside. The path to the house was curved back and forth like a snake. It led to a door that was large and ornately carved in strange symbols that neither Bina or Jewel had seen before. Welcomed into the interior of the house, they both stood in awe at the grandeur. Everywhere they looked, candles and oil lamps were lit, giving the house a strong smoky smell.

"The master will see you now," announced a house official dressed in braid trimmed uniform. Jewel and Bina looked at one another in puzzlement. "How did he know we were coming?"

"Welcome! Welcome! Do come in!" urged the jocular master. He was as round as he was tall and covered completely by a magnificent robe of fur. Tiny stones were dotted closely on the fur to pick up the light from the myriads of candles causing him to sparkle and glow. "I have been expecting you. Yes, indeed—I heard that you need help. And I am just the one who will help you. Oh yes, that is my specialty, helping. If you are in trouble, I will rescue you."

Jewel and Bina were speechless. Jewel had never seen the face of the one who had saved them, or the one who had met her in her strange dream. Somehow, this didn't seem like that same person. His light had come from somewhere inside him and radiated out. Could there be another ONE who helped people, who rescued people from danger?

"Tell me now. From what trouble do you wish to be rescued? How can I help?" Jewel thought to herself, *If he was the one wouldn't he know what our problem is? He should know we are seeking a home? He should know what he already promised?*

Bina finally spoke. "Master, we are your humble servants. We have come from a country far away looking for a place to live and be at home."

"And what was wrong with the place you came from? Perhaps you need to return there and try again to get along," said the master. He could see right away that this answer was not going to do so he tried again. "Ah, I see it now. A home and a family." The faces of the two women brightened. "What you need is a…a home…and a family. I have the very place for you. But first you must do something for me."

"What is it, Master?" asked Bina.

"As a matter of fact, my servants have had the day off and my scullery is in quite a state. You clean it for me and then I give you the good news about your future." Bina frowned but looked resigned. Jewel scowled and was confused. She turned to Bina and said softly, "This can't be right. We didn't come all this way to become servants again, did we?"

Bina replied, "Look. Anything we do here is better than where we came from. So what if we have to work for our keep."

Jewel was deeply disappointed but, in the end, they agreed. "Thank you, Master. We will report to you tomorrow if you will allow us to stay the night."

The butler showed the two to the scullery, bowed, and left them surrounded by a mountain of pots, pans, bowls, plates, and cutlery that reached to the ceiling. They stood dumbstruck in the doorway. Where had Master Perphidius even gotten so many pots and pans? His servants had to have been gone for more than a day. "Bina, I think we have been deceived. This man is not capable of helping anyone. He is lying to us. I think we are his new servants."

Jewel turned to go back out to the hall but found the door closed and locked behind them. It grew darker each passing minute. Only a dim lantern burned over the wash basin. Water would have to be hauled from outside and there was no possibility of completing the task before dawn the next day. Jewel began to sob. Bina hung her head and agreed with Jewel that they had been duped. "It had all looked so hopeful. How did we go wrong again?" howled Jewel. "We have to get out of here. And this time we are going the *other* direction, the way I wanted to go."

Rummaging through the piles of greasy plates, they were able to scrape bits of leftover food and ate greedily despite the odor of decay. Once they were satisfied, they changed again into their brown, work clothes and headed out the back door to an ancient well where they began to draw buckets of water.

The noise of buckets banging against the sides of the well and the squeaking of the turning handle brought the dark yard to life. Two growling dogs edged closer and closer with fierce glowing eyes. "What do we do about them?" asked Bina in a shaking voice. Both women backed into the kitchen and began searching for more scraps of food. When they had filled a plate they approached the well again. The dogs began to drool.

Jewel looked around to see a way of escape. "I think we can climb over that wall."

Bina rolled her eyes. "Short people have limitations, you know. Maybe you can climb over the wall. How am I going to get over before becoming dinner for those dogs?" Jewel surveyed the grounds and spied a wooden crate. "When I put this plate of food down, we have to make a run for it." Each woman tied her cloak in a bundle that was slung on her back. "Are you ready? Now!"

Bina scrambled behind Jewel who quickly shoved the crate next to the wall and then heaved Bina up and over. The dogs inhaled the food and weren't far behind, lunging at Jewel's foot as she scurried to the top. She looked back and saw that the light in the scullery window brighten. Hurriedly ducking her head, she crouched with Bina close to the ground.

They walked away from the house of Master Perphidius as fast as they could and headed north through the dark of night.

"I can't see," complained Bina who kept stumbling over loose stones. Jewel could hear the frustration and anger in her tone. "Your eyes will adjust. There is a moon rising." She reached out and took Bina's hand and led her forward down the lonely road, once again, into the unknown.

Exhausted, they finally stopped and sat beside a lake. Bina opened her bundle. Wrapped in her red tunic, she had hidden a two ends of a sausage salvaged from the evening before. "Not much, but better than NOTHING," Bina spat out the words. They shared the simple meal in silence.

The sky grew lighter around them. A mist rose from the lake giving the site a mystical quality that became more beautiful as the day dawned. Nothing was heard but a frenzy of waking birds, whose morning chatter sounded like the clinking of metal cutlery.

Jewel stood to her feet and walked mechanically as if in a daze away from the lake through trees and brush looking for some place to sleep. The discovery of ripe succulent berries brought a smile to Jewel's face. They would eat, though she knew they still needed something more substantial.

A large tree had fallen against another forming a small space. Jewel tugged another smaller fallen tree and some dead limbs into place and smoothed out the surface of the ground with last season's leaves. "Bina, come on. We can sleep here," called Jewel and the tired woman did not hesitate or question the arrangements. Their only thought was to sink into the oblivion of rest.

Mosquitoes buzzing in her ears woke Jewel and, even though she was wrapped in her cloak, she could feel a damp chill that got colder by the moment. The day was spent. It was too late to begin walking. Would berries sustain them sufficiently to keep up the pace, especially as they approached the northern mountains? Warm tears spilled over her cheek.

Please help us. We are hungry and weary and we just want to find a home.

Nostrils flared on neighing horses as they anticipated the digging of spurs into their sides. Leather saddles groaned under the weight of heavily armed riders who mounted and prepared for the long ride out of Bellicosa. The entire country and the desert had been searched extensively and now it was time to go beyond the borders into the surrounding small kingdoms in search of the fugitives.

Legerdemain headed the pack and shouted orders, "Forward, men. For the honor of the king!" The men shouted gleefully. Excitement was in the air as this was a chore all anticipated for more than one reason. The town of

Bellicosa was a dull place and this was an adventure to win the favor of the king and the chief of intelligence. Wearing their smart gray uniforms, each with the green dragon on the front, and armed with swords, spears, and a host of minor bludgeoning instruments, they galloped up the mountain in a cloud of dust before the fawning crowd.

Ladies fainted at the sight of the courageous heroes who protected their land from those who defied the king. Hadn't Chief Legerdemain himself just declared before them, "The king will find the criminals and they will confess that they assaulted the guard themselves and escaped. They will tell you that no mysterious freedom fighter was involved. The two shall be punished with death by hanging for trying to deceive the people of Bellicosa! Justice and truth will prevail!"

CHAPTER 35

Cavilton

The people of Carpville were very helpful once it was clear that Diamond and Gem intended to help them gain mastery over their archenemies, the citizens of Cavilton.

"Time to eat, boys," Hurla called from her tiny kitchen window. Diamond and Gem were amazed to see the collection of plates on the table, each steaming with a local delicacy. "Did you cook all this food, Mistress Gripe?" asked Gem. "Oh, no. I had lots of help. The zinger berry pies are from Letty Dumble. The balder nut and corn pot surprise was baked by Dory Grit. Looks like every girl in Carpville wants to impress you two handsome fellers." The newcomers looked at each other and grinned. "Not only that, but Nelda Snivel left some of her handiwork." Hurla pointed to a neatly folded pile of clothing. "I guess she thought you could use a little sprucing up."

After the meal, the satiated and well-dressed duo returned to work. Gem spent the day learning to work with leather and amazed everyone with his skill at the forge. Diamond tried his hand at the manual jobs but was able to offer more help in developing better ways to run the business.

"For a sailor, you sure know a lot about horse trading," said Gripe jokingly. Diamond was glad to be able to do something profitable and amazed even himself at his abilities.

"Gripe, I want you to have this sheath. I have no sword for it and I see that you could use it more than I. Please take it with my gratitude for all you and your wife have done for us."

Gem was in the middle of creating two small pouches, one for his key and one for Diamond's stone. Upon hearing his companion's offer, a knot formed in his stomach.

"Looks like a genuine Chiselstone. Are you sure you want to part with such a valuable piece of work?"

"A Chiselstone, is it?" asked Diamond. Gem stiffened and held his breath for a moment. "If I had a better memory, I'd appreciate it more than I do now. It is all yours," concluded Diamond. Gem exhaled and continued cutting the leather circle under his knife.

The day ended with a loud argument across the road. "There's rumors of a fight!" said Gripe to his hired hands. "There was a cow found in old man Gruesome's garden. No one knows who it belongs to. We know. It is a Cavil cow put there to bring him to starvation, no doubt." Gem then asked, "Could it be just one of their cows that got in the garden accidentally?"

"You're not from around here, are you? Cows don't get into the garden of Carpville folks by accident. It was a planned assault. There has to be retaliation or they will try it again." Diamond thought to try another approach. "What if someone like me was to take the cow back down the road and just point out to them that it was found in a garden. Wouldn't they take it back and apologize?"

"You ARE a numbskull if you think they will take their cow back just like that. They will insist that it isn't their cow and start calling us names. Once they do that, it's fists and clubs, hammer and tongs, swords and daggers."

"Isn't that a bit of an overreaction, Gripe?" The muscles on Gripe's neck tightened and he said emphatically, "No! We know those brutes. They would stop at nothing to make us look bad. Fighting is the only thing they understand."

Diamond motioned to Gem to follow him outside and they headed down the narrow main road. "I think the time has come that we must do something to prevent more bloodshed," said Diamond. "Let's talk to Constable Clam and see if he agrees."

The constable's office was a small cubicle in back of the bakery. A desk and a rough, locked closet for a jail cell was all that was needed in Carpville, as the only criminals were the ones who lived down the road and seldom wound up under his surveillance.

"Clam, we have an idea. We will go to Cavilton and ask about the cow. Perhaps it was an accident and can be easily cleared up. What do you think?"

The constable exploded from his desk pointing an accusing finger in Diamond's face and shouted, "I knew it! You are a Cavil spy. Only a Cavil would say that. Here we trusted you and what do you do but try to trick us into passing up a good fight." Diamond and Gem did not know what to reply to the outburst.

"We only want to help and it seems like the logical thing is to try to find reasons NOT to fight." Gem added, "Forgiveness. Maybe that's what's needed." Hearing himself say the word forgiveness, he wondered how such a foreign concept had entered his mind.

"You get out of here right now. Get down that road and go where you belong—in Cavilton with yer pals. That's what you are, underhanded, conniving cronies of those Cavils."

Gem and Diamond backed away into the street as Clam advanced with finger pointing and threats pouring from his mouth. A crowd gathered and the men became the center of attention once again. Scandal and dismay registered on faces and all became intent on running the Cavil sympathizers out of town.

Giving up when they saw there was no use in trying to explain again, the two backed down the street until they were beyond the main buildings. As they turned to continue, Gem felt a thud on his back and then Diamond had the same sensation. Looking back they could see small boys throwing vegetables and, from the look of the remains, determined they were tomatoes. They began to trot along, not wanting to take any more direct hits.

"What happened?" asked Gem puffing down the lane. "I thought we were helping. That's the last time I try to be a nice guy. The one time in my life I felt like I was making it on my own and being a man, look what comes of it."

"Sorry, Gem. I didn't expect this either. I wonder what the Cavils will do when we get to Cavilton. There is no way around it," observed Diamond.

The afternoon was warm and sunny. It hadn't rained again since the storm and the road was drying rapidly.

"I was starting to like the place," said Gem.

"Yes. It had great possibilities. You are a fine craftsman, Gem."

"Hmm," Gem responded wondering if he would ever get a chance to prove he could be somebody.

The mood was somber between them. Both knew that the Cavil vigilantes would show up at any moment. A wagon pulled by two sad-looking horses slowly made its way toward them. The driver was jolted from a stupor when he spied the travelers. He pulled up on the reins and cried, "Whoa." Diamond continued walking, and greeted him with a smile and wave; the farmer sat in stunned silence.

"Good day." There was no reply. The farmer quickly turned his wagon around and whipped the horses into a canter. Soon they were left in the wake of dust and dreaded of what might be waiting for them once the town's people were informed about their approach. They didn't have to wait long.

A brown cloud could be seen long before the horsemen arrived. The animals were pulled to a halt and a dozen men dismounted to face Gem and Diamond who now swallowed hard before speaking.

"Hello, friends," choked out Gem.

"Who's he callin' 'friend', Bludge?" asked one of the men to the leader.

"I'll ask him, Fester. Who you callin' friend, boy?" asked Bludge. Before Gem could answer, he asked, "You a Carp?"

Diamond responded as best he could, knowing the deep-seated hatred each group bore for the other. "We are neither Carp nor Cavil but simply travelers who wish to help both parties find a basis for peace between your clans." At the word "peace" a whoop and holler went up from the men.

"How come he knows so much about the Carps and Cavils, Bludge?" asked Fester.

"How come you know so much about Carps and Cavils? You a spy?" asked Bludge. He spit a dark liquid from the side of his mouth and it hit the dust with a splat.

"No," replied Diamond. "We lived in Carpville for a short time and became aware of the grudges born by both sides."

"You LIVED with those buzzards?" Bludge paused and then said, "Go get 'em, boys!"

Hours later, Gem and Diamond awoke in a dark place. From the smell, they guessed it was a barn. Cows could be heard munching hay not far away. They tried to move but found themselves tied securely.

"Hey, sailor boy, how are you with untying knots?" asked Gem, barely able to get his breath. "Great. But I never mastered the skill with no hands," replied Diamond.

"Are you all right?"

"I've been better," admitted Diamond, straining against his bonds.

"There are usually tools in a barn, maybe even sharp ones. Shall I find out?" asked Gem.

"How will you do that tied up?"

Gem began to rock back and forth until he was able to roll, groaning as he successfully completed the first full turn. He continued in the dark until a shudder and exclamation came from his lips.

"Agh!"

"What?" asked Diamond.

"I think I rolled in something. My new clothes aren't going to be quite so nice after this."

"Worse than rotten tomatoes?" asked Diamond.

"Oh, yeah. Lots worse," came the reply as he struggled on toward the door of the barn. Diamond heard shuffling and movement of unseen objects.

"I think I found a shovel," Gem quietly groaned. He began rubbing his bound wrists against the blade. It seemed like hours before he heard Gem sigh and whisper, "At last." More minutes went by as Gem worked the ropes back and forth, up and down, trying to free himself.

Diamond had all but fallen asleep by the time Gem crawled over to him and began untying more knots. It was painstaking work in the dark, but at last, they were both standing up and ready for their next move.

"Ouch. I hurt all over." said Gem curtly.

"I think we took a beating all right. I don't remember. They must have knocked the sense out of us," said Diamond feeling his sore jaw.

"How do we get out of here? Which way do we go? I never want to see another Carp or Cavil as long as I live," admitted Gem.

"You are the escape artist, you tell me."

Together, they snuck quietly out the barn window and crept along the side of the low structure under the thatch eves. An open field could be seen in the moonlight with a forest on the other side. "I say we head for the forest." Gem studied the position of the stars and moon.

"North...let's go."

Down the mountain and into the quiet town of Credulos rode the Bellicosan horsemen. Paramount Harbinger met them and was dumfounded to hear of their quest.

"We are looking for two women who escaped from Bellicosa."

"Was one of them tall and the other a short, older woman?" asked the paramount who officially represented the town in such queries. Legerdemain smiled and said to him, "Tell me everything you know about them." The paramount escorted the black-caped man into his office.

"Yes, we have quite a tale to tell about those two."

CHAPTER 36
Gem's Dream

Silvery-leaved corn stalks shone in the moonlight providing cover for Diamond and Gem to flee from Cavil territory. They needn't have worried. A deathly silence signified the deep slumber of all but the escapees. Gem wondered if his body could possibly survive any more bruising than it had in the last week, feeling painfully the jarring of every step. Diamond brushed against him in the dark and heard him moan.

The gray of dawn appeared and the men were stumbling along a game trail that wound back and forth. In the light, they could see that they hadn't fared too badly in their last stand. Black and blue on top of the yellow-green of older bruises was easier to manage than cuts in their hasty escape. After hours of continual walking, they were desperate for sleep and were overjoyed at finding a small lake where they could refresh themselves.

"Diamond, come and look at this," exclaimed Gem. "Here is shelter someone has made under this fallen tree." Diamond stooped down and observed that it was dry and matted as if someone had slept there very recently. "I haven't seen any signs of habitation for miles. I wonder if a hunter was sleeping in the woods way out here."

"Hey, look at this!" continued Gem, holding up a red tunic. "I wonder who left this behind. Not your usual hunting attire." He stripped off his vest and shirt and donned the red tunic. It was short but would keep him from the chill of the morning while he scrubbed his own clothes with sandy soil in the lake and laid them out in the morning sun to dry.

"I could swear I smell sausage." Gem sniffed the air and finally traced the odor to the red garment. "Man, someone left the tunic and took the sausage. Too bad it wasn't the other way around."

"I guess we hunt. There must be something to kill if the hunters built a shelter here."

Gem walked around the perimeter, careful to detect anything left by a hunter to help with their dilemma. "The berries have been stripped off these bushes. Maybe our friend wasn't successful with his bow."

"It is getting cold. What are our chances of getting a fire going," asked Diamond, "with no flint or coals? I've heard that you can start a fire by rubbing sticks together, but it is difficult." Gem did not relish the thought of trying this method.

"What about your stone?"

Diamond took the diamond from its pouch and held it in the sunlight. "It's worth a try." He set about to see if it would work. He gathered a large pile of the driest leaves and twigs he could find, held the stone close to the top and waited. The minutes dragged on and his arm grew tired. He was about to quit when a small swirl of smoke rose from the tinder and caught the others alight. Gem ran off and, before long, returned with a freshly killed rabbit.

By evening, they sat beside the lake, one on each side of their fire, eating rabbit—tired, yet feeling good about the day. "I guess my lucky diamond worked. You ever had any luck with that key of yours?" Diamond knew there was a story behind it and hoped that Gem trusted him enough now to tell it.

"Yes. I have." He paused, deciding whether or not to tell the whole story. With their pasts so far behind them, he thought little harm could come from it now, so he began.

"The key is much more than a luck charm. It was like you said. I was in prison. Not just any prison, but the granddaddy of all prisons that they said no one had ever escaped from before. Not sure I believed them but it was tough. I didn't do all that much to get there either. I stole something and then found out it was more than I had bargained for. Then I tried to get a free ride on a ship and got caught." Gem glanced at Diamond's face to see if this brought back anything to him. His face was clear and curious, so Gem went on.

"I tried to escape—pretty stupid. I got beat to a pulp and thrown in the dungeon. Foul place. Rats, food that would turn your stomach in knots, and some old fool telling me if I behaved myself I might get to go out in the corridor once in a while. I was beat up bad and could hardly sit up, let alone walk. It was darker than any dark I've ever known."

"I lost control. I mean I finally broke down and cried like a baby." Gem laughed nervously at the memory. Diamond didn't flinch. "I hit the bottom. Life was over for me. I wanted to end it and planned to eat or drink nothing until I died. But I couldn't even do that. I cried. I screamed for help and begged someone to hear me, but all I heard were rats lining up to make a meal out of my toes. I have never felt so alone or empty or useless."

"I fell asleep and had a frightening dream. I was standing in a circle of fire, flames shooting up very high on every side. On the other side of the fire were creatures out of the worst nightmares imaginable. They were trying to get me." Gem began to choke up and he stopped. He was not accustomed to losing control over his emotions and it surprised him that he felt like crying again as he recounted the awful dream. He shook off the sadness and went on.

"I saw a key on the ground in front of me and bend down to pick it up. When I did, the flames began to get closer and closer, closing in on me. I was terrified that I would be burned alive but, as they got closer, I did not feel the heat—must have been because it was only a dream."

Diamond interrupted, "Like protection. You were protected by the fire barrier." Gem hadn't thought of it that way, "Yah, I see what you mean."

"The key I picked up was bright with a blue stone inserted in the place where the hole should be. The flames finally touched me and then it was like I was a pillar of light and it was inside of me. A voice said, 'Gem! Be free and shine!'" He laughed again. "I know this sounds crazy."

Diamond then asked, "How did you get the key then if it was only a dream?"

"I can't explain it. I woke up and dug around in the dirt and there it was." Gem could see that Diamond was waiting anxiously for the next part of the story. "I tried the key in the leg chains and manacles and," he shrugged, "it worked." At the last word, tears erupted from his eyes. Rubbing his face with his hands, he tried vainly to stop, but the tears flowed. "This is stupid I know. But it was such a rotten place and I was pretty happy about that key. It was much more than luck; it was a miracle."

"That is an incredible story, Gem. No wonder you carry it with you. It will always remind you that you were bound unto death but were set free. You said the creatures on the outside couldn't get to you because of the fire. Maybe some power was trying to show you that you are protected from even worse things than have happened to you already. You screamed for help and it could be that that power heard you and sent the dream to let you know that you were not alone."

Gem had thought about the dream and the key in his cell but could not make any sense of it. He was amazed at how quickly Diamond had come up with these notions.

"We must talk of this again. I feel there is a meaning and a purpose for this "miracle" as you call it, and together we will discover it," Diamond said confidently.

He scratched his head and said, "Why me? I have not been a very upstanding character. Not like you. You seem to know a lot of things. I have just been a troublemaker all my life—pretty worthless."

"Someone is giving you another chance, Gem. Let's see that key." Gem fished in the pouch and brought it out into the firelight. The blue stone was deep in color and reflected light rays into their faces that were almost too bright to look at.

"Who would want to give someone like me another chance?" asked Gem.

"I don't know," Diamond paused as he turned the key over and over in his hand. "I'm sure getting tired of saying that. But I do know one thing. I was helped too. I have the strongest feeling that I was pulled out of the sea and guided to that beach. I should have been dead like you, but instead I was saved from drowning. Someday I'll know for sure."

A look of fear crossed Gem's countenance and Diamond saw it. "Well, don't you want me to find out? You look like that's not a good idea. What are you afraid of? If they find me, they will find you too? I won't give you away, Gem. I promise."

"Why?" asked Gem.

"There must be a purpose. Both of us have an enchantment on our lives. It is up to us to find out who and why?" Diamond reached in to get his diamond from its leather pouch and held it up to the firelight. "Look, Gem! It is clearer than it was. I can see reflections in it where before it was cloudy. This is more than a good luck charm! But what is it?"

Chief Legerdemain emerged laughing from the paramount's office. "You have helped our cause tremendously today. I can't thank you enough. These criminals we seek have a history of deception and deviousness. I can't believe you fell for their act but what a story this will make when King Ironfist hears of it."

"Well, I am sure you are right. I still can't believe that they took advantage of a people who only wished them well. How they knew of our legend before arriving and how they convinced those silly women of their credibility, I have no idea. And for that tall one to insist that we find her a wealthy, land-owning husband, well, I am flabbergasted that it got that far. It is just fortunate for us that Master Karakul discovered the ruse in time and chased them out of town," said the haughty paramount.

"Tell me, Paramount Harbinger, which way did they go when they were chased away?" asked Legerdemain.

The official hesitated then spoke nervously. "They headed back up the mountain toward the sacred waterfall."

"I think we shall be traveling along the river to the west then. In their cunning and cleverness, I think they will try again to swindle unsuspecting innocents." Chief Legerdemain strode out into the street and mounted his horse. "Forward!" he motioned the company to move ahead, and they galloped out of sight.

CHAPTER 37

The Vision

The gray dawn was cold and crisp in the mountains. A shudder woke Diamond and he felt a cold that would not retreat, though he tossed and turned. The two men had traveled through the woods moving north. No farms or towns had been encountered and he began to wonder if they had made the right decision about their route. Diamond had been willing to travel with Gem away from his home, but what was he to do about finding out his own identity?

He squeezed out of the shelter Gem had made out of branches, ferns, and moss. It kept out the rain but it was not much help with the cold. Eating berries and rabbits was getting tiresome as well. Thoughts of bread, cheese, and fruit only made his rumbling stomach ache for relief.

Trying not to wake Gem, he crept some distance away and jumped up and down to get his blood moving. He needed to move about to warm up so he looked up the mountain and sized up a dash for the top. Once he got back to camp, he thought, he should be feeling more like hunting for breakfast. Scrambling over rocks and brush, and darting in and out of depressions in the side of the hill made him feel alive and invigorated. The top was in sight and he felt better with each upward lunge.

He finally made his goal and saw that he was not at the top but only at the base of yet another precipice. Breathing hard, he stopped and considered the extra climb. Looking up, he saw something move. Not far from him was a sight that he did not understand. *What is it?* he wondered.

A girl was standing at the edge of the cliff with arms raised toward the rising sun. As it rose, she glowed with an unearthly light. A dark cloak was fastened at the neck but pushed back behind her shoulders. Her green dress with threads of gold picked up light from the sun. Outshining that was a green stone hanging as a pendant on her chest that spread rays of brilliant green like a halo around her body. Diamond drew in his breath with surprise and held it until he nearly passed out for lack of air. By the time he remembered to breathe again, he fell backward and caught himself against a tree.

Then to make the scene even more eerie, a soft, moaning tune reached his ears that sounded sad and lonely. He closed his eyes and braced himself, then opened them again, and she was gone. It had been a vision. So many strange things were happening to him and to his friend. He was dizzy with the memory of what he had seen. Turning around, he carefully let himself down the hillside.

"Gem, wake up!" Diamond urged the sleeping man as he shook him inside the cave of branches.

"What?" groaned Gem who had not slept well and needed all the rest he could get.

"Gem, I saw a vision up on the mountain. What can it mean?"

"What are you talking about, a dream?"

"No. This was more real than a dream," and he carefully described what he had seen.

"You say a girl was up there? Let's go see if she is still there," replied the sleepy Gem. "Was she pretty?"

GEM! It was a vision of a girl."

"I thought you said she was real. Maybe she needs *help*," Gem said with a twinkle in his eye and arms raised in a flexed position.

"Oh, stop. Let's get breakfast," said Diamond in disgust.

"I'm going up there to look for a rabbit for breakfast. You can stay down here and make a fire."

Gem took off at a run with a makeshift spear. He quickly got to the place that Diamond had described and looked up to the next level of cliff. Seeing a place on which a person could stand, he made his way up until he stood on that spot. In the quiet, he heard voices coming from back in the trees and decided to investigate. His heart beat with excitement. With every muscle tensed, he prepared to meet Diamond's flesh and blood vision.

"I'm sick and I'm hungry, Jewel. We have nothing to eat. Look at me! I'm wasting away to nothing before my very eyes." Bina held out her clothes, which were fitting more and more loosely each day they traveled further into the forest.

Gem recognized that whining, nagging voice. *It couldn't be,* he thought. He broke out into the clearing and there stood two women. Gem fell backwards with shock and sat on the ground, mouth hanging open, barely able to speak.

"Mother, is that you?" Then his eyes went to the strange woman standing before him. Jewel had changed into her green dress briefly to beseech the unseen One, and was about to again put on her dingy tunic and trousers. Her hair had not been dressed and its bulk framed her head and shoulders darkly. Gem asked, "*Who* are you?" ready to believe that Diamond had been right about her being more mystical than real.

Bina screamed at the sight of the ghost who had jumped out of the bushes. She ran to him and burst into tears. She held him around the chest for a moment then backed away holding him at arm's length.

"Jip, they said you were in prison!"

"Mother, they told me you were hanged!"

"What are you doing here? You are the one who started all this. I should kill you now on this spot. Do you realize what you did? You ruined my life forever. How could you dare be alive and show up like this?" She began to pound on his chest as she sobbed with joy and pain.

"I'm sorry. I know what I did was wrong. Can you believe that?" confessed Gem. Bina stared in amazement. Her son who had been so haughty and cruel was apologizing.

"The name is Gem now." He looked at Jewel and inquired tentatively, "Julen? Is that you?"

"No, that's not Julen, imbecile. That is the Goddess Remora. No, that is Jewel, the delusional follower of the Knight of the North," she screeched. "Why is everyone so intent on changing their names around here? Take me away for I am going mad. Do you hear me?" She pushed on his chest to beat the words into his consciousness.

Ignoring his mother momentarily, he turned to Jewel and asked, "What is she talking about? What's with the dress and the fancy necklace? My friend down there thought you were a ghost."

"What friend?" asked Bina, frantically hoping to be rescued from their futile plight.

"Oh, boy...have I got a story for you. And I can't wait to hear yours! But first you had better hear mine because, if you don't listen carefully, we will be in serious trouble." With that, he quickly gave them the highlights of his escape, the discovery of Damon, and their travels since.

"And he doesn't remember anything before washing up on the beach?" asked Jewel.

"No! And don't call him Damon. We are calling him Diamond because he has this lucky charm...well...diamond, so we agreed to be Gem and Diamond. Get it? Oh, never mind."

Bina put her hands over her ears and pretended to scream, then muttered unintelligible words to herself. She had hoped that deliverance was in sight at last, but now, they had to continue with some kind of act before the dangerous son of Master Chiselstone. Their position was worse, not better.

"Mother, take it easy. I can at least help you get something to eat." At this, the crying lessened and Bina brightened. "What are you waiting for then? Go!" she commanded, and he headed back over the rise.

Gem tried to think, as he came down the mountain, how he would explain the two women without giving away who they really were. He could trust Diamond, but how far, he was not sure. What would happen if his friend remembered that he was the son of the very master who owned the three runaways? Not being very good with creative ideas had Gem at a disadvantage. *Diamond would think of a great story*, he thought. Then he remembered that he was supposed to be getting breakfast. After a small diversion, he returned to camp with two large squirrels.

"Well, what was up there? Anyone?" asked Diamond, trying to sound disinterested.

"You aren't going to believe this but, you did see a girl. And guess what, there are two up there—one girl and one older woman." Diamond jumped from his seat on a log and exclaimed excitedly, "I was right? Where are they? Who are they?"

"One said she was the Goddess Remora, but I think she was kidding me—that must have been the one you saw on the cliff. Impressive, I must admit. The other is her, ah, handmaid, yah. They have run away from a cruel family and are on the run just like us."

Gem was proud of himself for thinking up this much. He tried to remember the details so he could tell his mother and Jewel the same story.

"How can they be surviving in this northern cold with summer finished? We must help them." Both men agreed this was a good idea.

"I told them I would cook up some food and they could join us but, I see I'd better get more than these two squirrels. This would be a great time to find a bobbit if they only lived around here," and Gem and he was off again.

CHAPTER 38
Surprise Meeting

Diamond paced nervously as the visitors were due to descend at any moment. He spit into his hands and smoothed down his wild hair. He straightened his clothing and dusted dried moss off the vest. Then, like a butterfly flitting down from the sky, Jewel seemed to float down into the camp. She no longer glowed as she had seemed to do in the first light of dawn, but her dark skin and black halo of hair, her dress and exquisite necklace, gave her an ethereal presence that took his breath away. *Her eyes*, he thought as he looked deeply into Jewel's eyes. *They are exotic and mesmerizing.* Something else about her was fascinating. She was beautiful, but more than beautiful. Perhaps she WAS a goddess.

Jewel was afraid to look into Diamond's eyes for fear of seeing once again the distain and anger. For so long, she had imagined him looking at her with kindness and caring. The habit of her servant days remained with her in the presence of the son of the master of the house, so she bowed her head as he spoke to her.

"Are you the Goddess Remora?"

Jewel looked up with shy grin and laughed, "No. Who told you that?" Gem tried to cover the mistake and interjected, "I told you she was kidding." Diamond smiled at her, relieved that she was not a goddess, but intrigued at the mystery of who she really was.

"My name is Jewel and I hear you are Diamond and this is your friend Gem." They all laughed as they realized the meaning of their names. Bina showed her disgust in a sneer and looked away from the group. Diamond turned to her, picking up the play on words, "And you must be Sapphire."

Bina did not laugh but shot back, "Forget the jokes. I'm just Bina to you and I am hungry, so let's get on with it." Gem was embarrassed for his mother and thankful that Diamond didn't know of their relationship.

He put his hand to the side of his mouth and told him quietly, "I told you about the old woman. Did I forget the part about *crabby* old woman?"

"HUNGRY old woman!" returned Bina whose hearing was better than they thought.

Sunlight pierced the forest, sending soft bands of warmth through the trees. The afternoon was pleasantly cool and the four busied themselves preparing food and conversing lightly about their experience in the woods. The two women had decided it would be safer to have Gem build them a shelter on the same level as the men's, so branches were gathered and placed a short distance away. At the end of the day, at least three of them were tired but happy.

It began to grow dark. Above the trees, a heavy blanket of gray clouds covered the sky and the women wrapped up in their cloaks against the cold of the evening. After they ate the roasted game and had washed their hands in a small stream nearby, there was nothing to do but sit around the fire and talk.

Jewel sat on a fallen log trying not to look at Diamond who had hardly let his gaze wander from her since their meeting. She finally broke the silence, "Why are you staring at me?"

"Lady Jewel, I always know what to say when I meet someone new, but you leave me nearly speechless. It is a great disadvantage to have no memory beyond my appearance on that beach, for if I had a memory I am sure I could honestly say that I had never met anyone as beautiful or wonderful as you. But if I now said such a thing, you would know it to be meaningless because of the brevity of my experience." Diamond was trying his best to say what he felt, but it was not making the impression he had hoped for.

Little did he realize the effect his words had on Jewel. She could hardly believe her ears. Longing to tell him how only a short time ago he had run over her and never looked back, she sat in amazed silence.

She looks embarrassed, he thought, *like she wants to hide away. Why is that? Don't women enjoy being admired?*

"I am not a Lady, Diamond. I am not anything."

"I can't believe that. You are obviously a person of great wealth and fine family. Though I hear from Gem that you have had some unpleasant times at their hands. Tell me your story and I will drink in every word, cherish every thought of who you really are." Diamond hoped he wasn't exaggerating his thoughts and feelings. He actually was enthralled with her and hoped to know her heart and mind, imagining it to be—and hoping it to be—like his.

Jewel felt a pang of sadness knowing that if he knew the truth, they would be parted immediately never to meet again. She couldn't let this happy moment end. Searching through her mind, she sought something to tell him that would not link him with her past.

"I am a woman who once had a father. He was wonderful and kind and I loved him dearly. He was taken away from me and I have been sad ever since. But I met someone who has taken my sadness away for he promised me a home and all the love of his heart."

Diamond's heart fell with a thud. *She is promised to another who is able to provide for her what I can never.* "That is wonderful, dear Lady. When will you wed this fortunate man?" he asked, trying to hide his disappointment. Jewel laughed,

"You mistake my meaning, Lord Diamond, for I shall call you that if you insist on calling me Lady. The one I spoke of is not to be a husband. I don't know how to explain it but I will try if you allow me."

"Speak on, for I am listening," said Diamond with new energy. Gem nodded his head in agreement, wondering what she could be talking about. Obviously, his mother and her protégé had had some interesting adventures since he last saw them.

Bina rose suddenly breaking the spell. "Are you going to fall for this rubbish as well? I can't listen to more insanity," and she walked away in a huff and went to try to sleep in the makeshift hut. Gem paid no attention to his mother and followed the conversation with great anticipation.

"I was in great need, feeling more lonely than I had ever in my life. I had a dream." At this, both men leaned forward. "In my dream I met a stranger in the dark as I walked in a desert land. He was someone I think I had seen before under certain bad circumstances," said Jewel, trying to pick her words carefully. "He had given his life so that I could go free. I felt his blood running down on me."

At this, both men leaned away frowning.

"It was good. It wasn't bad," she assured them. "Oh, how can I explain? The blood was like a healing medicine poured over me and I knew that he had forgiven all the bad things I have done in my life. He changed me from being an orphan to being his own daughter, the daughter of the king."

At this both men leaned forward again." "I knew it," said Diamond. "You are a Princess!"

"I hope you're not making fun of me," said Jewel, "for I am quite serious."

Both men sat straight up and looked serious.

"In the dream, I was absorbed into the inside of the man and the whole of him was filled with light. Inside was glittering treasure, jewels spread all around my feet, jewels that sent their beams of reflected light out into the dark night beyond me. Each one held a promise that was just for me—a promise of love, a home, a future. He named me Jewel, for in another life I had a different name. He said, 'My precious Jewel.'" Tears slid down Jewel's cheeks and she raised her hand to brush them away. "When I awoke, I had this necklace around my neck as a reminder of all his promises and love."

Both men sat in silence entranced and brimming over with emotion. Diamond was hypnotized, somehow feeling there was a connection between his own rescue and Jewel's. But he couldn't remember. Oh, why couldn't he remember?

"Do you know who the man was?" he asked, thinking back to the discussion he had with Gem about their rescues.

"He is called Prince, the son of the king in the Kingdom of Light. This kingdom is far to the north and we are going there if we can find the way."

"And the necklace, does it have magical powers?" asked Diamond, who had read of such things in his younger years.

"I am not sure. In the desert I found food and water, but it was not magical," replied Jewel. "On another occasion it seemed to have magical powers but I think it was more on the order of being miraculous. You see I believe it is a person who has done the miracle and not the jewel itself. The jewel is just a reminder of all the promises that the prince has given me."

Both men were deep in thought. "Yes…miracle. That is what you told me wasn't it Gem?" asked Diamond. Jewel looked at Gem in surprise, as she had not expected that type of sentiment to come from him.

Gem saw that her curiosity has been roused and spoke with a husky voice, "Jewel, I must tell you my story as I have told it to Diamond. He knows that I was in prison for reasons I haven't shared in detail, but he knows that I did bad things I regretted after spending time in the deepest dark dungeon in chains." Reaching into the tiny bag tied to his neck, he brought out the bright key.

Jewel was amazed as Gem shared the story he had told Diamond. Upon hearing it, she threw her arms around Gem and embraced him tightly, "Oh, Gem. I am so glad to hear that. I thought I was going crazy at times, but you have met the same man."

When she released Gem, he sat in shock, as the Julen he knew had never before taken him seriously. To his amazement, being touched warmly by another person thrilled him in a wonderful way he had never experienced. Diamond too was astonished at her reaction to the story. *She acts like Gem is her long lost brother,* he thought, feeling a twinge of jealousy.

Both men leaned back again, thinking about what Jewel had said and realized she might be right. They all looked at Gem's key with a new appreciation.

Diamond wondered if the stranger was the same one who pulled him out of the waves. But what were the chances of that being true? At that moment, he desperately wanted it to be the same man and he longed to tell her every detail of his rescue.

Gem spoke his friend's thoughts out loud, "Diamond was rescued when he was blown overboard, or shipwrecked at sea. He should have drowned, but someone pulled him up and made sure he got to shore." Diamond nodded in affirmation.

"You remember that much," asked Jewel, "but nothing more?"

"Unfortunately, true. Why I lost my memory I do not know, except that I had a knot on the back of my head the size of a balder nut."

Jewel and Gem did not wish to question him any further and he was disappointed. Somehow, he thought if they persisted it might bring his memory back and he could finally get on with his life as it should have been. But most of all, he wanted to share in the same experience that seemed to bond a budding friendship.

The evening became cold. Gem put more wood on the fire and Jewel pulled her cloak tighter. Neither Gem or Diamond seemed bothered by the cold, as they were deeply intrigued by their conversation. Despite Diamond's lack of details, their common experiences had brought them together in a way that none of them had imagined possible.

"What about Bina?" asked Diamond. Jewel looked at the ground and sighed, "She won't listen to me. I have tried to tell her but she thinks I have lost my mind. All she wants is to find some niche where she can be in charge and she thinks that will make her happy. She will never be happy," lamented Jewel.

"How did she ever manage to be appointed your caretaker?" asked Diamond. The other two just looked at each other knowingly. "What did I miss?"

"You didn't miss anything, Diamond. We all know she is a hard woman, bitter about her past and not hopeful about her future," replied Jewel before Gem could say something incriminating.

"Does she want to go to this Kingdom of Light?" asked Diamond.

"No. I'm afraid not. She is getting more and more difficult to live with." Gem just nodded and said, "Mmmm." The conversation wandered back and forth, sharing details of recent times until Gem's head bobbed forward and he admitted his need for sleep.

Diamond and Jewel sat close to each other and continued to talk. The clouds eventually cleared and a full moon sent dull light down upon them. Even in the moonlight, Diamond stared at the luminescent beauty of the woman next to him and couldn't believe his good fortune at meeting her in the cold north woods.

"Diamond, there is something else I wish to tell you. In the house where I lived, I found a hidden room through the back of a closet that no one else knew about. In that room, there was a strange message written on the wall. I am not very good at the art of deciphering letters as I was taught so long ago and never practiced when I grew up. But I could make out the words "Cry out to THE ONE and he will rescue you." There was a symbol at the bottom—perhaps it was a signature." Diamond hung upon her every word.

"I saw a book in the room which bore the same symbol and I opened it. The writing was in someone's own hand and was very strange. I was unable after many tries to find its meaning. Do you, per chance, read well?"

"Why do you ask? Do you have the book with you out here in the forest?" he asked in reply, assuming a negative answer.

"As a matter of fact, I do," she admitted softly. "I am very curious as to its meaning. Will you look at it for me and tell me what it says?"

Diamond's jaw dropped in surprise. "Of course, where is it?" Jewel reached into the folds of her cloak and found the inner pocket in which she had been keeping the book. Diamond eagerly reached for it and opened it to the first page. After a brief moment of studying it, he began to read aloud.

"Today is the first day I have attempted to write a full account of the strange things that have happened to me in the last few weeks..."

Diamond's curiosity was engaged as well, so he continued, shivering slightly in the cold. Jewel saw his plight and offered part of her large cloak to warm his shoulders. The two sat huddled together listening to the recounting of the life of a stranger by the dim firelight.

Unable to stay awake any longer, Jewel's eyes grew heavy as his voice lulled her into rest. Soon she fell fast asleep. Diamond looked at her but was too interested to stop. He continued to read to himself straining in the poor light. The stranger's story grew more and more interesting. The fire died down and he managed to throw two chunks of dead wood onto it with his free arm.

"I was trapped and could not escape and I knew that I would soon be found. Overcome with fear and dread, I called out for help to any god who might hear me.

Diamond's heart began to pound. He continued. After a few more sentences he read,

"A man I had never seen before was there suddenly. I don't know how it happened, but I was free. Those who sought my life were gone."

He wanted to wake Jewel and tell her but she was soundly asleep. It would wait until morning, but not a minute longer.

The sun was about to rise before a clear, crisp morning when Diamond jolted awake. He and Jewel had been huddled together sitting on the ground with their backs to the log. Jewel woke when he moved and was shocked to see that they had spent the entire night together under her cloak. Diamond rose to his feet and stretched. Jewel wrapped up tighter and pulled her feet in close. "When's breakfast? Is it squirrel and rabbit, or rabbit and squirrel this morning?"

"Could I offer you some snake on the side?" joked Diamond as he began to stir up the fire. Jewel shuttered and pulled the cape over her head.

Bina crawled out of the shelter but said nothing. She headed into the woods without a word. Gem stirred and came out automatically grabbing his spear and dumbly sighing, "Weren't there any leftovers last night?"

"I have to talk to you both. You won't believe this. I read this journal most of the night and it contains things we all need to know."

"What do you mean? Isn't it someone's meandering thoughts from years and years ago? What does that have to do with us?" asked Jewel.

"Last night we all told our stories of how we were rescued by a stranger. Jewel, yours was the most stirring, as the stranger came to you personally and spoke to you. You knew exactly what he was doing in your life and what things he promised you. Gem, you were given the means to get out of the prison. The stranger gave you the key so you could boldly escape. For me, I did not see anyone but just knew from a faint memory that I had been rescued." The others nodded in agreement but still wondered what Diamond was trying to say.

"This book was written by someone who knew the prince."

Jewel and Gem together cried, "How?"

"This person—I don't know who it was—not only knew him, but knew his whole story. Look here at these places I have marked." Diamond held up the page for them to see.

His father in the Kingdom of Light sent him here for the very
purpose of rescuing people who were in bondage to an evil power."

Gem heard this and wanted to ask why Diamond had been rescued when he hadn't been a slave, but he knew that was too much information to give away. "Were we *all* in bondage?" he asked instead.

"Yes. You see the evil power must be a king of some kind who rules over a large part of the known world. He stole his kingdom away from the king of Light. It's all here."

"Diamond, please tell us the whole story. We need to know every detail," pleaded Jewel. Diamond smiled at the thought of spending long hours together going over every page.

From somewhere in the forest, they heard a strange noise. It was Bina and she came running into camp out of breath. "What is it, Bina?"

"Men! Men on horses coming!"

CHAPTER 39

Capture

"Are you sure?" asked Diamond. "Maybe they are hunters. You needn't be afraid of hunters. We will just let them know not to mistake us for deer and all will be well."

Jewel and Gem jumped up and asked Bina, "Where did you see them? Could you make out who it was?"

"It's him!" cried Bina, and all the color drained from the faces of the two escapees.

"Who is 'him'?" asked Diamond cheerily. "You act like you know someone down there." Jewel turned to Diamond and said carefully, "I am afraid we do know someone down there and it isn't good. We will have to run into the forest and hide. If he finds us, all is lost!"

"Gem, do you know what she is talking about? I get the feeling you two have talked about this already." Gem said, "Yes, we have. The man leading the horsemen is their enemy, seeking to do them harm. We must all run away quickly. Will you help?"

"Where can they hide? Maybe if you and I can lead the men in a different direction, they will be safe. If they find us, they won't do us any harm will they?" Diamond thought his reasoning was sound, but all three cringed at his suggestion.

"They are seeking me as well, I'm afraid. I can't go with you. Come with us, Diamond!" This new bit of information was confusing and Diamond thought of questions he wanted answered. But there was no time. He looked into the sky and saw the narrow plume of smoke from their fire rising up like a banner waving to those below.

"Quick, put out the fire."

"It's too late. We must run!" cried Gem.

The three took off into the trees as Diamond tried to scatter the embers and kick dirt on them. Satisfied that the smoke was no longer a threat, he chased after them. The forest was dense with low branches, fallen trunks of ancient trees, and outcroppings of mossy rocks. Jewel stumbled and hastily got up to keep running. Diamond stayed by her side, helping her up when she fell, pulling her up when the steep ground was difficult to climb. Gem saw to his mother as best he could. She was more fit than she had claimed and, with trousers instead of a skirt, she was able to make good time.

All four stopped abruptly, hanging on to one another. They had come to the edge of a cliff with a raging river below. They looked at each other in dismay, not knowing which way to turn. Going in either direction might bring them closer to their pursuers.

The sound of neighing horses was not far behind them now. Jewel was breathing hard, but shouted over the sound of the torrent, "Call for help! Here. Now. The prince will save us!" Diamond and Gem stared in disbelief, but there was little else to do. They were trapped. Jewel raised her hands to the heavens and shouted, "Please hear us! Deliver us from these men. Show us a way of escape!" They stood still in expectation of what would happen next.

Capture

Looking from one side to the other, they saw only soldiers surrounding them and closing in quickly. Should they jump? The water was too swift and they would all surely drown if they tried. From behind them, they heard the voice of Chief Legerdemain.

"What have we here?" he asked in astonishment and began laughing until he could hardly stop. "This is simply too much good fortune. Close the net and catch, not two, but four!" There was silence from the fugitives. Soldiers dismounted and approached holding chains and manacles.

"If I am not mistaken, we have an unexpected addition to our little troop of vagabonds," said Legerdemain from atop his mount. "Master Damon Chiselstone is it? Remarkable! Did you know you were thought dead? How did you get yourself involved with this riff raff?" he continued, with thorough amusement, and waited for an answer.

"If you mean me, Sir, I was lost overboard from my ship but washed up on the shore near Carpville. So that is my name, Chiselstone?" The master laughed again, "This is beautiful! You mean you don't know who you are? Did you not ask these three. They all know quite well who you are, is that not true, Bina? Bina, the slave, and her skinny accomplice, Julen. And you, Jip! Slave, thief, and deceiver, and son of that curmudgeon, Bina?" he said, pointing to Gem. "You were locked up in the dungeon, last I heard. How you got out will be interesting to hear."

Diamond was stunned when he finally understood the meaning of Legerdemain's words. "She's your MOTHER?" he asked Gem. He turned to Jewel searching her face for answers. "Have you known all along who I am? Why did all of you keep this from me?" They looked at the ground and could not answer. The soldiers clapped on the irons and led them away into the forest. Bina swore loudly and cursed the soldiers, screaming and crying out things that no longer made sense.

Diamond stood before the last horseman who leaned over and spoke to him, "Do not concern yourself over these low-born slaves. They have deceived you in everything they have said. All three of them are known for their great deceit." Legerdemain noticed the small pouch around Diamond's neck similar to the one that Jip carried but said nothing.

"Your father, Master Chiselstone, will be very glad to hear you are alive. I will order my man here to carry you back with all haste to your home in Bellicosa," said Legerdemain.

"Thank you. What will happen to…" he started to say "my friends," but changed his mind, "to these prisoners?"

"Oh, we have big plans for them, but that is no concern of yours, my boy. Go home now to your father's house and find your life again."

Diamond felt the outline of Jewel's journal he still carried in his pocket and knew that whatever life he would find, it would never be the same as it had been.

Days of riding on the back of the soldier's saddle made Diamond sore from head to foot. He was relieved that the man assigned to his transportation was not one for words. There was a lot of time to think. He ignored the book, as it was too confusing to put the pieces of the puzzle together.

As they galloped over the terrain that it had taken Gem and him days to traverse on foot, pleasant memories came back. His mind was clearing some but he still didn't have a picture of his home and family. All would be put to right soon enough, he knew. As they drew nearer to Bellicosa, hard memories burned his conscious mind as well. He thought of the loveliness of Jewel, the close, sweet friendship he had with both her and Gem—Jip. *Is my name Diamond or Damon?* he asked himself.

My name is Damon.

He wondered what his real family was like. He would soon see. Once with them again, maybe the memories would burst into life.

How he missed his friends. He turned his "diamond"' over and over in his hand and noticed that is was cloudy again. How had he thought it was turning into a real diamond? *I must have been under some kind of spell.*

Why had they lied to him? How did such a conspiracy take place right under his nose? What a fool he was to believe everything they said. Vacillating between anger, joy, and sorrow, he spent the days of riding in the silence of his thoughts.

The rider began the assent into the dry mountains of Graystone that dropped down into Bellicosa, and Damon wondered at the barrenness of his home. Was this the land of his birth?

No word had gone before this surprise arrival, so he knew there would be a shock for those who believed him to be drowned at sea. As they arrived at Arcana, he dismounted and was thankful that the torture of the trail was over at last. He stretched and prepared himself for the revelation to a family he longed to meet.

A doorman opened to Diamond's knock and stood mouth agape. "Master Damon. Is it you?" Other servants overheard and ran to the door to confirm what they had heard, then set at a dead run to all parts of the house to declare the news.

Violencia perked up her ears and felt her heart drop in her chest. *No! It's impossible!* she said to herself. She made her way down the stairs to the Great Hall. She stopped short of the tall figure before her and said, "Damon?" He stepped forward and asked, "I'm sorry. Who are you?" Violencia recoiled in shock. An odor of unwashed body and clothes met her nostrils and she put her handkerchief to her nose while saying vehemently, "You know very well who I am…don't' you?" she looked into his face and saw ignorance. "What has happened to you? Don't you know who you are?"

"I seemed to have lost my memory, but was hoping that the sight of my loved ones would bring it back to me. Can you direct me to my parents, please?" Violencia did not know what to think at this bizarre twist in her plot. "Your father is upstairs. He is not well and is sleeping. You had best not disturb him now. I can take you to your mother, if you wish," and she ground her teeth with anxiety at the thought of all Dismalia would tell her son.

CHAPTER 40
Chief Legerdemain's Revenge

The journey back to Bellicosa was agonizing for the three. Manacled while riding on the back of a horse wracked their spines and, as they neared home, the animals sped up making it worse. Chief Legerdemain had given orders that they should be treated well, "We want them in good shape for the celebration of their coming deaths," he cackled in triumph.

No matter what food or drink they offered Bina, she refused and fought her guards. She made so much noise, they tied a gag around her mouth. But it was no use. She screamed and cursed despite the restraint. At night, she wailed a mournful high-pitched tune that convinced everyone she had lost her mind. During the day, she refused the stale bread and bitter tasting water. She knew what was ahead and preferred to die of starvation rather than give Legerdemain the pleasure of hanging her.

For Jewel, it was a time of questioning and doubt. She had called out to the prince of Light for help, and yet, no one came. They were going to be hanged for crimes not of their own invention, but only committed as unwitting participants. Why did he not miraculously rescue them? Perhaps it was all a dream, a fantasy of her own making, just as Bina had accused.

But then, there was the book. What had Diamond seen there that he did not have the chance to tell them? Jewel realized she would not have the opportunity to find out and grieved the further loss.

Arriving at the prison, they were led to a large central room. Legerdemain stopped the procession that led them up a flight of stairs to their respective cells. He faced Jewel first. "I'll take this, little thief!" he said as he snatched her necklace from her neck, "and this as well!" He grabbed the pouch from Gem's neck. He looked inside and produced the key.

"What have we here? Is this how you managed to escape from our prison? Guard, try this in every lock!" he commanded. He looked at Bina and realized she had nothing valuable so he allowed her to be shoved into confinement before the others. Without further word, he marched out, commanding the doors be double locked.

King Ironfist was in a good mood when Legerdemain strode proudly into the upstairs receiving room of the castle. "Well, old man. I hear you have obeyed your king." Legerdemain bowed with a contented look on his face.

Standing behind the king, he noticed a stranger trying to look inconspicuous. The fellow visitor wore the fine clothes of an emissary from a foreign king. His face was devious and shrewd, a man Legerdemain should relate well to.

The king saw that his chief was intrigued by the presence of another during the report and explained, "This is Regent Incubus Pestilent from the Kingdom of Cimeria. You may not have heard of it as it is far from here.

I told you, did I not, that this was a bigger problem than you understood. The regent informs me that there are those beyond our borders who have an interest in seeing Bellicosa succeed in quashing this malevolent deceit. Your success means the success for greater powers than our lowly kingdom knows."

"I am honored to serve whatever powers furthers the reputation of my king," said Legerdemain, who modulated his tone with appropriate humility.

"If I may," added the regent stepping forward. "What your king says is correct. Rumors of this 'prince,' as he calls himself, have had a very damaging effect. Our ultimate ruler has decreed that anyone calling on this fictitious character will be punished with death. He is very powerful. At his word, kingdoms rise and fall. All are advised to heed his warnings."

Legerdemain stood in surprise, having never heard about an ultimate ruler before. In all of his experience, there had only been one ruler, and that was Ironfist. His success suddenly took on new importance as he mentally calculated his future service.

"Tell me, have the prisoners denied any knowledge of the rumored accomplice?" asked Ironfist. A pang of anxiety shot through the chief as he admitted, "We have only just returned and I have not spoken to them yet about this. But do not fear, Eminence. One of the prisoners has gone raving mad and the other hardly speaks."

"I have heard that there were four brought back."

"The others were merely a bonus, my king. The young Master Chiselstone was among them, having washed up on a foreign shore after an accident at sea. I'm sure you have heard of it. He has lost his memory and has no idea who he is—most amusing. The other is just a common slave who has nothing to claim for himself. We will hang him, of course." Legerdemain braced himself for further interrogation but none came.

"That will be all then. Report to me when you have finished with our little problem," and he turned and smiled cunningly at Pestilent.

The dark gray prison walls were damp and moldy and the floor cold. Despite having cloaks wrapped about them, both Jewel and Bina shivered. The younger woman was very worried about her companion. She had not eaten or drunk for days. Her face was emaciated and pale; her hair was stringy and matted. She had lost interest in living.

"Bina, don't leave me this way."

Bina raised her head slightly and looked fiercely into Jewels eyes, "You made it all up didn't you, the whole thing about the prince, the One, the stranger who rescues! You know, I almost believed you. The three of you almost had me convinced that there was a person out there who cared about what happens to people like us. But no. It was all a lie. And where is Master Heart-of-Stone? All that mushy stuff about you being so wonderful. Where is he when you need him. Men! They always let you down!" she recoiled as she retreated again into her self-imposed death watch.

"It can't end like this, Bina. It simply can't."

CHAPTER 41
The Son Returns

Violencia rushed up the staircase after Damon walked away toward his mother's quarters. Entering the master suite, she did a quick search for cups, potions, bottles, anything that would give away the fact that she had been administering certain medications to Damon's father. The master was due for another drink, but she would have to forego and allow him to come out of his stupor. Damon must not suspect anything.

Damon followed directions down the long corridor, following the twists and turns, and came to the door of his mother's apartment. He rang the bell and waited. There was no sound inside so he opened the door and entered. He walked quietly into her bedroom and saw her shrunken form lying on the vast bed.

"Mother? It's Damon," he said cautiously not wanting to cause her to die of fright upon seeing him.

Dismalia opened her eyes and looked in his direction, moaning softly. "Oh, no." she cried, "I am hallucinating, or is it a ghost?"

"No, mother. I'm not a ghost. I have come back. I didn't die." Damon was shocked at her appearance. He had imagined that his mother would be vibrant and full of life, but it appeared that she was close to death. She sobbed, "Damon, Damon. My son! Can that really be you?"

"Yes, mother. I am sorry to surprise you but I just returned home. It is a long story and I will be glad to tell it if you want to hear."

"Damon, I am sorry. My life has fallen apart. Everything has changed since you left. Yes, tell me your story for I have nothing left in life and I need to hear how you have been saved to come back to me," she said in such a sorrowful voice that Damon almost cried.

"First I need to tell you that I have no memory of my life before my accident. I must have been hit on the head by something because everything from the past is gone. I have only the memories of the last few weeks and those have mostly been wonderful."

"Oh, Damon! You came to visit me before you left and said you would return. I am overjoyed to see that you kept your word." Dismalia reached out for him and he came to her and held her hands in his.

"Captain Fairway said you stood on the deck of the ship waving your sword for some reason. A boom broke loose and hit you on the back of your head and you went overboard. They gave you up for lost in the raging storm. Oh, Damon, I cried and cried. I missed you so much. Please never leave again. I couldn't stand to lose you again." The son could see glistening tears roll down her cheek in the semi-dark room.

"Mother, the earliest memory I now have is being pulled from the water by someone. I woke up on a beach. A young man happened to be there and he helped me get back on my feet. We traveled together until I was found by Chief Legerdemain way off in the north woods." Damon skipped some of the details, as he knew of no reason for her to be interested.

"Why on earth would he take you to the north woods?" asked Dismalia.

"Mother, it is a long story and I fear you will not like parts of it. I don't like it either but I must tell you. You do know now that I have no memory of my past. When I met this young man, I didn't know who he was and I assumed he didn't know who I was. In that I was wrong, for it turns out that his name is Jip and he is the son of your servant Bina."

At the mention of Bina, Dismalia put her hand over her mouth and wept. The thought of her long-serving slave Rubina brought a wave of memories back to her. The sight of the young woman working in the castle gardens, pregnant and alone touched her heart. Dismalia had seen her later with a young child in tow and felt sorry for her and had asked her husband if she could take Bina on as a maid and helper with her own young children. She remembered how her husband had laughed his devilish laugh, and agreed that the mistress' boudoir was a good place for Bina and her son.

"It is all so terrible. It was my fault they hanged her. Oh, Damon. I have been so bad. Will you forgive me for what I did?"

"She hasn't been hanged yet as far as I know, though that event is not far from happening now."

"What do you mean?" cried his mother in alarm. "Violencia told me she had been hanged, as well as my lovely Julen. I had such hopes for her."

"Oh, where to start...I don't know—this is very complicated and I fear there are things going on here I can't explain. I only know that I met Bina and Julen—she calls herself Jewel now—in the woods and we shared a most heavenly evening together. She is the most wonderful woman I can imagine existing in all the world."

Dismalia was horrified and sat up straight in the bed. "Damon, you can't be serious. I am very glad to hear that she is still alive, but she is a slave in your father's house. She is low and...." she sought for a demeaning enough word.

"Mother, I understand now that she is that. But something changed her. She isn't like you think—a slave—she's different." His mother's tears continued to drop wetting her drab dressing gown.

"My son, what has happened to you? You have changed too. Don't you remember the way you treated her only a few months ago?"

At this question, Damon sat back waiting to hear what he knew must be the truth, but it was painful to realize that he had known Jewel and treated her badly. In his thoughts, he concluded that his abuse of them gave the three reason to conspire against him and draw him away from his family. Anger and confusion mingled in his mind and kept him from gaining a clearer picture of his previous life.

"What was she like?"

"Who? Do you mean Julen? She was ordinary, my son, very ordinary. And she was always bothering me, wanting to know if I felt all right."

"She had such beautiful eyes, didn't she, mother?"

"Stop it! I don't want to hear this. I want the old Damon back, please," his mother begged.

"The old Damon can't come back. I don't even remember who he was. I came back thinking I had a happy, loving family in Bellicosa, and I find my father upstairs, ill, with a strange woman, and you here in this cave of an apartment pining away, close to death. Is this the kind of family I have?"

"My darling, I am sorry for that too. You have no idea what has happened since you left. I...I broke the law, dearest. Bina and Julen helped me. I was told I deserved to hang for my crime. Your father was merciful and convinced the king to let me live here as punishment instead of going to prison. But I am no longer to be Mistress Chiselstone. That title has gone to Violencia who has probably seen all this happen by her own design. She is an evil woman, Damon. Watch out for her."

"I met her in the Great Hall, I think. So she is Mistress Chiselstone now? And my father is very ill, and the son and heir has died! What a coincidence. Mother, I shall want to look into this."

"Oh, son. Be careful. I believe Chief Legerdemain knew all along that the powder he gave me was going to be found. He tricked me, and that is why my poor servants were taken from me."

Hearing the name of the chief of intelligence, Damon's mind reeled even more. The information he received from his mother appeared to be a complex conspiracy in which everyone was involved, from the highest in authority, right down to the slaves in the house. Damon contemplated how he would sort out the truth and find out what was really going on and wondered where he would start.

"Sleep, mother. I will come later and we will talk more. Right now rest in the knowledge that your son has come home." He left Dismalia with her head aching but her spirit much improved now that her beloved son was alive again.

Damon retraced his steps down the stone-walled corridor wondering why his mother had chosen to spend her life is such a depressing part of the house. He concluded that it was better than prison. He found the Great Hall and started up the stairs.

"Good Day, Master Chiselstone. We are all glad to see you have returned." The head housekeeper bowed as she passed.

He stopped and looked into her face and said, "I am sorry to have forgotten your name. Can you remind me?" Coldstone was taken aback at this unexpected question.

"Why Master Damon, I have served in this house for twenty years. Of course, you remember me, Obdura Coldstone," she asserted before recalling that the master had lost his memory. She did not believe the rumor but now saw for herself. Worry lined her face as the truth sunk in, and she realized that Damon's return would be no hindrance to those who plotted against him.

Damon moved upward and tried to guess which was his father's room. Stopping an upstairs maid, he asked for directions. She pointed to the double doors down the hall and he continued purposefully. He knocked and thought he heard rustling and shifting noises within. The door opened and Violencia stood beckoning him to enter as she bowed respectfully.

Damon could see the luxurious bed with a long, rounded figure upon it. He crept forward and whispered, "Father?"

"He knows you have returned," offered Violencia and he is happy to hear you survived your harrowing accident.

"Is that what he said?" asked Damon waiting still to hear some response from his father's lips.

"He has been very ill. News of your death hit him hard and he has never recovered from the shock. Those who have seen this kind of thing before say he will not survive long." Violencia tilted her head assuming a posture of sympathetic concern.

"I have spoken with my mother and she told me the circumstances that bring you to my father's side. I am shocked at my mother's behavior. Surely you have done the right thing." He knowingly lied, believing his mother's warning about his father's new wife. Perhaps if she thought he did not suspect anything, he could get to the truth behind the mysterious changes in his family.

"Your sisters, Alumina and Nichola, come regularly to see their father. They both will marry soon, you know." said Violencia with a look that told of her cunning participation in the matches.

"I have sisters, do I? I look forward to meeting them." His frankness about his memory surprised his mother's usurper. Little by little, she was seeing what he was capable of and it wasn't as much as she feared.

"Father, can you hear me?" asked Damon trying again to communicate. The master opened his eyes and fought to stay awake.

"My son, it *is* you. How long have you been here? I've been asleep but I will wake up soon...." He drifted off again, emitting a loud snore.

"The poor dear. He has not been able to do much since the fits began. I have been treating him with a potion that my grandmother taught me to mix for such spells. He has responded well to the treatment and has been calm. When the fits take him, it is terrible to see. I must continue with the medicine so he doesn't tax himself too much." Violencia looked at Damon to see if he believed her and saw no doubt in his eyes. The way was open for her to continue her regimen.

"It seems to make him very sleepy. I would like to talk to him. Why not skip the potion for a few days and let's see how he feels."

"I fear for him, Damon. I have seen these fits and it is most frightening," she said hoping her plan would not be interrupted.

"I can stay with him then and you may go. You can find another room to sleep in if you are afraid of his fits. I want to see what happens to him when it comes on him."

Violencia moved to the next level of action for getting what she wanted. Surely he would back down if she chose assertiveness and anger. "I think you are not in charge here, Damon," she said glaring at the incursion on her sphere of control." I am his wife now and I shall stay and take care of him."

Damon realized that a battle of wills was playing out before him and chose to call her bluff. "No. I am the heir and *I* am in charge. Go and find another place to sleep until I call for you. Do you understand?" Excitement rushed through every pore as Damon spoke the words of power to one he was sure had some evil scheme afoot. Violencia tried to cover her anger but her red face, rapid breathing, and dilated eyes gave her away. She spun briskly on her heels and left the room. Damon bristled with exhilaration having faced a formidable foe and won the first round.

"Now, father, we will see if you are dying or not."

Chapter 42

Ruby

Inky darkness filled the prison cell that was now cold and deadly silent. Jewel lay awake shivering in her cloak on a skimpy mound of hay that only slightly insolated her body from the floor underneath her. She could not sleep. The sensations experienced in her dream eluded her now, but the memory was strong. What had gone wrong? Why were they not rescued? What was happening to Diamond? Did he think of her at all and, if he did, was it as a runaway criminal or as a friend?

"Uraaaghh." Jewel heard Bina making noises in her sleep. *I hope she isn't dreaming about walking up the scaffold to the gallows,* she thought. Her mind had snapped. It was surprising that Bina was still alive. She had actually gagged at the sight of food. *She may not ever have to hang. It will be me there alone before all those people, with Diamond standing in the back, waiting for "justice" to be meted out.* Tears started down her face. After a while, she fell into a dreamless asleep.

"Uuuuuuuu." In the blackness, Jewel became aware that she was hearing a soft, beautiful melody. She opened her eyes in the dark but could see nothing; she could only hear the heart-stirring tune rising in the stillness. She trained her ears and realized it came from Bina, who lay close-by.

"Bina, are you awake?" The singing stopped and she answered weakly, "Yes."

"Why are you singing?" asked Jewel, and the only reply was, "I think I want to eat something."

"What? Here, have this," and she passed Bina a hunk of dried crust saved from the last meal. Jewel fumbled in the dark and located a cup filled with water. "Drink this first. It has been so long since you ate, you won't be able to swallow."

The famished woman obeyed, drinking the water and eating the bread, then lying down again in the cold. "Bina, you were making noises in your sleep. Did you have a nightmare?" Choking with emotion Bina replied, "He is real, Jewel. I am sorry I doubted you. Forgive me for being such a… how did Legerdemain put it…a curmudgeon. That should be my name, Jewel, Curmudgeon." She started to cry.

"Instead, he gave me a new name, it is Ruby. Can you believe it? A complete set. Diamond will be pleased." Jewel noticed that her voice had lost its harsh tone.

"Who are you talking about, Bina, ah, Ruby?"

"I did have a nightmare. It was a nightmare about an ugly, senseless person—me. Do you want to hear about it?"

"Don't be silly! You know I do." said Jewel excitedly. Despite great weakness and tears, Bina shared her story with Jewel whose goose bumps now were more from astonishment than cold.

"I was running in the dark trying to get to a light in the distance, but it never got any closer no matter how hard I pushed myself. I tossed aside and kicked at things in my way when they slowed me down. I got so tired that I couldn't go on. I stupidly tried to run but, when I tried to lift my legs, they were too heavy." She wept quietly before starting again.

"I woke up and thought about the dream. I felt cold and dark and ugly. I did like you said, Jewel, I cried out for help to the prince. I knew he was real. I could see that in you, but mostly in Jip, I mean Gem. He is a Gem now. He has changed so much, I hardly recognize him. There was only one explanation."

Jewel shivered with excitement as Bina continued. "In my mind I saw a man. He forgave me for everything, and it was as if he held me in his arms." Jewel reached out in the darkness and took the crying woman into her arms.

"He said to me, 'Ruby, my precious child. My kingdom needs you.' Can you imagine that? Then he said, 'You must sing what is in your heart,' so I sang. It felt so good to sing joy and forgiveness," and she continued to hum as they rocked back and forth.

"Ruby! I love that name. I am so happy for you."

The two sat huddled together until it was light. When vision was restored and they could see each other's faces, Jewel was stunned to see the change in her fellow slave. Her sunken eyes and wasted limbs were pink and full of life. She had lost some of her girth from both the life in the forest and the self-inflicted fast, but did not look like someone on the verge of death by starvation or madness. The prince had not only forgiven her but he had restored her in body and mind.

Prison guards approached the cell bringing bread and water. They recoiled at the sight of the woman who had been shriveled and dying the day before. How had she been transformed from a groveling lunatic to the smiling, radiant woman they now saw? Leaving the food, they backed away hurriedly, running to report to their chief.

In a lower level cell, isolated from his mother and Jewel, Gem sat glumly stewing about his predicament. He had been freed from prison only to wind up back again. Now he faced death along with the others.

If Diamond had been there, Gem thought, he would have gone through all the information and put it together for him in a way that made sense. But Diamond was Damon again, and his friendship was lost forever. Memories of running through the forest hunting for small game, bringing it back and together, skinning and roasting it over the open fire, filled him with warm feelings. Though Jewel was obviously more interested in Diamond, Gem treasured the time they had had around the fire recalling the miraculous events they had encountered. He realized that he loved her, and he loved Diamond, and this was in itself miraculous, as he had never loved anyone before, not even himself. It had been worth it to be free for that short time if for nothing else than to have friendship and meaning in his life that had never before existed. He ached to have it back again.

Where was Damon right now? Had he learned about his vicious father and reclusive mother and realized his family was not the idyllic fantasy he had made up in his head?

Where was the prince that Jewel told them about? Why didn't he show up when they needed him most? What did it matter now?

"Hey, you in there," shouted a guard, banging his truncheon against the metal bars in the door window of Gem's cell. "Here's your grub. Eat up, for tomorrow you die," he guffawed spewing saliva across the brown crusts.

Gem took the food saying, "Thanks."

"Did I hear 'thanks'? That's a first in this place. Sounds like you turned all sweet like that mama of yours," and he turned and walked away. Gem jumped up and yelled after him, "What about my 'mama'? Is that supposed to be funny?" He plunked down on the floor and began to tear the bread with his teeth.

CHAPTER 43
A Fortunate Fall

The chilly air of Bellicosa was dry and filled with dust blown up the hill in a stiff breeze from the sea. Damon pulled his cloak collar up and shaded his gaze with a broad-brimmed hat he had found in his father's room. Descending into the town, he passed gray-washed building after gray-washed building. All the homes and shops were mixed and joined together. The only way to tell one from the other was a flower box here or a decorative tile arrangement there. The plaster on the outside of the some walls had fallen away revealing their stone construction. It was shabby, but he knew he would have to call it home.

It had been a strange day. After leaving his father's room, he gave orders to the servants that Violencia was not to go in under any circumstances. The butler was to stand guard over the older man until whatever concoction she had given him had worn off. Coldstone had winked at him and smiled as he left and he wondered why.

Diamond dashed quietly down the stairs, not wanting the treacherous wife to know of his departure. That plan did not work as, at the bottom of the stairs, he slipped on a newly scrubbed surface, falling hard and hitting his head on the stone floor of the Great Hall. He instantly saw stars and bursts of light and struggled to stay conscious.

As he lay on the floor, he opened his eyes and found himself staring at a sight that sent a shock wave through his body. It was a large wall-hanging, prominently displayed above a small table. His eyes focused on the green dragon in the center, its hungry mouth showing fangs and tongue. Its eyes flared with anger and threat.

Instantly Damon was aware that he had seen this image before. And then it came back to him...the storm, standing on the deck waving his sword wildly as if the dragonish apparition would take any notice of it and be frightened away. Shame washed over him remembering his foolhardiness.

His eyes wandered around the Great Hall, the staircase...he recognized them all. The dragon was the dragon of Bellicosa, god of the sea, who had come to kill him. But someone in the dark snatched him from the jaws of Leviathan and saved his life. He did remember now. His memory had come back!

"Master Damon! Are you hurt?" he heard from behind; a servant came running to help him up. Brushing himself off, he stood unsteadily and found that Violencia was watching him from the balcony above. She sneered and disappeared.

At a much slower pace, the young master walked to the door and continued on his errand, not telling anyone about his recovered memory.

As he looked around at the town from high up on the steep, winding street, he remembered it all—the bay and ship he loved, the business and his earlier longing to prove to his father that he could succeed. Worst of all, he remembered his father. What a disappointment it was to remember that mordant man. How he had hoped for a wise and loving guide and mentor.

Other memories came back to Damon as well. He remembered Jip, the odious boy who ran the streets. Gem had been right; he was nothing but a troublemaker. *Was that the person I befriended on the beach?* he wondered. *How could Jip and Gem be the same person?* He wanted to go to the prison and see for himself, even though he had been deceived by the three. And Julen, what of her? She had been just a slave that moved quietly about the house serving his mother. Was this the beautiful Jewel he had confessed as one who held a place in his heart after such a brief friendship?

He pushed aside the thoughts and turned his attention to something more pressing.

CHAPTER 44
A New Discovery

In the upper level of the prison above the common room, Jewel and Ruby passed the time talking about the common threads of their experience to try to bring meaning to the present. Below, they could hear rattling of spears and low voices. Jewel heard the sounds of someone coming up the stairs. Bracing themselves and clinging to each other, they were ready for whatever was to happen to them.

A company of soldiers advanced in front of Chief Legerdemain and stood on guard in formation as he came forward to speak to the prisoners. He immediately detected a change in the women, how they clung to one another. Looking into Bina's face, he saw that she was unrecognizable as the person he had arrested in the forest. Where was the rage and the fear? Where was the weakness and insanity? These were dangerous signs.

"Greetings. I have come to prepare you for an event very important for the stability and unity of our Bellicosan society. You will shortly have a chance to find favor with the king and redeem your memory, once departed, if you do as I request."

Ruby retorted, "You want us to help you and you are going to kill us anyway?"

"I see you haven't lost your sharp tongue, Bina, though I must say, you are looking…changed…this morning." Legerdemain tried to think of how to convince the women to cooperate. "You have committed crimes worthy of death. The king has spoken. All I need from you is a simple statement and you will find that you will die very comfortably. An uncomfortable death would be much worse, don't you think?" It made sense to Chief Legerdemain. Why shouldn't these women see the logic?

"What is the simple statement you wish us to make?" asked Jewel who was now standing tall and confident.

"You will state that when you escaped from my soldiers that you over-powered them by yourselves, without the help of an accomplice. It's that easy."

"But we did have help. A man stepped in front of the soldier's blow of the sword and your soldier killed him," said Ruby.

"Killed him? We found no body. That cannot be true. Now tell the truth!" demanded Legerdemain.

"We are telling the truth. The truth is that he was killed, but he didn't stay dead. He came back to life and then disappeared from sight," declared Jewel realizing that it did sound fictitious.

"You want us to say he wasn't there, that he doesn't exist? You are wrong. He does exist. You may kill us to keep the news quiet but he will come back again and again to help people who are in desperate need. They will call out to him and he will be there and you and your soldiers will not be able to stop him." Jewel listened to herself speaking and wondered where she got the nerve to speak so strongly.

Chief Legerdemain had not prepared for such a response and was caught off guard. Before he could devise more threats, Jewel continued, "What's more, those the prince rescues will follow him right out of Bellicosa, and out of Graystone, and King Ironfist will not able to stop them! And if you do try to stop them, they will not be intimidated, for their allegiance to The One is greater. Send them to the gallows and you will not stop them. Make their deaths *uncomfortable* and you will not stop them. You will not stop us!" Jewel yelled. "We will not make any such statements because it would not be true!"

The enraged chief pulled the necklace and key out of his pocket and waved them before the women. "Your story is as worthless as these market trinkets. They are fakes, counterfeit, junk! The green is poor quality glass and the key fits no lock in the kingdom! Even now, they rust and spoil before my eyes. You will perish with them at sunrise tomorrow!" and he threw the necklace and key in Jewels face.

"Where is your prince now?" he snarled.

Jewel's face stung from the blow, but she caught the treasures and held them tight.

"The ultimate ruler has spoken. You will have no more opportunity to pass on your malevolent lies about a rescuer." The chief narrowed his eyes to slits and spit on them before turning to leave.

Jewel and Ruby stood still, shocked at what had just taken place, but were satisfied that they had spoken the truth. The future was bleak and their cries for help had not brought any relief. Still, peace reigned and they were not afraid any longer.

Looking down, Ruby and Jewel saw the gifts lying in Jewel's hand gradually turn from base metal to shining gold; the jewels sparkled once again and cast blue and green light around the room. They knew the One was there with them at that moment.

"Look! He gave them back to us!" They turned to each other in amazement as they witnessed the transformation.

"If only I could get this key to Gem," said Jewel quietly.

"Who is the ultimate ruler?" asked Ruby. They both shrugged their shoulders in silence.

Damon returned from his day out and hoped that his father would be able to talk. There was much to tell him now. He mounted the stairs and felt the venomous presence of Violencia as she lurked in the shadows.

"Father," began Damon once he had found his father sitting up looking dazed.

"Damon, my boy. You look well. Did you have a good journey? That's it, isn't it? Or was it, you had some kind of accident. You are looking fit enough, so it must not have been too serious."

"Father, I died! I was washed overboard and drowned, remember?" Damon shouted at the outrage of his father's state of mind.

"Died? I can't remember. Did I know that? Well, you look all right now, so what can I do for you? Where is Lency? She is your step-mother now, you know…long story."

Damon did not know where to begin. "I was on a journey and I went overboard and nearly drowned. I washed up on shore and a young man found me. I think you remember Bina. The man who helped me is her son. He helped me stay alive, father, when I was nearly dead."

"Remember Bina?" he laughed. "I should think so. And that brat of hers…you would think that some Chiselstone blood would have improved the stock, but as you can see, he is a loser like his low-bred mother."

Damon was not sure of his meaning. This was not the issue he came to discuss, but from the sound of his father's unguarded answer, Damon now knew that Gem was more than a friend. He was his half-brother. Once again, his world was turned upside down by yet another revelation. At least this one was one he was overjoyed to hear. It was hard to focus after that, but Damon brought the conversation back to discuss his own revelations.

"Father, I have some very important things to tell you so you must listen carefully. I have proof that the woman you call your wife has been robbing your estate of money. She has left the business in a state of near collapse with her debts and spending. Father, she is an evil woman!" Damon waited for some understanding to sink in.

"Nonsense! Who told you that? I've been ill. She has taken care of business for me. She has a shrewd head on her but she is all goodness to me."

"Here are the documents proving what I say," and Damon brought out of his coat a folder filled with papers. "There are more that have gone to a magistrate and he says this will be reported to the chief of intelligence. Father, I think the chief of intelligence is in league with Violencia so we must take the case to the king."

"Ridiculous! Whatever accident you had has touched your brain. Didn't you hit your head or something? I thought I heard that somewhere." Damon was frustrated and angry. He could see that he would have to find another way to save his father from sure destruction. As he rose to leave the room, Harrasster said, "By the way, can you find Lency out there and send her in. It's time for my afternoon potion. I feel a fit coming on," and he laughed a foolish and senseless laugh.

Damon rang his mother's bell and found her looking more like her old self, which pleased him. "Mother, I have to warn you about what is going on with father and Violencia." He carefully explained all he had learned in his day of investigation. She was understandably alarmed and this too pleased him after seeing how his father failed to understand the danger they were in.

"I believe you are right. I have suspected as much for a long time, but I have no position, no power. What can I do?" asked his mother. Damon didn't know how to help. He realized that the dilemma was of their own doing and their world was going to collapse around them.

"Damon, there is news from the prison." Damon's attention was wrenched from the family crisis to that which was equally, if not more, dear to him. "What have you heard?" Damon wanted to see the three he had called friends more than anything.

"The king has ordered a public execution for high crimes against the kingdom. It is to be tomorrow morning at sunrise."

"High crimes? What is high about escaping and running away?" asked Damon alarmed.

"I heard from Bessie that they are charged with breaking the king's law. I think that means they helped me get the sleeping powder. It is illegal. That is why I am sentenced to be imprisoned in this room. But that is not all. When they were being taken to prison, they assaulted a soldier and lied about some accomplice helping them escape. The story is all over Bellicosa. The king is furious," replied Dismalia.

"Shouldn't they be trying to find the accomplice and punish him?" asked Damon, feeling panic rise in his chest.

"Bessie says there was no accomplice. Julen and Rubina lied to make it look like they had been helped by the one they call the prince of the Northern Kingdom. The whole thing seems to be about the rumor going around about this prince saying that he rescues people. The king is determined to eliminate any such talk, but Julen, and now Rubina as well, have taken a stand and will not budge. Jip will be hanged for being part of the conspiracy. I am sorry, Damon. I know you made friends with them, but they will be gone very soon. You must try to get over it and forget. You have friends here who are worthy people and not slaves."

At the mention of worth, Damon flew into a rage. "I can't let them do this."

"Damon, son, calm down. It is what the king wishes. I don't want you to risk your life for rabble. Julen was sweet in her own common way, but there are many finer, nobler girls for you to attach yourself to. And that young man Jip is a horrible creature."

Suddenly, Damon remembered the story Jewel had told him about the house where she lived. Did she lie about that or was she telling the truth?

"Mother, where is your closet?"

"I'll show you, but why do you want to see my closet?"

"I have to find out something for myself." He followed his mother and went into the back, feeling along the wall as Jewel had described. His hands found the metal hinges and the latch just as she said. His heart skipped rapidly as he pushed open the door and found the hidden stairs. He rushed up in the near dark and stood in the doorway. There it was. He saw the tapestry and the books. One was missing from the shelf. Then he saw the dusty hand prints and raised the cloth to see the hidden message.

"Mother, look at this," he yelled. She came into the room and was astonished.

"What is it? Has this been here all along? How did you know it was here?

"Jewel told me about it. Everything she said was true. She did not lie!" Damon rose to leave, but turned to his mother first, "Mother, there is one thing I forgot to tell you. My name is no longer Damon. It is Diamond."

The day was getting late. If he wished to see his friends before sunrise the next morning, Diamond had to go quickly. There was nothing he could do, he knew that. It would be only to say goodbye. But he had to do that much. He held the small pouch in his hand that Gem had made for his diamond then tied the strings firmly around his neck.

He pondered his mother's words as he ran the distance down the hill to the prison. Could it really be that they were dying because they would not recant their story about being rescued by a stranger? How could this possibly be a cause to die for? He himself had probably been rescued by the same stranger, supernatural though he was. All their stories had been supernatural and beyond belief, but true nonetheless. He knew the prince was a real person and he did rescue them all, from a wealthy son to lowly slaves. As they talked about him around the fire, he had seen it so clearly. He had felt the bond that bound them together more firmly than any family in Bellicosa. What he had experienced could not be denied and he understood why the three would not recant their beliefs.

If I admitted that I had met the rescuer, would they kill me too? he wondered.

CHAPTER 45

Last Goodbyes

Clanking of iron meant only one thing. Gem sat upright and wondered if his time had come. Either he would be moved to the lowest level of the prison again or he would be led to the gallows. He was not sure which to expect. Either way, it wasn't good.

"Someone to see you, Scum," the guard hissed through a small window. Gem stood and held his breath momentarily, as the visitor was allowed to enter his cell.

"Diamond! Or is it Damon?" asked Gem. Diamond threw his arms around Gem and said, "It is Diamond!"

"Forgive us for the deception. Do you understand why we didn't tell you who you were?" asked Gem anxiously. Diamond moved away and replied, "I do."

"We had no choice if we wished to survive. You know that, don't you?" implored Gem. Diamond was filled with an unfamiliar emotion. Here stood his own flesh and blood, more family to him than any at Arcana. He wanted to cry out against the injustice of the imprisonment and the sorrow that his loss would bring. Helpless, he stood there and finally said, "Gem. I prefer to call you that. I understand why you deceived me. At least, I think I do. I've never been in your place and it is hard to know what it feels like. I know I can't do anything to help you, but I had to come to see you again. Have you heard anything about your mother and Jewel?" Diamond asked sympathetically.

"No, but there was a jest that the guard made this morning, something about my mother being sweet. He could have been meaning just the opposite, but that is all I've heard. I am sure they are still alive. What have you heard?"

"Gem, tomorrow at sunrise you are all scheduled to hang for crimes I don't fully understand. They say Jewel and your mother have taken some kind of stand and will not change their story. The story is that someone helped them escape and they say it was the One that Jewel told us about. Someone in high places sure doesn't like that prince. I read the story about him, Gem. I think I understand but I don't have time to explain. I just have to tell you to trust him."

Gem bit his lip and winced at the thought of his short future. "Tomorrow is it? If I had my key I'd change that in a hurry, but Legerdemain took it away from me. I see they let you keep your diamond, but you weren't the one they were after."

"Maybe I can find it for you. Where do you think he might have put it? They have not connected me to the crime yet so perhaps there is a chance I can move about freely to find it," said Diamond.

Gem shook his head. "I don't know. Hey, that's your line isn't it?" They both laughed despite their sorrow.

"Gem, I have things I want to tell you, but there is little time." Diamond looked directly at Gem before proceeding, "This one is important; are you ready?" Gem nodded in the affirmative and waited excitedly. "I found out who your father is." Diamond waited.

"Tell me! What are you waiting for? It must be bad. Then don't tell me. I don't need any more bad news today."

"Gem, we have the same father. You and I are half-brothers."

Gem choked back a cry of disbelief, then a muffled laugh. As the implications sunk in, his face flushed with anger. He thought of his mother, young and vulnerable all those years ago. Was that why she was so bitter? How had it happened? He would never know.

"That...why that...despicable old...!"

"Hush. They will hear you. He is your father. Make the best of it while you can. I knew you would want to know and I'm glad, Gem. He may be despicable but he did us a favor." The brothers clasped hands tightly and said an emotional goodbye. Still looking intently at his brother, Diamond yelled, "Guard, I wish to visit the other prisoners. Take me to their cell."

"Yes, Sir. But this is highly unusual. I'm not sure I'm supposed to be doing this," lamented the troubled guard.

Diamond was led up the stairs to the main floor and then another flight of stairs to the upper level of the prison. The large open room was bordered by cells on all sides, all but one of them empty. Resisting the urge to rush forward, he made himself walk sedately toward the door of the cell and commanded it to be opened. The worried guard complied. Diamond entered and stood. Jewel studied his face for a moment trying to see if it was Master Damon or her cherished friend, Diamond.

Deep sadness and anger of injustice flooded his heart and drowned timidity and fear. He stepped forward and held out his arms looking at his friends, wanting only to pour out his own love and compassion.

Jewel rushed into his arms, "Diamond."

"Jewel."

"I'm so glad you came. I was afraid you hated me now. I didn't want to lie to you." He returned her embrace and then pushed back her hair with his hand gently. "I know, Jewel," he replied with a voice strained with emotion. He held her at arm's length and said, "I have something I want to say to you. I remember everything. I hit my head today...stupidly tripped on a wet floor…and it all came back to me." Jewel searched his face to get some idea of what he meant. "I remembered knocking you down, running right over you. I was such an odious character. There were probably countless times when I saw you but didn't see you."

"I saw you," she said smiling.

He bowed his head in shame, "Can you forgive me for being such a clod? I was so blind."

Jewel leaned forward and kissed him on his cheek. His face flushed with color and they pulled each other into an embrace once more. Diamond turned to the other person in the cell and was not sure who he was seeing.

"Bina, is that you? You look so different." She beamed with the joy of seeing him again.

"I've seen Gem and he is fine. I told him some news, Bina." He looked at her intently. "I told him who his father is and he was glad. Just like me; I'm glad." Ruby drew in her breath, shocked that he knew. She looked away momentarily, afraid to look Diamond in the face.

Jewel saw the interchange and didn't know what they were talking about. "What is going on here?" she asked.

"Jewel, Gem and I are half-brothers." Jewel laughed. Remembering all the clues she had seen, Jewel asked herself why she had not known before this.

Suddenly realizing that there were other new developments, Jewel said, "Diamond, Bina is gone. This is Ruby." Ruby flashed a glorious smile that had behind it a tinge of doubt, "Are you really glad to be related to that half-wit son of mine?" she said as she hugged Diamond with all she could muster in her petite frame.

"Whoa! What is this? What happened to you?" asked Diamond floored by the change in looks and attitude.

Ruby quickly told him about her rebellious fast, her near brush with death, and the nightmare from which she realized her true condition. Then of her encounter with the prince who named her Ruby.

"Remember how you teased me about my name being Sapphire? You weren't far off. All it took was a touch of miracle. Get us out of here and we'll turn the world upside down."

"I would give anything to get you out of here. Gem said if he had his key, he could do it in no time. But Chief Legerdemain took it from him." Jewel reached into her cloak and took out the key, holding it up for Diamond to see.

"Do you suppose it will work for us?"

"You have it! How?" asked Diamond.

"Chief Legerdemain 'gave' it back—I still have the scrapes here on my nose—saying he had tried it on every lock in the prison and it didn't work. Look, he gave me my necklace back too." She held it up as well. "Once we held it in our hands, it returned to being bright and shiny again," she said, as she tried to find some light to reflect.

There was no light in the cell. The only window in the upstairs showed that it was getting darker as they spoke. It was time to say goodbye. "Give me the key. Maybe I can get it to Gem. He has done this before so he must know the way out." They handed over the precious key.

Standing in a tight circle the three held each other one last time. It was too painful to say goodbye so he turned, walked away, and did not look back. With a lump in his throat, he solemnly trudged back down the steps and out of the building. He heard the bang, clunk of heavy locks as he passed out of the main floor room, out beyond the fortress gates and onto the main road back up to Arcana. Tormenting thoughts whirled in his mind. *How can I get this key to Gem in time?*

CHAPTER 46
Final Departure

Diamond looked out his window and saw no moon. Untold numbers of stars shone brightly in the chill night air. Pacing back and forth in his room, he wondered how he could endure the coming hours knowing his friends and brother were suffering and would soon die. He opened a drawer and picked up the journal, momentarily staring at it. He opened and began to read the words again that had amazed him so while he sat by the fire next to Jewel. The words filled him with hope and courage.

"The king sent his son and equipped him not with horsemen and weapons. He had given him Treasure, bright, sparkling, and very powerful—Treasure hidden in secret and dark places that only the ones he called forth would find. With this Treasure he would win back his father's real Treasure."

Diamond was near tears. Everything in him told him this was the truth. The necklace, the key, the diamond—they were all part of the Treasure that the Prince was using to bring them back to the rightful king. He looked again at the word "powerful." Jewel had told them the truth. The power was not in the Treasure itself, the power was from the One. He was the One who made Diamond's jewel cloudy or clear. It was not to confuse him but to show him when he believed in the prince and when he was losing heart.

Gazing up again, he imagined an unseen force somewhere out there, someone who was looking down and who understood his anguish.

"You are there! You are real!" he heard himself declare to the open expanse. "Each one of us has faced a life-threatening crisis. Each one of us cried out for help. You saved us. You have been with us in some invisible way. Even this trip to prison had the positive result of bringing Ruby back to her senses—Ruby, the stubborn; Jewel, the lonely; Gem, the bound; and Diamond, the proud. Can all this be for no future purpose?"

"Please hear me now! I know who you are and I cry out to you to save my friends!"

Diamond stood motionless for what seemed like a long time. He heard and felt nothing. Fingering the key in his pocket, he remembered Gem. *If only I could get this key to him.* He looked at his new sword in its sheath and started to pick it up. An image came back to him of his waving his old one like a mad man, standing on the deck of a ship tossed in waves as big as mountains. How little his sword did then to ward off the ghostly Leviathan, or the storm that almost took all their lives. Would it do him any good now?

This was a battle not for one sword but for a legional force with power greater than Ironfist and all his armies. His hand went to his throat and felt the diamond within the pouch Gem had made for him. He took it out and it was sparkling brighter than he had ever seen it. Diamond threw on his cloak and flew out of his room, racing down the stairs to the door.

"Damon, wait!" came a voice from the shadows. Diamond recognized her voice and stopped. She approached him warily in the half light of a single lamp that burned in the Great Hall. "Mother, what are you doing up so late?"

"I couldn't sleep. I am worried about you, Damon. You look troubled. I think I know where you are going and I don't want you to go."

"I have to go, Mother. I can't let them die. I don't know what I will do but something will come to me," said Diamond frantically, but with great confidence.

"If you go, you throw everything away, everything you have a right to—your name, your future, your inheritance, and your parents. Surely, you can stay and take back your rights as a son! You are the only who can save the house of Arcana from destruction!" she blurted out in anger. "Once you walk out that door, you leave everything behind. Do you understand? You will not be welcome back!" she fumed, her face hardened with disappointment and disgust.

"Thank you for putting it so well, Mother. You are right. I have no claim here anymore. I have been called away by One who is greater."

"Who do you mean, that slave girl? You think she is greater than me, your own mother?"

"No, I mean the prince, the ONE. I believe in him and I am going to go and take my chances following him. The inheritance he is offering is far beyond this crumbling old house."

Dismalia's brow wrinkled, her eyes were set and her lips tight with determined anger. She turned and walked away, leaving Diamond standing alone, staring at her back.

"I'm sorry. Goodbye, Mother," he said and strode away from the House of Arcana for the last time.

CHAPTER 47
Weapons of Light

The prison yard was dotted with small, tight groupings of armed men, each made visible by faint lantern light. Chief Legerdemain took in the sight with smug approval. His prize catches would not slip through his fingers again. Diamond hunched in the shadows, waiting, not knowing for what.

Inside the upstairs cell, the two women were spending their last hours trying to console each other. Ruby seemed troubled by something and at last confessed, "I feel like I should explain some things. I know we only have hours left to live, but I will feel better if I tell you."

"What is it, Ruby?"

"I have never told you much about myself, as I was afraid. It is true that I am the daughter of servants" Jewel silenced her and said, "I know. Bessie told me. You are an orphan and came from another place. She even told me about the master winning you in a game." Ruby looked a little surprised but said, "Well that is the way of the kitchen isn't it? No secrets. But that is not what I wanted you to know. You heard what Diamond said. Master Chiselstone is the father of my son."

"It's all right, Ruby. That was a long time ago. I am sorry for what happened to you."

"No. You have to hear me out. It wasn't all his fault, in a sense. I worked in the garden and it was backbreaking work. I hated it. I was very young and wanted to have a higher position and be important. The master offered me more. I talked myself into believing that he really loved me and wanted to help. I knew I might live to regret it, Jewel, but I was very ambitious. In the end, he broke his promise and did not bring me into the house. Instead, my life got even harder with a young child to look after. It wasn't until his wife, of all people, saw me and brought me in to be her personal maid. She never knew about...me and the master." Jewel sat close to Ruby and tried to comfort her as she relived the painful past.

"The mistress did not like having my son around so sent him away and he lived on the streets. I could do nothing about it except go back to the garden work, and that was unthinkable. It was my fault that he turned out like he did. I grew bitter and angrier with each passing year."

"Ruby, I am sorry. Please don't punish yourself for that. Gem grew up. He didn't have to do the things he did. You have been forgiven." Ruby wept. "Ruby, what was that song you were singing when you woke up in the night? Can you sing it again? It was so beautiful."

Ruby couldn't remember but said, "The One told me to sing what is in my heart."

"Sing then, Ruby. But don't sing sorrow of the past, sing the joy of right now, knowing he has healed you and given you what you needed the most."

Ruby closed her eyes and began humming, and then crooning a haunting melody. Jewel listened and imagined she saw restful scenes of beauty in the darkness of the cell. The music grew stronger and soon Ruby was putting words to the tune. She sang of the wonder of life, of joy inexpressible, of gratitude to the prince of Light. She sang of the treasure of his promises—ruby, diamond, and sapphire promises. Both women sat with eyes closed swaying to the music of Ruby's voice.

Sparkles of colorful light appeared as the words of the song grew in volume. Shapes formed and danced around the room as she went on. Soon the room was alive with jewels flitting like fireflies, lighting up every dark corner, swirling in dizzying circles. Jewel opened her eyes and looked up in wonder. She nudged Ruby. "Look! What is it?"

Outside Diamond grew weary and momentarily closed his eyes. He did not want to fall asleep, but he was very tired from the exertion of running between the prison and the house. A hum of voices stirred his conscious mind and brought it back to respond to his ears. He listened. Voices called out in the night, "What's that?" "Huh?" "What the...? Get it! They are alive!"

Looking hard into the compound, Diamond saw a stream of light particles flowing through the air in circular patterns, growing and filling the night sky. It streamed down from the small cell window above and over the heads of the guards causing them to look up and follow the flight. As the men watched, some became quiet, staring with dilated eyes, unable to look away from the hypnotizing light display. Others saw the lights as aggressive bees flying in menacing circles to aim their stingers. Screams could be heard alongside men who stood perfectly still.

Diamond quickly discerned that something miraculous was happening. "Thank you," he whispered, and quickly rose to see what advantage he could take. Approaching the stunned gate keeper, Diamond found the keys were easy to snatch. The man never blinked or looked toward the one who lifted them from his open hand. Quick as a wink, Diamond was inside the gate. He expected to be stopped and asked his business at this hour of the night. No one spoke; all were transfixed except the screamers who were randomly running in circles, unable to see anything but the threat over their heads. Diamond kept slowly making his way to the main entrance.

At the door, guards were violently waving their spears in circles to ward off the threat. As the weapons flew, Diamond ducked down and crawled underneath. He lifted the heavy latch and pushed open the door, all without a bump or interruption to the light show.

Diamond stepped inside the common room. It was filled with the same dancing lights of every color of the rainbow, flickering in shapes and blinking in rhythms. Every eye in the room was directed up and stood or sat completely engrossed.

Stopping, he listened. A clear, beautiful melody wafted down from the upper chambers and with it millions more of the bright patterns of light. Diamond realized that the prince of Light could not be far away.

Reaching for his neck, he took the diamond from its bag and grasped it in his fist. A surge of energy flowed through his body. "Keep singing, Ruby!" he whispered then hurried down to the lower level.

Gem's cell was the first on the left. Banging on the door, he called out, "Gem, wake up! It's Diamond." After a few moments, Gem's face peered out of the small, barred window.

"What are you doing here in the middle of the night?" he yawned. Diamond slipped the key in through the bars and said, "This is what I'm doing. Now you do the rest! I'm going upstairs to try to get Jewel and your mother."

"You'll never make it!"

"Then get out of there and help me."

Gem obeyed. He put the key in the lock and it worked perfectly. They snuck cautiously up the stairs when suddenly the singing stopped. The two froze between steps and looked at one another in horror. Men began to stir and they could hear, "What? What was that?" "Get back to work! Who opened that door?" There was a rumble of talking men, the volume rising every second.

"Get downstairs and check those prisoners."

Gem and Diamond fell over one another as they ran down the stairs again and hid in the cell. The door has just creaked shut when the guard made his rounds and went back up to report.

"Now what?" whispered Gem.

"Sing, Ruby, sing!"

"Sing? Ruby? Who is Ruby?"

"Your mother!" proclaimed Diamond. Gem grinned broadly.

"Yes indeed. You may have the locks covered but she has the distraction."

"Sing, mama, sing!" pled Gem trying vainly to transfer his message upward.

Again, the enchanting sounds floated down to them and they both jumped for joy. After a few minutes, the men resumed their attempt. As quickly and quietly as they could, they went up the flight of stairs and across the room to the second set of stairs. The guard on the second floor was leaning against the wall and slowly sliding down, gazing into space.

"Keep singing! Keep singing!" he commanded, as he came into view of the two women looking through the small window. Ruby looked puzzled but kept up the song. Diamond waved his hands as if he was leading her in the music. Gem came forward with a key and soon all four were standing in the room.

"We have to get to the dungeon!" exclaimed Gem.

"The dungeon! Why? There is a front door right there and we can take it easily." "Trust me!" barked Gem, who motioned for them to follow. As they trailed cautiously out of the cell, only Ruby's soiled apron remained discarded and balled up on the prison floor.

Diamond waved his hands at Ruby, who kept singing until they were clear of the main floor, and headed down to the lower level. After that point, her voice could not be heard so she stopped and the foursome ran with all their might down the last stairs to the dungeon.

As soon as she stopped singing, the guards began to stir again. They quickly realized that the prisoners had disappeared and pandemonium spread throughout the whole building.

"You! Check the stairs! You, check the gates! If they have gone out the front, we will find them easily. They can't possibly escape." The muffled sounds reached the four, but they kept going.

"Where are you taking us, Gem? The corridor is getting darker and deeper. I can't see where I am stepping," cried Jewel. Centuries of accumulated effluvium assailed their noses. Moldy slime under foot threatened even the most sure-footed. Diamond took Jewel's hand, and soon, all were holding hands in a line to guide them along.

Gem could not see either, but he knew the gate was at the end of the corridor. They kept going and then abruptly stopped.

"We are here," said Gem.

"Where?"

Gem reached out and felt for the gate. His fingers soon told him something had changed. His hands felt in the dark for the lock but found instead that the bars had been permanently embedded into the portal. Legerdemain had found the gate and the tunnel and had made sure it would not be used an escape route ever again.

"We have a problem," said Gem.

"What now?" they asked in unison.

"It's just a matter of cutting through these irons bars. Any suggestions?"

"Ooohhh," they collectively sighed and collapsed to the floor.

"I have an idea," said Diamond. I have heard that diamonds are the strongest of all substances. Mine may work as a cutting tool. Shall we try?" They all quickly agreed, as there were no other options forthcoming. Diamond took out his jewel and began to saw at the bars. He could feel scratches on the surface, but nothing more. He kept up the sawing motion until the groove was deeper. "Sorry. This is going to take a while."

Diamond's arm grew tired so Gem spelled him. "Here let me have a go at that thing," Ruby volunteered. Jewel contributed what muscle power she could muster. They were all exhausted.

A rustling noise was heard down the dark corridor. "Are they coming? We must hurry." Diamond took his jewel and smashed it against the portal in frustration and was astonished to hear portions of the stone falling away. He did it again and again until all the bars were exposed and had been removed.

As they passed through the portal, Diamond gave it one last smash with his gem stone. The entire portal fell behind them blocking the door for all time.

"We are almost free," said Gem as they rushed on. After a long slow journey, they neared the opening of the tunnel. Gem stopped them and all were quiet. Did he hear voices at the other end? He crept forward trying to hear over the roar of the distant waves. Two small boats had been pulled on shore where the tide had gone down. A group of soldiers led by Chief Legerdemain were making their way toward the tunnel opening.

CHAPTER 48
The Tunnel

Gem withdrew from the edge and reported the news to the three. "Will they leave?" asked Ruby.

"I doubt it. They are sure we have not escaped through any other route," replied Diamond. Gem thought for a moment and then said, "There is one more possibility. Wait here and I'll be back."

Gem felt his way along back into the tunnel, periodically tossing a pebble toward the ceiling.

"Hello," he called out.

"Helloooo," a voice echoed back to him. He found what he had been seeking. Bending over, he tried to gather loose stones from the floor of the tunnel and piled them up at the edge to mark the location. It was easy to get turned around in the pitch black, but Gem's sense of direction was acute. He returned to his nervous companions.

"This is a very long shot," he said, asking them to follow him back the way they had come.

"Maybe we should go in there and get them," said a voice from outside the opening of the tunnel, accompanied by the sound of rattling swords. It had been a long and eventful night for the soldiers. The four could not make out the mumbled response, but shrunk back into the cave at the thought of being pursued.

When they arrived at the spot Gem had marked, he said to them, "I remember when I came through last time. It sounded different here—like an echo. Maybe it's nothing, but what do you say we see if there is anything up there?"

Diamond bent over and picked up a small stone. He tossed in up toward the direction they imagined a possible way out. They all heard the stone strike rock a distance up and beyond them. Diamond agreed to stand on Gem's shoulders and explore the top of the tunnel with his hands. Moving up the wall, Diamond felt for any changes in the surface. There was a ledge just above their heads that felt wide enough for them to lie on. He crawled up upon it announcing to the others, "I feel a cold breeze up here. It is coming from...what's this? I'm sure there is another opening past this ledge. Is anybody up for going into uncharted territory?" Realizing how close they were to being discovered, everyone agreed and began hoisting and pulling one another up. Gem was last. As he bent down to scatter the small pile of stones, a jumble of voices echoed down the tunnel. Leaping phantoms of light appeared just as he scrambled up the wall and fell forward. The four flattened themselves against the ledge and froze.

"I know they are in here, chief. There was no other way for them to go," echoed a voice from the long tunnel.

"Look for footprints. Is there another way of out here?" It was Legerdemain. "They blew up the tunnel entrance at the prison with some powerful explosive, so we know they are here."

The men were standing directly beneath the ledge; their torch flame burned, producing foul smelling fumes that wafted past the four. To cough would be fatal. They waited. If the soldiers looked up, they would see that the cave roof was high. Would they raise their eyes and see the escape route? Jewel's hand was on her necklace, Diamond held his clear stone in his fist, and Gem grasped his pouch as all three remembered how they had been delivered in the past. Each now silently called out for help. Ruby began to gag as the smoke filled her lungs.

"Keep going! They must be up ahead closer to the prison. We will drive them back until they are pinned against the entrance." Legerdemain laughed and lunged forward, the flame and smoke drifting away with the squad of soldiers.

At last, the air was clear and they could breathe again.

"It should be interesting to see what happens when they reach the end of the tunnel with all that acrid smoke. I'll bet they don't stay long," observed Diamond.

"I'm too tired to find out. If it's all the same to you, how about we all try to get some rest," suggested Jewel.

It had been a long night and Chief Legerdemain was exhausted. His eyes were wild and his usually neat clothes were disheveled, giving him the look of a mad man. He could come up with no way to explain the escape of the prisoners, whose execution would have been the capstone of his career. Dread filled him as he awaited his escort to the second floor reception room once again. As he presented himself, he bowed deeply before King Ironfist.

"My king, we return empty handed. My men searched the whole length of the tunnel and have found no one."

"How is it possible they escaped?" the king exploded. "Are you sure there wasn't another way out of the prison?"

"It was a work of sorcery, Your Eminence. The soldiers reported seeing an army of fierce fire flies that swarmed like angry bees. They were frightened beyond imagination," Legerdemain offered as his only defense.

"This is insanity! What will I report to the ultimate ruler? The word will quickly spread. Of course," he interjected casually, "you will have to hang in their place. But that hardly solves the problem, does it?" Legerdemain cringed as the palace guards were summoned and he was yanked out of the presence of the king and led away to his own prison cell shouting, "No. There has to be an explanation. I can find them. Wait!"

From behind King Ironfist's regal cabinet appeared the solemn person of Incubus Pestilent. The king felt the threatening presence and trembled. All his strategies had failed. His best man had let him down, and now what was to be done? Standing alone in the room with the man he had hoped to impress, the king felt like prey stalked by a hungry lion, waiting for the final pounce.

"Ironfist, you have failed. The ultimate ruler will not tolerate this."

"I don't understand," he stammered. "Who is this ultimate ruler, anyway? I thought...."

Pestilent bowed to someone behind the king. Ironfist turned and beheld the banner behind the royal chair as it morphed into animation. The green dragon leaped into full size, with red eyes blazing and a wide-open mouth closing jagged teeth around the tiny robed figure, swallowing him in one bite.

The royal guards stiffened in horror and waited to be similarly punished. Pestilent rose reverently and smiled. The dragon leapt back into its colorfully-framed threads, looking as it had before. Pestilent dusted off his hands as he turned to the guards, "I guess I have to do everything myself?"

The guards ran for their lives.

The four had rested as best they could on the uncomfortable stone floor of the upper tunnel. No one wanted to move but at last, they began to talk to one another and plan for continuing to seek a way to the outside world.

"Isn't it true that the prince is the prince of Light? If that is true, then he can give us light to see our way out of here," said Diamond. "We can't see him, but he seems to work through the treasures he gave us. Let's see if he can use them again." Diamond held out his jewel. Gem held out his key, and Jewel touched her necklace. Ruby hummed softly. It remained dark, but a luminescence appeared ahead of them. They all stood and walked into it, stepping over stones, and finding the way smooth and clear. A gradual upgrade raised hopes that they would come out on land above the cliffs.

The breeze brushing past encouraged them to keep going. It began to grow lighter, and as it did, the glow inside the cave gave way to faint starlight. Gem peered into the heavens and recognized the signs of the impending new day. "The sun will soon rise. We will have to find a place to take cover."

"Anyone have an idea where we are?" asked Ruby. They all shrugged their shoulders and gathered close together against the chilly pre-dawn breeze. No one spoke, but each reflected on the day and night that had now drawn to a close.

"This was to be the hour of our death, but it has become the hour of triumph," observed Jewel as she put her arms around her friends.

"What do we do now?" asked Ruby.

"Where do we go? Diamond, will you return to your family?" Jewel looked tensely at him, awaiting his answer.

"I will not be going back. That part of my life is over," said Diamond sadly. He looked at Jewel and smiled. "A new chapter is beginning—one in which I am following the prince."

"How will you do that?" asked Gem. Diamond brought out a worn book from inside his vest. He said nothing but held it out for all to see.

A gray mist swirled around their feet and rose around them in a cloud. Diamond opened the book. A flash of thunderless lightning swept all four off their feet and before them an enormous white horse reared high. They all ducked beneath the mighty hooves that struck out against the air just over their heads. The hooves came down to the soft earth and stood still. The four looked up to see the shining figure of a man seated upon the steed. He had the bearing of a great warrior, but he had no armor and held no sword. On his arm was the band of a simple slave. He raised his arms in triumph and shouted, "Well done, my dear ones!"

The four needed no introduction as each one recognized him. Jewel's heart felt like it would burst with joy and excitement as she exclaimed, "It is you—the One whose blood washed me clean!"

Gem's mind went back in an instant to his dark prison cell and a strange dream. He raised high his jeweled key and yelled, "It is you—the One whose fire set me free!"

Diamond hardly heard the others because his own amazement overwhelmed him. At last he knew the truth. "It is you—the One whose hand pulled me from the depths!"

Last of all, Ruby cried out, "It is you—my song in the night!"

The horse panted with loud breaths, threw its head from side to side, and stomped the ground with impatience. Restrained by a strong arm, it waited for the signal. Leaning forward, the rider waved his farewell with a final shout,

"Go and tell others about me. But don't worry. I will come back and take you with me to the kingdom of my father and you will live with me forever and ever."

The four stood stunned and speechless, doubting the reality of what they had seen and heard. He was gone. The horse had leapt away and out of sight in a single bound. Diamond still held the book in his hand and now they all turned to face one another. "What does this mean?" asked Ruby.

"I am not sure but I think the answer might be in this book," Diamond answered. "Let's start our new adventure here."

Epilogue

Cheering, dancing crowds lined the bright lanes, waving banners of every color of the rainbow. Smiles, tears, and shouts of "Congratulations!" and "Bravo!" met the prince who was returning from his conquests in the Dark Lands. Passing by the jubilant throng, he reached down to shake the hands of those who wished to greet him. As he did so, many saw the deep scar and knew he had paid a great price for his obedience.

His pure white horse trotted rhythmically, its shod hooves making loud clacking sounds against the golden pavement. With great dignity and beaming triumphantly, the son of the king carried his trophies and rode toward the castle. He dismounted and signaled his servants to shoulder the prize he had brought with him. The servants carried an enormous chest and followed the prince as he walked into the castle. They made their way to the throne room, and into the presence of the king.

"My son!" said the king, who tenderly reached out to embrace the prince. "You have come at last. I've been anxious to see how you have achieved the

task for which I sent you." The father saw the scar and wept in sorrow realizing what the mission had cost his son. After releasing the younger man, he
sat once again upon his throne with a look of great anticipation on his face.

"Father, I am thrilled to show you what I have brought back!" said the
prince and motioned for the servants to bring the chest forward. They gently placed it on the marble floor. The prince opened it, shooting his father
a sidelong glance, and said, "Wait until you see this!" Reaching inside, he
picked up a precious jewel and held it out to the king. The king bent over and
looked closely, seeing into the very heart of the gem to see its story.

"Remarkable! Unequal in value to anything else," said the king shaking
his head in disbelief. "Son, you have done well. I am very pleased."

"Wait until you see the rest." For the next several hours, the prince
showed the king one jewel after the next. Each one the king inspected to
see inside it.

At one point, the prince said, "Look at this one, Father," and held out
a shimmering emerald that was so bright it looked alive. The king looked
deeply into it and said, "Amazing." Then with a twinkle in his eye he
continued, "Two stories lie within this stone!"

The prince then placed beside it a large, clear diamond and held the two
in his palm together. The King smiled and said, "Perfect!"

Fetching a deep blue sapphire, he placed it alongside the other two.
The King nodded in understanding and a tear of joy fell from his eyes as
he looked at the story deep within the jewel. The prince retrieved yet one
more, a bright red ruby, and made the four a complete set. The king roared
with laughter and said, "Wonderful! My precious Treasure has been brought
back from the darkness."

The prince returned the jewels to the chest and commanded that they
be displayed before all the people of the kingdom. Everyone who saw them
was struck with awe and delight. Returning to the throne room, the prince
took his place seated beside his father.

"Is that the end of the story?" asked Jubilee to his fellow attendant.

"No, of course not," replied Mirth. "It is just the beginning."

Made in the USA
Charleston, SC
11 February 2012